SOMEWHERE OGRE THE RAINBOW

THE HIPPOSYNC ARCHIVES
BOOK 6

DC FARMER

WYRMWOOD
BOOKS

COPYRIGHT

This edition published by Wyrmwood Books 2025

A CIP catalogue record for this book is available from the British Library

eBook ISBN - 978-1-915185-40-2
Print ISBN - 978-1-915185-41-9

Published by Wyrmwood Books.
An imprint of Wyrmwood Media.

EXCLUSIVE OFFER

WOULD YOU LIKE A FREE NOVELLA

Please look out for the link near the end of the book for your chance to sign up to the no-spam-guaranteed Readers Club and receive a FREE DC Farmer novella as well as news of upcoming releases. HERE ARE THE BOOKS!

FIENDS IN HIGH PLACES
THE GHOUL ON THE HILL
BLAME IT ON THE BOGEY (MAN)
CAN'T BUY ME BLOOD
TROLL LOTTA LOVE

CHAPTER ONE

KENT, ENGLAND, THE HUMAN WORLD

Motorways, by and large, tended to be roaring arteries where engines throbbed above the backdrop thrum of rubber on asphalt. When silent, the quiet sat uncomfortably; an all-too-familiar soundtrack to death and destruction. Covid had taught everyone that. But not that day. Not entirely.

On a silent July morning, with the sun already warming the Kent air, the mangled steel and rubble-strewn carriageway that had once been the M20 portended lurid headlines and a list of obituaries. Death, however, had decided to take the day off, sending Injury and Fear instead, and allowing their feckless cousin Luck to tag along unsupervised. Granted, the collapse of a passenger bridge onto a major motorway would not normally have been considered fortuitous, but with no fatalities and only half a dozen people hospitalised, that fact remained a matter of debate.

In the twenty-four hours following the incident, the roads had been cleared, traffic turned around and evacuated, diversions posted, emergency services had come and gone. All that remained were the roadworkers and forensic engineers, galvanised by a need to reopen as quickly as possible. And, of course, the inevitable burger van, whose presence in situations where men with hard hats, pneumatic drills, and dumper trucks worked, was a statutory requirement.

Explosive experts had ruled out a bomb. CCTV footage had revealed no collision from TikTok-distracted drivers or sleepy travellers. The cause remained a mystery. Yet the two people in conversation at the edge of one of the buckled pillars identified as the cause of the collapse wore grim expressions of people whose worst fears had been realised. They both squatted low as one pointed a finger at a dark smudge near a crack in the concrete.

'Sulphur,' he said, brushing it with his finger and raising it to his nose. He had short dark hair and an easy smile that hadn't yet found a reason to appear that morning. Like his colleague, the dark suit and white shirt under his hi-vis tabard seemed out of place in this windy outdoor location. He shifted his position for a better view, and his wiry body moved with an easy fluidity.

'Definitely.' His colleague nodded. Her voice had a throaty edge that might have suggested a tobacco addiction. But she was not a smoker. It was a habit that disgusted her. Drawn by a movement at the edge of her vision, she glanced over her shoulder with eyes that appeared almost flecked with gold. A man wearing a hard hat and holding a clipboard approached.

'Oi, you need to wear head gear if you want to be this close,' shouted the man.

The two people inspecting the pillar stood and turned to face Mr Clipboard, whose short-sleeved shirt stretched tight over a bulging belly. The tie he wore ended two inches above his sagging belt. His white safety helmet sat squarely on his head atop a jowly face. Someone had scribbled Attila in blue felt-tip pen just above the helmet's peak.

The black-suited man apologised. 'Sorry. Should have realised. Doesn't matter now, though, we've finished.'

'Attila' continued to approach. He wore a suspicious expression mingled with fatigue. 'Who are you two with?

Traffic?' He paused before adding, more slowly and with narrowing eyes, 'Manufacturers?'

The dark-suited man reached into his pocket, pulled out a wallet, and flipped it open. It revealed a badge showing a shield and the letters, DOF. He smiled. It was disarming. 'Matt Danmor. And this is my colleague, Kylah Porter.'

Attila ran a pencil down the list bulldog-clipped to his board. The permanent frown on his face deepened a notch. 'I don't see those names here.'

'Ah,' said Matt, 'you wouldn't. No. Special arrangement. Government business. Security stuff, you know.'

Attila wasn't buying it. 'You're not trying to tell me this was a bloody act of terrorism?'

Matt shrugged, and it might as well have been wearing a striped shirt and a beret. 'Let's just say we're not ruling it out.'

'Rubbish. See that?' The pencil was thrust towards a crack in the concrete pillar. 'Classic concrete stress fracture. This bridge was badly built. End of.'

'And you'll be putting that in your report, I take it?' Kylah asked evenly.

Attila's aggressive stance eased somewhat. Kylah's voice, both in timbre and the easy confidence that came with years of command, had that effect.

'Preliminary report. Yes.'

'So if we told you that we think the bridge collapsed because of a transdimensional energy strike, possibly a wand-generated and deliberate curse, we'd be wasting our time?'

The man stared at the serious faces before him, looked away, and dropped his chin. He did a magnificent impression of an exhausted mountaineer dangling fifty feet above the ground with only ten feet of rope left. He sighed a pantomime sigh. 'The 250-tonner that was supposed to lift this thing is stuck in traffic on the M-sodding-25, the minister's having kittens, and I forgot to bring my missus' idea of a packed lunch—a bloody rice cake and two tomatoes. The last thing I need today is a couple of jokers like you two.' He looked up, pierced them both with a glare, turned, and walked away, saying over his shoulder, 'I'll send someone over with a couple of hard hats and some red noses for you clowns.'

He strode ten paces, stopped as if he'd remembered something and pivoted. 'And another thing…'

His words tailed off. The two people he had been addressing moments before had disappeared.

He opened his mouth to complain but realised no one was listening. His shoulders sagged, and he pulled a shortwave radio up to his mouth.

'Jill, I've just had two people tell me the bridge collapse was due to a bloody wizard attack, and guess what? They've disappeared into thin air. I must be hallucinating from all this stress…and hunger. Mainly hunger. Sod it. Get the bloody tea on and crack open those biscuits. I need two sugars and a hobnob right away. Sod the diet. I might even have a burger from that van. For God's sake, don't tell Dorinda.'

CHAPTER TWO

LONDON, ENGLAND

The Director General of MI5 sat in his office overlooking the River Thames on the Embankment. Below him, a barge tugging scrap slid along and a glass-topped tourist cruiser churned up the water. He had another office in the guts of the building where the real work was done. But the one with the view was used when he needed to officially meet and greet those colleagues from other institutions involved, like him, in overseeing the security of the country. There were a few nice touches in the room: polished wood, thick carpet, a drinks cabinet and, to ensure everyone's safety while they chatted, bulletproof glass windows. The guests the DG hosted always had targets to meet and MI5 wanted to ensure that they did not become one themselves. Sniper rifles these days could split a seagull's tail feather like a spaghetti strand from well over a kilometre away. The DG did not want anything like that to happen. Not on his watch. Nor his tie, shirt, carpet or wall.

Besides the door leading to the corridor outside, there were two more in the room. One led to a small bathroom and the other to a stationery cupboard. Though the DG inevitably had a lot of paperwork to deal with, the presence of a stationery cupboard might have been considered a tad incongruous. But the fact was that every DG insisted upon it and insisted that it was swept for surveillance bugs at least twice a week.

Just in case. Of emergencies. Like the one he was having to deal with currently.

So, though it was not often that the DG needed to open the stationery cupboard door, he needed to this morning.

Paunchy now that he was past fifty, Sir Bernard favoured thick-rimmed glasses and liked walking the dog and attending Twickenham on international days, though it was getting insanely expensive. But he wasn't thinking about rugby this morning as he informed his secretary not to disturb him and stepped towards the cupboard door and opened it.

Instantly, another door, not previously present, opened on the opposite side of the cupboard and the space both doors opened on to became…somewhere else. Somewhere unobservable and unreachable—even beyond the tentacles of GCHQ—where certain delicate matters could be discussed. The DG had just enough time to compose his expression into a smile as the doorway three yards away filled with a small figure.

Ogden Hamage, known affectionately as Magister Hamage, was an advisor to the government of New Thameswick on matters of state as well as being the chancellor of New Ron university, a seat of learning still on a ten-week delay thanks to an unfortunate Krudian physics experiment on temporal displacement fields gone wrong. Or, right, depending on which way you looked at it.

Unlike the DG, who was a big man in all senses of the word, Hamage was small, with sharp eyes the same colour as his sky-blue robes, and a face that would need a half gallon of Botox to have any effect on the many centuries-old lines crisscrossing it. He held out a hand. The DG shook it, flicking his eyes down to make sure he still had the requisite number of fingers, having previously been the butt of one of Ogden's little jokes involving painlessly removing one or more digits and repositioning them on the shaker's other hand, by way of greeting.

It was something one tended never to forget as first impressions went.

'Bernard, good of you to come at such short notice.'

'Not a problem, Ogden. Any time.'

'Shall we?'

They stepped through a third door and out onto the open deck of a huge wooden yacht moored in a pristine bay surrounded by lush vegetation. The sun was hot and high above them. Under an awning providing welcome shade, a table was laid with cups and a pot of coffee.

'Is this the…Royal Yacht?' the DG asked, eyebrows an inch from his receding hairline as he clocked firstly the colour scheme and then the flags fluttering above.

Hamage nodded.

'Wasn't it mothballed in '97?'

'It was. So we got it cheap. We'll probably re-gift it. There's a potentate in Blip we owe a favour to and he's into royal merch. Said I'd glance over the refurbishments in case it's been hexed. You know the drill.'

The DG attempted a sage nod which, under the circumstances of his almost dropped jaw combined with knowing bugger all about anti-hex drills, was a pretty good effort.

Something large and green and amphibious leaped up from the water below to land on the deck with a mucoid flop not five yards from the table. It sat, blinking in the sunlight and turning its large head this way and that, staring at the men. The DG froze. The only noise came from the flags snapping in the breeze and the nervous rattle of the DG's coffee cup against its china saucer.

'Sniffer frog,' said Hamage. 'Ignore it.'

The frog croaked deeply and leaped up a deck.

'Where exactly are we?' asked the DG in a voice better suited to the female lead of *Madama Butterfly*. He cleared his throat and repeated the question an octave lower. 'Where exactly are we?' He'd learned to speak slowly and clearly to Hamage, who tended to mishear and sometimes used a cow horn ear trumpet that he carried jauntily attached to his belt.

'British Virgin Islands. Sea trials.' Hamage waved a hand vaguely. 'Thought we might as well get some sun while we're at it.' He leaned back and turned a face like a well-past-its-sell-by-date russet to the sky.

'I take it that this is in relation to the rising disaster count?' the DG ventured.

'What?' Hamage murmured, eyes closed.

'Rising count,' said the DG more loudly.

Hamage's eyes snapped open. 'There is no need to use foul language, Bernard.'

The DG pointed at the horn on Hamage's waist. Hamage lifted it to his ear and turned his head away.

'The rising number of disasters,' said the DG, slowly emphasising each syllable.

'Ah, yes. Indeed.' Hamage nodded. 'Rathkoorne. A carbuncle on the unwashed rump of the world. Well, our world. It is getting to the stage where it no longer even bothers denying its involvement.'

The DG sighed. 'Last week we had a bridge collapse on a major motorway. Confirmed as a wand strike by the DOF. Miracle no one was killed.'

'Ours was a mudslide. Many casualties.' Hamage shook his head.

'Is there any point me asking why?'

'The obvious answer would be paranoia. Such an abhorrent regime realises that it must arm itself. It is desperate and frightened of an invasion and the consequences. And then, of course, there is maintenance of the power base. Le Liare wants to appear strong and retain his god-like status in the eyes of his brainwashed people.'

'Le Liare. The cult of personality,' muttered the DG.

'Erthu Le Liare is certainly that.'

'No, I said cult…of personality. You know, where a leader deliberately creates a worshipful, idealised and heroic image backed up with unquestioned flattery and praise and underlined most often by merciless terror.'

Hamage waited a beat and then said, 'I think I prefer what I apparently misheard.'

'Even so. Such random acts cannot be acceptable.'

'Agreed. However, the Northern Wights have a vested interest in allowing this folly. They fear a change in the political landscape might end up with the whole starving population of Rathkoorne storming across their borders if Le Liare and his madness falls.'

The DG sipped his coffee. It was the best he had ever tasted but he knew better than to ask how or why. He simply accepted this little gift as a perk of the job. And anyway, even if he did find out and went back to tell his wife, she would not believe him. A minute ago, he was in his office on an overcast summer's day and now here he was, drinking a wonderful Java roast on a bloody yacht. The bloody yacht, to boot.

'What, then, can we do about it?' he asked finally.

'We have no plans to move against them because the consequences would be catastrophic. There is no doubt that Rathkoorne is flexing its biceps because it can. The Northern Wights would look at any overt aggression unfavourably. And Le Liare's defensive charms are extremely powerful.'

'By charms, you mean the magical stuff?'

Hamage dropped his chin. 'I would certainly not be hinting at Le Liare's alluring characteristics, of which I can think of not a single one. He rules the country with a fist of iron and a cauldron of fear. Anyone who disagrees with him simply disappears. Or perhaps their children first, then their parents. Somehow that makes it ten times worse.'

'Then must we sit back and accept this mayhem?'

Hamage sighed. 'It is set to worsen. We have evidence that Le Liare's chief weapons tester, his son, Gauinebald, is now dabbling in temporal displacement, as well as transdimensional targets.'

'You've lost me.'

'They are able and willing to fire their weapons into the past. Changing the future. Everyone's future. It has happened already.'

'How?'

'You lent me a copy of your history. It tells of a monstrous disaster in 1931 in your China. The Yellow and Yangtze floods.'

'Of course. Four million people—'

'It will be in every history book in your world. But in my other copy, given to me thirty years ago by one of your predecessors, it never happened. Le Liar's hands are bloodied to the elbow.' Hamage shook his head.

Above them, a flight of geese flew over, the noise of their powerful wings drawing both men's gaze.

Hamage smiled. 'Nature has a way of humbling us. Geese fly in formation to preserve energy, utilising the wake of the one in front to streamline. And they will rotate the leading bird for pacing. Cooperation wins the day.'

When the wise old man looked back down, the DG wore a look of grim determination.

'What do you want us to do, Ogden?'

'Let us take this little rowing boat on one trip around the bay while I tell you what I have in mind.' He stood and cupped both hands around his mouth. 'Sinbad, put down that rum and get your arse in gear.'

The DG looked impressed.

Hamage shrugged but proffered a knowing smile. 'One has to be firm with the younger generations, you know.'

The yacht's engines fired up, foaming the clear blue waters at the stern. Hamage offered up the still warm coffee pot. The DG held out his cup.

'Is the captain a youngster, then?'

'Barely two hundred years old. Now, where was I, Bernard? Ah yes, a plan.'

CHAPTER THREE

NEW THAMESWICK, THE FAE WORLD

IN NEW THAMESWICK, a place not a million miles away from where the DG was chatting to Hamage—so long as you knew the right interdimensional door to open—another meeting convened in Asher Lodge's office in the Bureau of Demonology. Five people were present: Lodge, an agent of the **BOD**; Professor Duana Llewyn, Lodge's head of department; Captain Kylah Porter and Matt Danmor, both of them DOF as previously described. Though Danmor was also considered an honorary **BOD** agent, having been seconded there for a year until just a few months previously. Additionally, there was Roberta Miracle, likewise a DOF agent and now a fully-fledged witch, pale of colouring and dressed in full-blown goth attire. At least, that was how it might be described in Oxford, where she was from. And no doubt there, her aubergine lipstick and green eyeshadow would, as it often had, draw stares and disapproving looks. But in New Thameswick, it was considered relatively conservative. Either way, Bobby Miracle owned it.

Though not exactly clandestine, no meeting minutes were taken. If they had been, quite a lot of black felt tip pen might have been used in crossings out if ever someone wanted to read them. Not that the topic was illicit. No one would have called it that. The better term might have been 'sensitive'. As in the don't-tell-anyone-or-we'll-have-to-kill-you type of sensitive.

With one exception, they all sat around a table, mugs of tea and plates containing the remnants of a coffee cake littering the surface. Behind them, Duana Llewyn stood with an unnerving stillness against a dark bookshelf: a blonde, alabaster snow queen in a pale cream robe. 'Your road bridge collapse was definitely wonderworking?'

'One hundred per cent certain,' Kylah answered. The sentence emerged as a virtual growl.

'And there was that cruise ship last week. Almost sucked into a whirlpool in the Indian Ocean,' added Matt.

Duana sucked in her to-die-for cheekbones. 'How was that explained?'

'The press needed something credible, so we put out a couple of explanations. One that it was an eddy phenomenon caused by unusual activity in the Agulhas Current, resulting in an anticyclonic core ring causing said whirlpool. The other that it was turbulence from the mating dance of two giant squid. I'll give you two guesses which one the press went for.' Matt waved his arms above his head in an attempt at emulating a cephalopod seduction ritual.

Duana exchanged a knowing glance with Asher. 'Then that makes four confirmed incidents in fourteen days.'

'Four?'' asked Kylah. 'I knew you'd had one.'

Asher shrugged and sat back, sending his long black hair cascading away from his angular face. A fashionable three-day stubble lent him a haunted look which, given that he was a necreddo and able to communicate with the dead, was pretty on point. 'You know about the avalanche in Tobler. Nothing unusual in that except for the fact that it's summer and there was no snow under 10,000 feet. But a whole village managed to get engulfed.'

'So, what's the other one?'

Duana sighed. 'This was a cottage at the side of a lake.

The people in it heard a ripping noise and woke up to find themselves at the bottom of that lake. Two people drowned. Of the three survivors, one happens to be the niece of the minister without a suitcase.'

'Shouldn't that be portfolio?' Matt asked. 'We've had cabinet ministers without a specific brief in the past and they're usually given that title.'

'Our lot don't work that way. Perhaps the better term should have been Home Affairs, but in an attempt at reaching out to the people of New Thameswick and its environs, they've renamed the government departments.'

Asher grinned. 'Education is now R and R. No one has the heart to tell them that writing actually begins with a W. Doesn't help that the bloke in charge has a speech impediment.'

Duana shook her head. 'It is nevertheless amazing how having a member of the cabinet's family embroiled in an "incident" galvanises an otherwise sluggish government into action. They have asked us to look into it and I do not like what I see.'

'You think there's demonology involved?' Matt asked.

'In a way. But we are looking at a demon once removed and very much in human form. Our colleagues in the department of Home Security—now renamed Iron Fence—tell us that they have been monitoring for abnormal and excessive thaumaturgical activity. There is no doubt that only one country is responsible and intent on developing new weapons.'

'New weapons? Surely that's a bit over the top?'

Asher expelled air in a mirthless laugh. 'Over the top is a very good description of this particular country.'

'Does it have a name?' Bobby asked.

'The Tobler gnomes have a good one for it. *Rückwärts Hölle Bohrung.*'

'Which means?'

'Backwards hellhole,' said Duana. 'And that is the polite version. The country itself prefers to be known as the Baronial Hegemony of Rathkoorne.'

'Everyone just calls it Rathkoorne,' Asher said.

'So why don't you open up diplomatic channels with Rathkoorne and let them know their experiments are pish?' Matt picked a crumb up from his plate and nibbled it.

'Because they enforce a blanket ban on any and all non-Rathkoorne citizens. Automated hexes. Anyone crossing the border is immediately wrapped in chains via a security curse. They won't listen because they won't let anyone in. The last time we sent an envoy, they simply sent him back, but in several different pieces and not all at once.'

'What's to be done?' Kylah asked.

'This is why we are here.' Duana pulled up a chair. 'We need to adopt a two-pronged approach. As mentioned, the main problem we have with Rathkoorne is that it is a completely closed-off society. We have very little intelligence on what actually goes on there.'

'Since the interloper curse is based on birthplace recognition, it excludes anyone from this world,' Asher added.

Kylah's eyebrows shot up. 'Are you suggesting Matt or Bobby goes in?'

Duana shook her head. 'Unfortunately, Matt has enough non-human DNA to be a trigger. And Bobby, I am sure, would not want to relinquish her persona.'

They turned to look at Bobby: long dark hair with one pink and one white streak, silver dagger earrings, dressed today in a dark puff petticoat dress and a black velvet hooded cape. Trademark black DMs completed her standard field-work attire. If there were a coven of widows in Scotland, Bobby would have been their poster girl. She returned the glances with large, challenging eyes. 'You know this is the way I roll.'

Duana continued, 'Besides, they still burn witches. No, we wondered if you might find us a completely human volunteer?'

'Hmm,' Matt said. 'You'd have to be someone pretty special to take this on. What would be the motivation?'

'Not to want to live a full life?' Asher said. 'The chances of survival are, at best, minimal.'

'I see. So we're looking at death row inmates, terminal disease sufferers or estate agents.'

'Okay,' Kylah said, as Asher giggled. 'We'll have a trawl. What about the other prong?'

'Ah, that too involves your department.' Duana smiled.

Matt picked up another crumb and waited.

'Specifically, we would like to set up an animorph squad. Send some volunteers in from our world disguised as animals.'

'Isn't it a question of Dolittle too late?' Matt asked.

No one laughed, except Bobby Miracle who was, like Matt, almost all human and steeped in popular culture.

'Since you will be back in Oxford coordinating the handling of your volunteer, we thought I'd better get to grips with the animal side of things. I have recruited an expert, based on one of your recommendations, Matt,' Asher said.

'Hang on, I don't remember recommending anyone,' Matt said.

'Well, recommend may be a little strong. But you have worked with him before, and in the files, you have mentioned him in despatches as being capable and motivated.'

'Really?' Matt said. 'I can't think who that could be…'

Kylah was looking at him with an expression of dawning horror.

'What?' Matt said. 'Do you know who this is?'

'I have a very, very bad feeling that I might.'

'He's been with us for a couple of weeks already and has begun to assemble a squad,' Duana said.

'Impressive.' Matt remained puzzled. 'Does he have a name?'

'Several. Though I understand he prefers his flock name. Rimsplitter.'

The crumb in Matt's oesophagus caused the tube to seize and set up a reflex splutter that had him purple-faced and tearing up within seconds. It took several deep breaths and at least half a glass of water before he was able to croak, 'Rimsplitter?'

Duana raised one eyebrow which, for her, was tantamount

to a chortle. 'He said you'd be surprised. When you're ready, we'll go and meet him and the recruits.'

She led them to a lift: a dark wooden box large enough for no more than six people surrounded by ornate ironwork that doubled as the balusters of a staircase winding upwards. A gangly, grinning boy stood behind the concertinaed cage doors.

'Afternoon, Prof,' Ned the stamp said. 'Where to?'

'Special ops training, please.

'Right you are.' Ned pulled the grill shut and pressed some buttons on a wooden console. There were no numbers on the buttons and the symbols they bore were unrecognisable to all but a few academics in the building.

And Ned the stamp.

As the Bureau of Demonology's post boy, Ned had an encyclopaedic knowledge of the building and its environs, some of which went well beyond the confines of New Thameswick and even known space. He beamed at the lift's occupants, his lopsided smile guileless under large blue eyes and a thatch of bleached-straw hair. But those features belied a talent for finding almost anything a BOD agent might ever need. So long as Ned's palm was crossed with silver, gold, or even the odd Victoria sponge. The lift jerked into motion and began to ascend…or was it descend…or was it move sideways? It was difficult to tell. Not that anyone in that lift was surprised by the disorientation, or the length of the journey.

Duana broke the shoe-gazing silence. 'You're quiet, Mathew. Looking forward to meeting an old friend?'

Matt smiled. At least he hoped that the frozen grimace he managed to force his lips to form might pass as one. He blinked, opened his mouth to speak, but found his voice had taken a minute or two to negotiate a truce with that part of his brain demanding that it laugh hysterically.

'Obviously, I've read the file,' Duana continued, 'but it might help if you explained to Bobby and Asher how you two met.'

'I…yeah…he…left in charge?' Matt's mouth opened twice as often as the words emerged, words that seemed to be the bastard children of incredulousness and gibbering nonsense.

Kylah sent him a sympathetic smile. She, of course, knew Rimsplitter too. Not as well as Matt did, but well enough to appreciate Agent Danmor's reaction to the news that Duana had seen fit to recruit him. 'Matt and Rimsplitter go way back,' she said. 'Right to the beginning of Matt's involvement with the DOF. They were both decorated for their roles in foiling the kidnapping and attempted murder of the head of DOF ops. And of yours truly.'

'Of course.' Asher nodded. 'The Ghoulshee uprising.'

'Exactly. I'll spare Matt's blushes by stating bluntly that the DOF, this lift, indeed the whole of New Thameswick and beyond would not be in existence were it not for their action. He and Rimsplitter forged an, um, unlikely alliance which the Ghoulshee underestimated very badly.'

'So Rimsplitter was a DOF agent, too?' Bobby asked.

Matt threw her a look that was difficult to interpret but might best be described as one someone walking in the grounds of an abandoned hospital at dusk might give if they happened to glance up and see a face appear at a darkened window on the fourth floor.

'Not exactly,' Kylah answered. 'He was in Uzturnsitstan on the transdimensional witness protection programme, having made a deal with the New Thameswick chief prosecutor after testifying against some pretty unpleasant people. He was offered immunity and an opportunity to hide out. As a vulture.'

'Rimsplitter is an unusual name,' Bobby said.

Matt, still wearing a rictus smile, let out a giggle that he stifled with a clamped-shut jaw. Kylah put a concerned hand on his arm. Matt shook his head and waved a hand in reassurance.

Kylah took a deep breath before answering. 'Think verb instead of noun. His role in the vulture community of which he was a part was to find a way into a corpse.'

'A way in?' Bobby frowned.

'Soft tissue ingress.' Duana nodded.

'Eyes for the brain, mouth for the throat and the remaining sphincters for the main body, if you wanted to avoid the dangly bits,' Kylah elaborated.

Bobby ventured. 'So, he was literally splitting—'

'Rims, yes.'

Bobby's expression did little to hide what her brain was being forced to imagine.

'What happened to him?' Asher asked, steering the conversation, along with everyone's thoughts, away from unpleasant imaginings. 'Did he stay in Uzturnsitstan?'

'He did,' Kylah said. 'Only no longer as a vulture. There was some morphic and status reconfiguration. Medals don't sit well on avian chests, so in return for turning state's witness, he now manifests as a crowned eagle.'

'A very noble bird,' Asher said.

This time the hysterical giggle that burst from Matt emerged as a peel of high-pitched laughter, stifled quickly by his own clamped hand.

'Do I get the impression that we're missing something here?' asked Bobby.

'Those are the facts,' Kylah insisted. 'It's just that as an individual, Rimsplitter is something of an…acquired taste.'

They all looked at Matt, whose face was now wet with tears of laughter. 'Rimsplitter. In charge,' he whispered, his eyes focused on some point in the cosmos invisible to everyone else, where fate was thumbing its nose at the universe. He came back to himself and looked around at the faces staring back at him before asking, 'Has anyone got a tissue?'

CHAPTER FOUR

PICT, THE FAE WORLD

THE LIFT TRUNDLED to a stop and the doors opened inside a room reminiscent of a steel shipping container. Duana glided along its length, her heels clipping on a chipboard floor. She pulled the door open to reveal a wide expanse of meadow overlooking an astonishingly beautiful landscape of valleys and gorges below. An alpine wind rippled the meadow's flora. The view ahead was breathtaking. It was a moment in which to contemplate the worlds in all their grandeur and wonder at nature's ability to paint a landscape worthy of any poet. But the moment lasted all too briefly. It was shattered by the loud fluttering of some very large wings. Before they could locate the source, a voice rang out from above.

'Stone me, if it ain't effin' Captain Kylah Porter. You are a sight for sore eyes. What you see in that skinny bee next to you is a mystery to me. I've said it before and I'll say it again. If you get tired of that human ay-aitch, you are more than welcome to enjoy a little avian fun. You know I would with me leg in a bear trap.'

There was a disturbance in the grass at their feet and suddenly, in front of an astonished group of faces, a very large bird touched down. It had mottled dark plumage and a distinctive short crest atop its head, the eponymous crown. It oozed power with a broad chest, massive talons and piercing yellow eyes.

'Wotcha.' Rimsplitter cocked his head, fixing two disconcertingly predatory eyes on Matt. 'Long time nosy, as me old gran used to say.'

'Rimsplitter,' Matt acknowledged the bird. 'How are they hanging?'

'Locked and loaded and fizzin' for action as usual.' The head turned towards Kylah. 'And you look as edible as always, Captain.'

'None taken,' said Kylah with an indulgent smile.

The eagle's head swivelled a little further. 'Prof, I know. But who's the Whovian lookalike?'

'This is Asher Lodge,' Duana said. 'He is one of my special agents. He can speak to the dead.'

'Strewth,' Rimsplitter let out a raucous caw which passed as laughter. 'Wouldn't fancy havin' a conversation with me dinner. Sod that for an effin' laugh.' Finally, Rimsplitter turned towards Bobby. 'And this young lady?' Somehow the absence of sarcasm and ribaldry made the question sound even more salacious.

'This is Roberta Miracle. She also works with the DOF and is a qualified witch.'

'Don't tell me, there's an effin' troop of bee-in' flying monkeys on its way?' Rimsplitter cawed again. No one else joined in, but that didn't seem to bother the eagle in the slightest.

'What's a being flying monkey?' whispered Bobby to Matt.

Matt turned to her. 'It's a flying monkey like any other, only an illegitimate one. You need to learn to separate the "bee" from the "ing". It's an adjective, not a verb. Rimsplitter here had a profanity gag in place when he joined the programme. I suggested we keep it running. It reduces the number of people he offends by at least ten per cent.'

'Yeah, thanks for that, you cee.'

'See what?' Bobby asked.

'Not see. Cee, as in the letter after bee,' Matt explained.

Bobby frowned.

Matt shook his head. 'Remember we're talking four-letter words here.'

Bobby's frown cleared, accompanied by a pink flush in her cheeks.

'Exactly,' Matt said.

Duana walked forward to survey the landscape. 'So, how is the training progressing? Did you decide on a name for the squad?'

'Yeah. Since there's four of 'em, we wanted something catchy and upbeat.'

'Like the famous four or the fabulous four?' Matt asked.

Rimsplitter turned his head slowly before blinking once. 'These sods are goin' in as animals wot can't speak, into a place wot treats spies like somethin' growing on furry cheese. TSD. Temporary Soul Displacement. Highly dangerous. They are not goin' campin', nor sailin' a boat on an effin' lake, you total tee. It's prolly suicide and they may end up bein' famous, but most of 'em would settle for alive and incog-effin'-nito.'

'Okay, so what are you calling them?' Kylah asked.

'The eff-eff,' Rimsplitter answered.

Several faces betrayed the workings of wary minds.

'I dread to ask, but I know I'm going to have to,' Kylah said. 'The, um, FF?'

'The eff-'em-effers,' Rimsplitter obliged.

'That's not going on anyone's obituary,' Duana said firmly. 'So, you'd better make sure they all come home.'

Rimsplitter let his head fall between his shoulders. Matt recognised it as a throwback to his vulture days. Not quite a sulk, but an avian grumble, definitely.

'I'll rally the troops.'

He took off with a slow and powerful stroke of his wings.

While they waited for whatever Rimsplitter had in store, Bobby, still intrigued by her surroundings, quizzed Duana. 'Where are we exactly?'

'We are in the highlands of Pict, which shares a narrow border with Rathkoorne.' She pointed towards a range of snow-capped mountains. 'There is but one pass and it is heavily guarded on both sides. However, birds can, of course, fly over any part of the mountain with impunity. There is also a little-known access way through a cave system. This is not guarded as it is far too narrow for a man to wriggle through. The same does not apply to small animals, however. Rimsplitter has named it the back passage.'

'No surprise there, then,' Matt said.

Above them, the huge eagle continued to soar, its plaintive cry clear in the thin air. A short while later, two dark specks appeared in the sky from the direction of the mountains, growing bigger by the second.

Rimsplitter landed, followed a few moments later by a large raven and a smaller magpie.

'Thanks for coming in at short notice, lads,' Rimsplitter said.

Neither bird answered.

Rimsplitter continued with the introductions. 'Prof, you already know these two and vice effin' versa, but for the rest of you lot, this is F1.'

The raven unfurled its wings.

'And this black-and-white beauty is F4.'

The magpie chattered a greeting.

'So, anything to report, lads?' Rimsplitter asked.

Both birds shook their heads.

Rimsplitter nodded deeply. 'We've been flying recon missions for a week now with no problems, apart from bein' effin' shot at by villagers wot consider anything with wings pie-worthy. But these bleedin' Rathkoorne ay-aitches are a bunch of prize cees.'

'If I may,' Asher spoke up, 'are we to take it that, unlike you, neither of them can speak?'

'S'right.' Rimsplitter nodded. 'Non ar-effin'-ticulate. Safer that way. If they're caught and tortured, I mean.'

Asher nodded. 'But then how do they communicate their reports?'

'We have set up communications nodes. Well-hidden points where messages can be sent back.' The eagle motioned the raven forwards. 'F1, 'ere, he's a siffo.'

'Siffo?' Bobby asked.

'Sith Fand,' explained Duana. 'We have three Sith Fand in the squad, volunteers from the Special Elf Service. One avian and two ground animals.'

'That'll be F2 and F3, the porcupine and the squirrel,' Rimsplitter explained. 'Or as we like to call 'em, Marshy and Nutty.'

'And the remaining member?' Bobby asked.

'F4, here. Constabulary, with a capital cee, volunteer. F4, I call Piano 'cos he's black and white and key to the effin' squad. Piano, see?'

'Very droll,' said Asher.

'Droll? Where are you from, *Downton*-effin'-*Abbey*? Anyway, Piano is our distractions expert.'

'What does that mean exact—'

Matt tried to stop Bobby's question with a desperate shake of the head but failed.

Rimsplitter was already warming up with his reply. 'Piano carries airborne artillery and loves a curry. So wherever he drops his lunch—on average sixteen times a day, 'cos 'e's a good eater—it always gets people's attention, if you know wot I mean?'

The expression on Bobby's face told everyone that she did indeed.

'What about you?' Kylah asked. 'Are you flying reconnaissance?'

'Nah. Not an indigenous species, your crowned eagle. I'd attract too much effin' attention. I'm forward ops first and foremost. Eff off, in other words.' Crowned eagles are physically incapable of grinning, but Rimsplitter made a good fist of trying. 'So, we've got F1 and F4 in the air, and F2 and F3 on the ground deep under cover. Now it's a question of lightin' the effin' bonfire.'

'Soon,' Duana said.

'Oh good, 'cos I got things to do once this little lot is over.'

Matt tilted his head. He'd long ago learned to mistrust anything Rimsplitter showed any enthusiasm for. 'Like what?'

'Like progressin' my career as a stand-up comedian, for instance.'

'You? A stand-up?'

'Yeah, go on, laugh it up, you bee.'

'I thought that was the point.'

'Back in Uzturnsitstan, Elvis—the recidivist dentist—and the rest of my crowd think I'm effin' hilarious.'

'Really?' Matt said. 'Give us a taster, then.'

Rimsplitter took a couple of affronted steps backwards. 'See, that's the trouble with punters. Think we can turn it on just like that. But we can't, us artistes, on account of our sensibilities. Take loads of effin' prep, does comedianin'. I got shedfuls of good stuff but it ain't like flicking a bleedin' switch, you know? Oh no. I'm like a singin' sheep wot wants to be a soprano. Forever raisin' the baa.'

Bobby giggled.

Matt stopped her with a pleading look.

Rimsplitter fixed Matt with another of his predatory glares. 'Okay, okay…um, here's one you'll like. People say I have me mum's eyes and me dad's brains. It's true. They're in the fridge next to the butter.' He convulsed with spluttering laughter while everyone else watched and waited.

In silence.

It took a while, but eventually Rimsplitter realised that they were not, like him, laughing hysterically. 'Oh, come on, you cees. That's genius, that is.'

'I did not find it amusing,' Asher said.

'Course not. You ain't a carrion feeder, are you? You got to look for the nuances. This is spot-on vulture culture satire, you tart. Guaranteed to get 'em rollin' in the aisles, that one is. Oh, yes. Once I hone me skills, I'm going to give it a go at the Comedy Store, suitably transformed into human form, of course. I can just see me live at the Apollo.'

'With that material you'll be dead at the Apollo,' Matt muttered.

Rimsplitter blinked. 'Hey that's not bad, you old cee. Can I have that one?'

'Feel free.'

'Cheers. See, I got ambition. Not like Elvis. All he wants to do is get back to normal life and follow in his dad's footsteps.'

'What did he do?'

'Upholsterer. But I told Elvis he'd be no good at that. Not got the temperament. Though he'd probably get away with specialisin'. He's already pretty good at stainin' chairs.'

Kylah giggled.

Matt grabbed her arm to steady her. 'Don't encourage him.'

'But what about the Rathkoornians?' Bobby asked. 'Have you had any sightings or reports of weapons testing?'

'Rumours only. And lots of 'em. But the trouble is, no one speaks their mind. They're vicious bees, them troops of theirs. Decimate you soon as look at you. Into limbin', they are. One step out of line and it's an all-expenses one-way trip to the copper mines. Steal and you lose an arm. Dance and they'll take a leg. Laugh at the wrong thing and you'll be wearin' your tongue as a necklace. An' God forbid they catch you buffin' your banana 'cos you'll end up peein' through a spigot.'

'Sounds idyllic,' Bobby said.

'It is if you're one of the nobs. They get to do double-you-tee-eff they like, bees.'

'You have an unusual way with words,' Asher said. A sentence, like Captain Oates's suggestion that he might be 'outside for some time', that dripped with understatement.

Duana sent the eagle an encouraging nod. 'You and the FF are doing fine work, Rimsplitter.'

'So, what are the chances of you gettin' someone in to work with us?' Bobby asked.

'Slim. But Captain Porter and Agent Danmor have a plan of sorts.'

Kylah lowered her chin.

'It's my plan,' Matt admitted. 'More a loose idea than a plan, in all honesty.'

'Thank eff. Love a bit of a read, me.'

'Read?' asked Bobby.

'Oh yeah,' said Rimsplitter with a swagger. 'Bonin' up on me Chitty.'

'Chitty?'

'Chitty chitty bang bang. Rhyming slang. Very useful when you've got a profanity gaggin' order. Helps me vocabulary.'

'So read means…?'

'Read an' write. Fight. Strewth, you don't go down the pub much, do you?'

'We will keep you informed,' said Duana, putting Bobby out of her misery.

Rimsplitter turned back to the two birds. 'Right, you 'orrible lot. Eff this for a laugh. We are goin' to do some behavioural trainin'. Spot the bottle top for you, F4.'

The magpie chattered excitedly.

'And some practise cawin' for you, F1. Get to it, I'll be there in a mo.' Rimsplitter turned back to Duana. 'Nice to see you, Prof. And you lot better keep an eye out for me. I'll be in my own sitcom before you can say fronds.'

'Fronds?' Bobby turned to Matt as the eagle took off.

'He means *Friends*.'

'That's quite funny,' Asher said.

'Only if it was a deliberate mistake,' Kylah said. 'Unfortunately, the chances are it wasn't.'

'I am still a little confused as to why he chose to call this tunnel the back passage,' Asher said. 'Surely the lower passage would have been more apposite.'

Duana sighed. 'He has called it the back passage because he wanted to be able to send the porcupine through by shouting into the tunnel. Some kind of ritual I was lucky enough to be present at. The words, if I remember them rightly, were, "Oy, you bees. Here is something prickly through your back passage from me and the rest of the effin' world."'

No one spoke.
Matt simply shook his head.

CHAPTER FIVE

MANCHESTER, ENGLAND, THE HUMAN WORLD

The streets around Deansgate were damp from rain. In Manchester, this was not an unusual state of affairs. Not even in July. If you lived there long enough, the absence of rain for more than a week was considered drought conditions. If wealth was measured in H2O, Mancunians would all be millionaires. And then there was that quote about the only thing Manchester needed was a beach because they certainly had enough water to fill a sea.

Trevor Reeves was, therefore, no stranger to the rain. Even so, tonight's downpour meant that a scooter was a less-than-ideal mode of transport. As a consequence, his legs were soaked from the dirty spray bouncing up from the street and the run-off from his anorak onto his knees and trousers. Despite the deluge, he'd not bothered to change his shoes and they were now sodden and ruined.

But ruined implied an expectation that they might be required at some future date.

Inside his helmet, he allowed himself the thinnest of smiles.

He braked at some lights and straddled the scooter. The city was 3.20 am quiet and there was only one vehicle, a taxi, behind him. The lights changed and he let the taxi go by, catching a glimpse of passengers in the back seat. A young couple, their faces animated. Reeves wondered fleetingly if they had jobs to go to in a few hours' time. Kids these days seemed to think nothing of getting home at some ungodly hour and then going to work with hardly any sleep. He had no idea how they did it, but suspected that it involved some sort of chemical help. Years as a probation officer had fostered a healthy suspicion in Reeves that people, in general, would try and get away with anything so long as no one found out. Or even if they did, so long as you could deny it, and keep on denying it, until the handcuffs were on and the cell door slammed shut.

He even envied the kids their energy. But it was an ephemeral thought. He let it go because, in the grand scheme of things, or even the not-so-grand scheme of things, it didn't matter a jot. And Reeves' current scheme fell squarely within the not-so-grand bracket.

By rights, Reeves—the name he'd been known by since schooldays and one he much preferred to Trev or Trevor—should have been falling down drunk, having spent the evening in a bar sipping nutty IPA. But his dark and roiling thoughts tumbling over and over seemed to negate the alcohol and he'd failed to numb his misery. The Kennel Bar was licensed until 4 am and he'd toyed with staying to the end, determinedly drinking with a view to getting thoroughly bladdered on the way to falling-over oblivion. But as he sat alone at a corner table, the beer had begun to taste sour and finally, much earlier than he'd planned, he visited the ammoniacal loo and hurled both abuse and stomach contents into the bowl. Appalled by his inability to even get drunk without messing it up, he paid the tab and left.

Wretched was a word that Reeves sometimes read in books but never, in his recollection, used in conversation. Yet it was the word that his brain plucked from his vocabulary and lit up in neon inside his head as he left the bar. Wretched summed up exactly how he felt, what his life had become, what was stamped on the tin of his continued existence.

He was walking, wretchedly, back to where he'd left the scooter near the pub when the idea came to him.

Or rather, if he was being honest, crawled out of the cage he kept it in and snarled at him.

Now he was on his way to the big multistorey attached to the Qibble hotel. Everyone in the city knew the car park because it was so big. It had even won an architectural prize for its design.

A multistorey car park winning awards? That was wrong on so many levels. He wanted to smile at that very old joke but he didn't. Couldn't. Funny was off the agenda. Reeves didn't give a hoot about the aesthetics, anyway. All he cared about was that this multistorey was the tallest in the city.

The empty road gleamed under the harsh streetlights. Though he had not achieved the state of bladderedness he'd been aiming for, he knew he was way over the limit. If he was stopped by the police, he'd be in deep shoeshine.

He smiled again. Mirthless and wry as a bone. As if he cared. Not even half a jot. But being arrested would be a damned inconvenience now that he was here. Now that he had finally made up his wretched mind.

He gunned the scooter's tinny 50cc engine and rode the empty streets. The entrance he was aiming for was on Barra-clough Lane and he made it in three minutes, saw no blue lights, heard no sirens. Luck, it seemed, was on his side. About bloody time, too, since it had avoided him like the black plague for the last forty-odd years.

He had to cross the carriageway to gain entry to the car park. He pulled across to the middle, balancing the scooter with one foot on the road. A woman wearing size twelve rubber boots with no laces and more coats than the Forth bridge was pushing a supermarket trolley along the pavement right in front of the car park entrance. The trolley's wheels squeaked as it trundled by. Despite the situation, despite

Reeves' desire to finally get on with…things, he waited, politely and patiently, for her to cross.

Whatever was in the trolley remained thankfully invisible, mostly contained in untied black plastic refuse bags. The woman, her face framed by a scarf tied around her head, paused in the very centre of the car park entrance and looked at Reeves. It was difficult to see her expression through his rain-spattered visor, but the woman's inscrutable face was the colour of an un-scrubbed potato, complete with tiny dark eyes and a wispy goatee of grey hairs growing out from a crop of warts on her chin. All in all, she bore a stark resemblance to a Maris Piper gone to seed.

But there was nothing wrong with her scratchy Lancastrian cackle, nor Reeves' hearing.

'Take what's offered, lad. Take what's offered.'

She turned back to the trolley and continued with her shambling progress, leaving Reeves to contemplate her words.

He did so for five frowning seconds, considered coming back with, 'That punchline needs a bit of work,' but then reality kicked in, and out came the standard, non-confrontational response to any mad street person's philosophising. 'Mind how you go, now.'

Reeves cringed. Damn those sensibilities. This was no time for sensibilities, but he was a slave to an upbringing that had drummed into him politeness and an awareness that a fall from grace was only a couple of good-idea-at-the-time decisions and a court case away for the best of us.

And he, of all people, should know that.

When the woman reached the central area between entrance and exit, where the cubicle became home for a bored attendant between the hours of 7 am and 7 pm, Reeves gunned the engine and buzzed through a narrow gap into the cavernous lower floor, conscious of the woman's gaze on his back. He reached the ramp and wound upwards. Overnight rates were not cheap in this car park and the floors were half empty, becoming emptier the higher he navigated. He should, by rights, have picked up a ticket on the way in and CCTV would undoubtedly have captured his rash act. He could expect a call from someone in authority.

Sod them and that.

He circled up the ramp to the tenth floor.

The top floor.

The minute he emerged into the open air, the rain recommenced its damp assault with a sodden vengeance.

CHAPTER SIX

He parked near the door leading to the lifts and stairs. A concrete overhang provided some protection from the rain. It was as he stood there taking off his helmet that his phone rang.

'You've got to be kidding,' Reeves said to the night.

The phone was in an inside pocket of his jacket under the sopping anorak. With wet fingers he unzipped and fished the phone out, half hoping that the ringing would cease. But this caller was persistent. When he finally got the phone free from his clothing, he read the caller's name and recognition made his insides shrivel.

Demelza.

His eyes went up to the black sky. He took two deep breaths. Really? Now of all times?

He needed this about as much as a coffee enema.

Reeves pressed the green button. 'Hello?'

'You took your time.' There it was. In that one harsh, carping statement. Demelza Galanis, dark of eye and darker of nature.

'It's half-past three in the morning,' Reeves hissed.

'So?'

'Some people might consider this an unreasonable time to phone.'

'I couldn't sleep.'

That was Demelza logic in a nutshell. Perfectly acceptable in her world view to disturb someone else because she was awake. A world where other people were actors in a play in which Demelza wrote, directed and starred.

'What do you want, Demelza?'

'To hear your voice and to tell you that you will never wake up next to me ever again.'

'It's been three months, Demelza.'

'Have you signed all the papers?'

'Yes, you know I have.'

'Good. But do you miss me, Trevor?'

His mother, his GP's receptionist and Demelza were the only people who ever called him Trevor. His mother because she had given him the name, the receptionist because of a touchy-feely faux friendliness that the practice holistically encouraged—even for people with an eye infection—and Demelza because she could. And because secretly she knew it irritated him. Secretly irritating was Demelza's specialist subject.

Did he miss her?

On one level, yes, he did. She was a second-generation Greek immigrant with dark Mediterranean eyes and olive skin. She turned heads. The trouble was she enjoyed turning them so much they often twisted right off. He sometimes wondered if she could turn her own all the way around through 360 as a party trick.

'No, not anymore.'

'I don't believe you. James comes home early from work every day to make love to me.'

'Good for him.'

'He says you're losing it.'

'Yeah, well, he's wrong. I am not losing it. He's way behind the curve. I lost it a long time ago.'

There was a pause. Reeves imagined her smiling. 'Trevor, you sound sad.'

'Do I? I wonder why? Maybe because my wife has swanned off with a toy boy half her age, chucked me out of my own house and keeps ringing me in the middle of the night to hear my voice. Forgive me for not doing cartwheels.'

'You know you didn't love me enough. There was something inside you that you couldn't let out. What was that, Trevor? What were you hiding from me?'

'I am not doing this now, Demelza. In fact, I'm not doing this ever again.'

Demelza laughed. It was deep and confident, full of the absolute knowledge that he was lying. Because even if he had no intention of talking to her at half-past three in the morning ever again, she clearly did.

'What is that I hear? Are you nearing a river?'

'Sort of. It's called the Manchester rain.'

'What are you doing outside on a night like this?'

'Go back to bed, Demelza.'

'I will. James is waiting for me there.'

'Good for him. I hope he's got some anti-venom by the bedside.'

'So funny, Trevor. Did I tell you my lawyer says that you still have to pay the mortgage on the house?'

'Yes, you did. But only if I'm alive to pay it, right?'

'What do you mean by that, Trevor? Surely not what I think you mean?' Her words petered out, silky and disingenuous. Reeves listened for any hint in the tone for genuine concern but what he heard was nothing but teasing and taunt. He could hear her breathing. Waiting. Eventually she said, 'Of course, the insurance will pay out if anything happens, right?'

'It will. Or rather, it would if I'd kept up the payments.'

He heard a rapid rustling. Sheets being thrown off, probably. 'Don't you dare!'

Reeves ended the call. His pulse was racing. Demelza could press all his buttons, including the big red one that said *FIRE*. As his wife of ten years, she had done exactly that on a depressingly regular basis. His phone rang again. He switched it off, placed it and his helmet on the floor, and walked across the length of the car park to the south side. The top floor of the multistorey was surrounded by a high and spiky fence, angled sharply inward around the entire perimeter. However, Reeves had noticed some workmen earlier cleaning the massive sign that read *NCP PARKING*. He knew precisely where they stored the ladder.

Perhaps because he was now higher off the streets and more exposed, or perhaps because the gods thought it an amusing wheeze, the wind picked up and began to pelt the rain into Reeves' face with a vicious needle-prick intensity. He dared, for one moment, to consider if this was an omen. Some kind of meteorological resistance to his plans. But then that sort of thinking implied that he believed in the supernatural. That the gods, or fate, or anyone or anything actually gave a tinker's cuss about what happened to him.

The thought was depressingly ludicrous. No one and nothing did.

Reeves reached the barrier. A metal ladder sat strapped to some brackets under a metal bar that ran at bumper level around the inside of the perimeter wall, attached by a couple of sprung clamps. Reeves put on one of his sodden scooter gloves and sprung the clamps open. He lifted out the ladder and leant it against the topmost strut of the tall fence at a point where a small platform jutted out. The top of the ladder fitted snugly into two indentations.

Made for the job. Well, perhaps not exactly this job.

Reeves took off his gloves and anorak and jacket, and stuffed them under the metal bar. Then, with the rain hammering against his shirt and making it cling to his flesh, he began to climb. Above the concrete parapet, the gusts were stronger, threatening to blow him back on to the car park floor. He bent into it, stepped over the topmost strut of the safety barrier and onto the small metal tread plate. Gingerly, balancing against the buffeting wind, he stood like a diver contemplating his final round attempt at the podium finish.

But there was no gold medal at the end of this tumble. All that awaited Reeves was a thud, an instant of pain and then darkness.

He looked down. Double yellow lines marked the road edge of a narrow access lane to the Qibble hotel's goods entrance. There were no cars parked. Nothing to impede his contact with the rock-hard road. He knew he was trembling. That it had come to this was something he had contemplated a thousand times already in the Kennel Bar, on the ride over, even as he spiralled up the ramp of the multistorey.

When did it all go so sour and why? Too many reasons to list them all now. Easy to blame just one thing or one person as the tipping point.

Screw you, Demelza.

But there wasn't just one thing. Or one person. Was there?

A name came to him, then. A name from twenty-plus years ago. And if there was a name he wanted to carry with him into oblivion, it was this one.

Rhiannon; of Celtic origin. A queen. A goddess. A famous and iconic pop song. A girl's name.

He hadn't thought of her in a while. Tried not to. Some things are too painful to recall. But pain was what he sought now. Pain and then release. So, thinking of her beautiful infectious smile, her laugh, her voice, was suddenly allowed.

He looked down. The road was still clear. The night black. The wind and rain slapped against his cheek as if in an attempt to wake him from this dark reverie. But this was an unending nightmare and he did not want to be woken.

'Rhiannon.'

He whispered her name, squeezed his eyes shut and saw her. Twenty years old, posing on the rocks of a beach with the wild sea behind her. Smiling. Wanting him to take her picture.

'Rhiannon,' he breathed, and dived off the metal platform.

He saw the bag lady emerge from the corner of the lane as he tilted forward. He screamed a warning. Screamed for her to 'LOOK OUT!' as he sped towards a slick, black, solid wall of death.

'LOOK O—'

He expected pain, noise perhaps, a crack of skull, oblivion. What he didn't expect was that everything would suddenly turn blue.

CHAPTER SEVEN

BLUE ROOM, THE FAE WORLD

BLUE WALLS, blue ceiling, blue floor.

Reeves blinked.

There was no pain, and his world was definitely…blue. An unremitting blueness broken only by the wooden door at the far end. But then he zeroed in on the 'no pain' bit and there followed an internal metaphysical reality check about how ridiculous he was being, since the likelihood of feeling pain was on the low-to-non-existent scale once you were dead.

But the blue room was something else. Nowhere in his reading had he ever come across a blue room playing any part in the transition across the River Styx. Unless this was a deluxe cabin.

But worse than the blue was the sensation that the blanket over him felt disconcertingly real, as did the canvas beneath him, and the floor he could brush his fingers against.

'How are you feeling?'

Reeves jolted up and pivoted in one movement, causing him to lose much of the blanket in the process. He grabbed desperately at the last few inches of material because he suddenly realised that beneath it, he was birthday-suit naked. Behind and slightly to his left sat two people on steel and leather chairs. Both wore dark suits and white shirts and both had coffee cups on the floor in front of them.

'Am I dead?' Reeves asked.

'Technically, no,' replied the man who had asked after his wellbeing in the first place.

'Technically? What the hell does that mean?'

'It means it's your lucky day.'

The woman nudged the man in a gentle warning sort of way.

Confusion threatening to overwhelm him, Reeves floundered for a toehold to avoid plummeting headlong over the white cliffs of madness, and managed to come up with, 'Why am I naked?'

The man shrugged. 'Because you were wet through and we didn't want you to catch your d—'

This time, the woman threw the man a full-blown glare. The sort that clearly meant business. He let the sentence he'd begun drift in the wind, as the metaphorical tumbleweeds rolled by.

'You were going to say death of cold, weren't you?' Reeves said, unable to prevent the challenge in his tone.

The woman stood up and smoothed down her jacket. Reeves put her at about thirty, trim, not tall, dark haired and with piercing, gold-flecked eyes. She stepped forward. 'The funny man next to me is my partner, Matt Danmor. I am Captain Kylah Porter.' She reached forward and held out her hand.

Reeves eyed it suspiciously, scrunched the blanket a little tighter around his throat and left the hand where it was. 'Captain? Am I in some sort of military unit?'

Kylah nodded. 'In a way, yes.' She withdrew her hand. 'I realise that all this must come as a bit of a shock to you.'

'Bit of a shock?' Reeves let his face assume a look of unbridled incredulity.

Captain Porter walked around to the end of the bed. 'It's a lot to take in, I know.'

'Is this what happens to everyone who jumps off a roof?' Reeves asked, his voice cracking.

Danmor joined Porter. He was slightly taller than the woman, trim but not skinny. 'No.'

'Then why me?'

'That's where it starts to get…complicated,' Danmor said.

Reeves' pulse accelerated. He looked around the room afresh. Why was it all so blue? And there were no electricity plugs on the walls. 'Look, where exactly am I? And, more to the point, why am I not dead? Technically or otherwise?'

Danmor pursued his lips, as if to imply that Reeves' question indicated a misplaced desire to not so much glance in the mouth of a gift horse as wear magnifiers and examine all its fillings. 'You sound disappointed,' he said, earning a WTF look from Kylah to which he responded with a silent, 'What?'

'Of course I'm bloody disappointed,' Reeves said slowly and deliberately. He clenched his fingers tighter on the blanket to stop them from trembling.

'Well, obviously, someone in your state of mind might find all this a little…confusing.'

'Thanks,' said Reeves.

'But it isn't quite as straightforward as being dead or…not dead.'

'I really do not understand any of this.'

'No,' Danmor said with a sigh. 'So, let's go through it one step at a time. You remember driving up to the top floor of the car park?'

'Of course I do.'

'And you remember climbing up the maintenance ladder?'

'Yes,' Reeves said, stretching the vowel out with exaggerated patience.

'You remember looking up into the night sky, mouthing a word, a name of some kind I think—'

'That's none of your bloody business,' snapped Reeves through gritted teeth.

'True. So, then you jumped in the hope that the fall would end everything.'

'Yes.'

'Well, what if I told you that it didn't end everything.'

Reeves stared back, shaking his head as if the words he was hearing were in some strange, incomprehensible language.

'When you jumped, did you notice Miss Fenella Whitney of no fixed abode entering the access lane from the right the second you became airborne?' Porter asked.

Reeves squeezed his eyes shut. 'The bag lady. Yes, I remember.'

'Exactly. You shouted a warning, but she doesn't hear so well.'

Reeves was shaking his head.

'Perhaps it would be easier if we showed you. And please, call me Kylah, and this is Matt.'

Reeves didn't respond. He didn't know these people and didn't trust them. He wasn't going to play their little game. Besides, everyone called him Reeves and they must know that, since they'd just dragged him from the blacktop of death.

'The head of the bed tilts forward. A bit like a sun lounger. It might make you more comfortable,' Kylah said.

Reeves fiddled with the mechanism and sat up. Matt returned with an iPad. He pressed the screen and held it forward for Reeves to look. 'The magic of CCTV,' he said by way of explanation.

Reeves' insides swooped. There it was in grainy black and white. Two views. One of the access lane and one of a man walking across an empty car park roof. He barely recognised himself. His short dark hair, normally flecked with strands of grey, was a sopping black cap on his head. The pale face murky with stubble glanced up at the camera. Reeves looked at his own haunted expression. Demelza had called him a bit of rough. Where she had once seen rugged attraction, Reeves now saw only gaunt despair. He'd lost none of the athleticism that had marked his early youth; regular swimming and punishing circuit training had seen to that. But Reeves barely recognised the agitated gait of the man walking towards the edge of that roof. He watched as he stood on top of the multistorey, rain pelting down around him. There was no sound and the silence somehow made it even worse. The split screen showed Miss Fenella Whitney entering just as he, Reeves, stepped off the tread plate. He fell like a stone, arms flailing, or was he gesticulating? Difficult to say in the three seconds it took for him to hit the ground. Or rather, hit the ground after flattening Miss Whitney.

Reeves hands flew to his face, palms over his eyes. 'Oh, please, no. Don't tell me that I—'

'You did,' Matt said. 'Or rather, you could have.'

'What do you mean?' Reeves said, very slowly.

'What you saw was…an extrapolation,' Kylah said carefully.

'You mean, I didn't hit her?'

'Obviously not, otherwise you would not be lying here and Miss Fenella Whitney would not be sitting under an archway on the Manchester ship canal, eating a four-day-over-the-sell-by-date cheese sandwich as we speak.'

'So, I missed her?'

'In a way,' Kylah said.

Reeves stared at the screen, mercifully frozen on a shot that showed two immobile bundles on the access road. 'In a way? What the hell does that mean?'

'Krudian bubble,' said Matt.

'What?' The word exploded from Reeves' quivering mouth.

'What Matt here is trying, and failing, to explain is that what you have just seen has happened in a car park in a Manchester somewhere. But not in every Manchester and possibly not in any Manchester.'

'Wonderful.' Reeves stared at her in open-mouthed bewilderment. 'Well, that's cleared everything up.'

'Okay,' Matt said. 'Let me try again. Imagine that what you've seen is what actually happened, but imagine we've got real-time temporal CGI—though we prefer to call it HTMHB—'

'How Things Might Have Been,' explained Kylah quickly.

'—which allows us to wind the tape back and, instead of letting you fall, pluck you from the air halfway down.'

Reeves frowned. 'How can that be possible?'

'Magoose,' said Matt, grinning.

'You're a goose?' Reeves said.

'No, Magoose. Krudian physicist. Genius. Recently invented Kwantum with a K.'

'Kwantum with a K?' Reeves repeated weakly. He could feel the sweat on his brow.

'Krudian Wave and Neospatial Teleportation via Unified Matrix.'

'Of course,' Reeves said with an airy jollity bordering on hysteria. He was beginning to wonder if, in fact, he hadn't died but was in some sort of coma and experiencing the most bizarre of nightmares.

'Anyway, Magoose has been experimenting with applications of Kwantum and has come up with the Krudian bubble, where he can grab a second of time and freeze it. We froze you 1.5 seconds into your fall. We had some people come up with proper CGI to see what would happen if you went on falling—that's what you see on the tape.'

'Okay, you saved me from death, why?'

'Well, saved you from death is an arguable point,' Kylah said. 'We have some very good links with forensics who've examined the speed and trajectory of your fall. And we also have some even better links with seers who can predict your future. The upshot is that you hit Miss Whitney headfirst, colliding with her shoulder. She is thrown backwards, hits her head on the road and is killed instantly.'

Reeves whimpered.

'You, on the other hand, get lucky.' Matt grinned. 'You collide with the trolley, snapping your neck, but paradoxically end up getting cushioned by several bags full of newspapers, magazines and filthy clothes. You suffer a C7 fracture and are rendered paralysed. You survive and spend the remaining ten years of your life at a rehab facility in Milton Keynes as a tetraplegic. You are also successfully prosecuted for manslaughter. So, strictly speaking, you don't die physically, but metaphorically, it could be argued that your life ends there and then.'

Reeves blinked and then whispered. 'Tetraplegic? How do you know that? How can you possibly know that?'

'Oh, we know lots of things about you.'

Kylah cleared her throat. 'I suggest we give you some time to absorb all of this. There's some bottled water. Have a drink and settle yourself and we can continue this in a few minutes?' She smiled. It looked a little forced. 'Mr Danmor, why don't you and I give Mr Reeves a few moments to gather his thoughts.'

'Sure. Great. Just give us a shout if there's anything you need.'

Reeves, shivering and naked under his blanket, watched them exit through a different door behind where he was lying. The door clicked shut and he heard a key turning in a lock. He looked down at the iPad and pressed the Replay button.

CHAPTER EIGHT

'Well, that went well,' Matt said.

'Really?' said Kylah. 'He's in shock. I'm wondering if he's taken any of it in.'

'Of course he has. Just needs a bit more time and explanation.'

'Like with the Krudian bubble, you mean?'

'Exactly.'

In the beat that followed, Kylah pressed her lips together and pierced Matt with one of her looks. 'Don't you think you ought to be a little less gung-ho? A little more…serious? I mean, he must be in a fairly fragile psychological state. He has just tried to take his own life.'

'Nah. He's a man that appreciates gallows humour. He's spent his working life around thieves and yobs, for crying out loud.'

She looked unconvinced, but Matt was adamant. 'Look upon me as the jolly facilitator. You'll both thank me for it in the long run.'

Kylah sighed. She spoke fluent sigh. Amazing how a deft expulsion of air could carry so much meaning. Each one came with a line of unspoken words attached that appeared in Matt's head as if in a speech bubble. Some were familiar like, *You're an idiot,* or, *Oh no, not the sausage joke again,* or *That drawer isn't going to tidy itself now is it.* But this one simply said: *I hope you're right. Because if you aren't, I am going to put your ear in a blender.*

Yet when she spoke, it was in a more conciliatory tone. Such was the chemistry of relationships. 'You still think he's the right man for this?'

Matt nodded. A straightforward response, but there was a lot to unpack from it. Working together in the DOF with the…being he was also living with, had proved challenging. Largely because Kylah Porter was a professional, a planner, someone who liked to weigh up the odds. And Matt, well, he was more of a pantser. It had caused enough conflict for Kylah to have wondered if having Matt in the field was a good idea because, when you channelled luck as a weapon, there was always the possibility of a 'unlucky' day. But he had proven himself more than once. And he had convinced her that this time, they simply had no choice.

But, of course, she had reservations.

'Yes, I am sure he's the right man. You've read the file.'

'I know, but—'

Matt picked up a manilla folder with a DOF stamp and read aloud. 'Trevor Cabot Reeves, born **20 February, 1982**. Only child, parents divorced when he was eleven. Father remarried, deceased. Mother divorced, deceased. Talented rugby player. Schools international. University-educated at York. No convictions. Engaged at twenty-one to childhood sweetheart. Hospitalised with two broken legs after jumping off a Welsh sea wall in an attempt at rescuing her after she was swept out sea. Girlfriend's body never recovered. Injuries ended rugby career. Dropped out of university and joined the police force. Commended twice. Left after clashing with authorities over stop and search policies. Joined the probation service. Well-liked by clients who consider him tough but fair and not someone to be messed with. Issues with management that have led to warnings. Two suspensions from work. One for six weeks after an accusation of assault. Reeves apparently found one of his clients, a girl, with a bruised eye. Exonerated after the accuser, the girl's stepfather, withdrew charges and left the country. However, this and other incidents have resulted in little or no prospect of promotion. Married to Demelza Galanis when they were both thirty-three. No children. Separated from wife seven months ago after discovering her having affair with younger colleague who had just been promoted over him. Suspended from work after "confrontation" with said colleague during office party. Hence the latest suspension. I tell you: this guy has seen it all.'

Kylah tutted. 'Sounds like he's the cause of most of it. And you have no doubts?'

'No doubts whatsoever. He's forfeited his soul, temporarily, of course. That'll make him completely undetectable in Rathkoorne. Reminds me of an older me. Plus, the long tail descendancy scan indicates he had some interesting ancestors.'

'That's not always an advantage,' Kylah observed.

'It can't do any harm that he has a touch of wonderworking blood.'

'Pretty dilute by now.'

'Just like me, then.'

Kylah thought about that and decided not to respond. She knew when she was being baited. She also knew that Bobby Miracle had told her in no uncertain terms that she needed to begin to trust Matt in the job. 'Then I suggest we go back in and stop pussyfooting around. Get right down to it.'

Matt grinned. 'I love it when you talk—'

'Stop it.'

———

REEVES DRANK the water and it had tasted good, and now he sat on the edge of the bed, mulling over what Danmor and Porter had told him. He concluded that there were three main possibilities that explained his predicament, though none of them fell into the realms of normality. In fact, they were all as far from normality as could be. The word "supernatural" oozed up through his cloudy thought processes and he cringed. He'd read about this sort of thing before and dismissed it all as tosh. The trouble being that tosh isn't that far removed from pish, and as a certain Scottish James Bond knew only too well, you ignore pish at your peril because before you know it, you're shittin' on the dock of the bay with a very nasty shtain front and back.

The first idea was that he was dead or dying and that this whole thing was some kind of pre-oblivion, out-of-body experience. Just a dream. A remarkably real and extremely weird dream, but a dream, nonetheless. And instead of waking up, it would all go very dark, very soon.

The second idea was that he was not dead but in a coma, and his brain was trying to rationalise his situation. In that scenario, the unpalatable possibility he had hit Miss Whitney on the way down was true. The tetraplegia was real, and his overloaded mind had concocted this whole elaborate shebang as way of dealing with that awfulness.

The third and most unlikely idea was that Porter and Danmor were real and they really had freeze dried him in a Krudian bubble. And if this was somehow his reality, then there was a chance he might be able to get away.

There was a knock on the door and it opened to reveal Matt Danmor, eyebrows raised.

'Decent?' he asked.

Reeves didn't answer that. As questions went, it was loaded with a whole refuse truck full of baggage that was almost begging for a smart answer. But he still felt disinclined to buy into their little games. Matt entered with Kylah in tow. It was she who now took the lead, pulling up the chair to sit.

'Trevor,' she began.

'It's Reeves.'

'Okay, Reeves. I don't think we've explained your situation very well, so let me start again. We've told you who we are, but not what we are.'

Reeves sat with his forearms on his knees, fingers loosely intertwined.

'We work for something called the DOF.'

'That's Department of Fimmigration, with an F,' added Matt.

'I can think of a word beginning with F,' said Reeves.

'Good one.' Matt grinned. 'Nice to see you've recovered some of your sense of humour.'

Reeves' expression remained flinty.

'We are a supernatural border agency,' Kylah went on. 'We monitor transdimensional flow.'

'Like what flows in the sewers?' Reeves asked.

Matt grinned again and said to Kylah, 'I'm beginning to like him.'

'That's what the Fimmigration bit means,' Kylah said. 'F for fae immigration.'

'Alright,' said Reeves. 'Let's say I accept that, preposterous as it is. What has it got to do with me?'

Kylah nodded. 'Good question, given what we've already gleaned about your circumstances. If you'll let me elaborate for a moment.'

'Oh, I'm all ears.'

'Imagine a place where humans don't exist. Imagine a world where *Homo sapiens* were replaced by *Homo elementus*— the fae—and a whole pick and mix of other beings as in anything and everything the Brothers Grimm could imagine to the power ten. That's where I'm from. That's the other side of the border. But, like all places where beings co-exist, there are tensions within and between countries, or in our case, city states. There is one spot in particular that has proven to be exceptionally troublesome. It has developed into an elitist oligarchy ruled by a powerful aristocracy. It maintains an iron-clad, rigid state control over its people, who have remained in industrial and economic isolation for decades. The power base of this state is the right to bear wands—'

'Whoa, wait a minute.' Reeves frowned. 'Did you just say wands?'

'She did. I know, wands, right? Takes a bit of getting used to, but go with it for the moment,' Matt said.

Kylah continued, 'This means that the ruling class has almost total power over the populace. It also means that, as a country, it brooks no interference from the outside. If change is to occur, it has to occur from within. But I can tell you there is a significant groundswell of concern over non-existent fae rights from everyone else in the fae world.'

Reeves stood up. 'Mind if I stretch my legs?'

'Feel free,' Matt said.

Reeves, with a blanket wrapped around him like a weird toga, started to pace. It helped him marshal his thoughts, which were threatening to run scream-leaping over the nearest cliff. After half a dozen lengths of the room, he pivoted towards Kylah. 'What exactly have fae rights got to do with me?'

'Ah, right. Quite apart from the internal issues, this particular city state has little or no rule of law. It appears that they have developed a weapon that allows them to inflict damage on this world at will. There is another video we could show you.'

Matt leaned forward and picked up the iPad, flicked his fingers over the screen and handed it back. This time the video showed a mountain road being engulfed in a rockslide.

'This looks like a natural disaster,' Reeves said, inching himself towards the end of the bed.

'Keep watching. We've slowed it down the second time.'

Reeves watched the scene replayed in slow motion. The trigger for the slide appeared to be a fireball on the end of a jet of purple light that emerged from below and struck the base of the stone cliff. The ball itself was red.

'That, Reeves, is not a natural phenomenon. It is not ball lightning, nor is it a warhead. It is what is commonly known as a destructor curse. Banned in most city states, except one.'

'That's worrying, then,' Reeves said, eyes on the door.

'Very worrying,' agreed Kylah. 'Small pockets of resistance have sprung up in this city state and there is one who we think has the potential to lead a revolt. This is where you come in. We have a proposition—'

Reeves lunged at the handle, depressed it and pulled.

Outside there was nothing but brick wall.

'Sorry, mate,' Matt said. 'We assumed you'd try.'

Reeves closed the door slowly and turned. 'That's a brick wall.'

'I know,' said Kylah with a grimace.

Matt joined in with one of those smiles that accompanied a brief nod of the head and implied complete and utter sympathy.

Reeves went back to the bed and sat. 'Okay. I've listened. I don't pretend to understand. Although the *Homo elementus* thing is extremely far-fetched, I am politically savvy enough to realise that lunatic states can and do exist. God knows we have some peaches I could name right off the bat. But I still have no bloody idea what any of this has to do with me.'

Kylah cleared her throat. 'Though we cannot be seen to be interfering directly for diplomatic reasons and because the rulers of this state have threatened all-out war if we do, we feel obliged to act. Via a more subtle approach. We have something very important that the resistance, specifically this one person, needs to facilitate the struggle. We need someone who is not allied in any way to any other faction in our world, ethnic or political, to deliver this item. The random attacks on your world and mine—that of the fae—are escalating, and we have been tasked with sourcing a viable solution.'

'And that's me, is it?' Reeves asked. 'The viable solution?'

Kylah nodded. 'We were hoping you might consider the job.'

Reeves stared at them. They were serious. At least five whole seconds crawled by before a laugh burst from his throat. 'You are kidding, right? Why on earth would I want to do that?'

'Krudian bubble,' said Matt. 'You are officially in limbo at the moment. That position remains frozen, awaiting events.'

'I just tried to end it all,' Reeves said by way of appeal.

'Exactly. And far be it from me to sound critical, but you cocked up big time. Should you choose not to accept your mission,' Matt segued into a dramatic theme tune, 'da, da, da-da, da, da, da-da.' He smiled and turned to Kylah. 'See what I did there?'

She rolled her eyes and thinned her lips.

'Should you choose not to accept it,' Matt continued, 'we can send you back to the bubble and forget any of this ever happened. But be warned, I think it's only fair you know that the outcome is not going to be what you'd hoped for.'

'Tetraplegia, you said?'

'And a very unpleasant court case attracting global media attention to boot. And you know how circumspect and respectful the media can be,' Kylah nodded.

Matt shrugged. 'Da, da, da-da, da, da, da-da. If, on the other hand, you choose to accept your mission…' He beamed. 'I just love saying that—and if you succeed, we will arrange for Miss Whitney to be delayed by a second or two in her passage across the access road. You will then miss her and succeed both in your attempt at ending your life and curing Miss Whitney of a severe bout of constipation.'

Reeves' eyes dropped to his shoes.

Matt added an encouraging tone to his final sentence. 'And, as an added bonus, the place we'll be sending you to is full of curse-happy Henrys who will strike you down as soon as look at you, and so your chance of getting wand terminated is extremely high anyway.'

Reeves looked up. He was a man whose reproductive organs were in a vice, who'd sold his right to be aggrieved by stepping off a tread plate on top of a prize-winning multistorey car park. 'If I say yes, am I going in armed?'

'No,' said Kylah. Rather too quickly for Reeves' liking. 'Other than with your wits.'

'Am I going to be one of the ruling class?'

'Definitely not.' Matt shook his head.

'Working with anyone?'

'No. Oh, except for the fact that we do have the odd mole—'

Reeves nodded.

'—or rather magpie, squirrel, raven and porcupine. Oh, and a crowned eagle.'

Reeves waited for the titter. It didn't come.

'Easier to hide as animals,' Kylah explained. 'Not so

useful when it comes to writing up reports, though. On the ground, intelligence is limited.'

Reeves nodded. Still no titter. 'Doesn't look like I have much choice, do I?'

'We can't force you to do anything. And, of course, should anything happen to you and you are captured, tortured and spill the beans—'

'I'll deny all knowledge.'

'No need, since we will render you partially amnesic for this little episode—for your own protection. If you do start to remember or are coerced or hexed into remembering, we'll insert a PD charm so that any mention of the DOF under duress will result in complete nonsense emerging from your mouth.'

Reeves frowned. 'PD?'

'Political debate. Some of our older spell-weavers have a warped sense of humour.'

Reeves took a deep breath. 'Let me get this straight. If I want to die, I accept. If I want to live, I decline but end up as a sentient mannequin. Pretty crap choice, isn't it?'

'But it is your choice.'

Reeves thought. After a few seconds, he said, 'Seems like the quickest way to finish the job is to accept, though I'll not pretend to be happy about it.'

'Great stuff,' said Matt. 'And we do have a charm for happy, if you want it?'

'Forget it. Not in my repertoire.' Reeves refused to recip-rocate the enthusiasm. 'You know, some might consider this blackmail, if not coercion.'

'Or, if you were Miss Whitney or the police, you might consider it crime prevention.'

Reeves inclined his head in grudging agreement. 'Okay, I'll do it. What happens now?'

Matt retrieved a small wooden chest from under the chair and opened the lid. 'Now we get down to business.'

CHAPTER NINE

Reeves wasn't sure what to think and therefore decided, for the moment, that it was best not to. He sat and watched Matt remove items from the wooden box like a conjurer at a children's party. All that was missing was jelly and blancmange.

'Firstly, in a nod towards modern wonderworking, we got the backroom boys to combine the PD hex together with a linguistics spell that'll make you fluent in Rathkoorne into one easy-to-swallow pill. Take with plenty of fluids.' Matt handed over a small yellow capsule and an unopened bottle of water.

Reeves stared at the little yellow oval in his palm. 'What's it like?'

'The language of Rathkoorne.'

'Rathkoorne?'

'Exactly. If we could relate it to something recognisable, it might be a combination of Croatian, Japanese and ancient Norse. Most of the aristocracy are descended from baronial landowning gentry. Unfortunately, their desire to keep the bloodline pure meant they were reluctant to branch out and so quite a few of their family trees are now stunted and bear little fruit.'

The pill sat in Reeves' open palm. 'Why do I need to take this now?'

'Because everything I tell you from now on is highly classified. This way we can be sure that you are not a security risk.'

Reeves popped the pill and swallowed some water, then put the bottle down.

'We'd prefer it if you didn't keep the pill under your tongue,' Matt said.

Reeves smiled and took another swallow. This time he opened his mouth for Matt to inspect.

'Excellent. If you were a horse, you'd be worth a fortune. Now, a brief rundown of Rathkoorne's geopolitical landscape.' Matt handed over a pile of postcards. 'Study these as I speak. It'll help.'

Reeves looked at the cards and listened.

'The current ruler is Erthu Le Liare, who holds sway over a loose collection of feudal baronies. His approach has been ruthless, both to those whom he taxes and to his fellow barons. He is stubborn and obsessed with justice—so long as that justice perpetuates the ruling class and the Le Liares in particular.'

The card baring Le Liare's name showed a lifelike drawing of a man in his late fifties with long grey hair and dressed in a dark embroidered tunic with silver clasps. The face was strong, the nose broad, the eyes unsmiling.

'No photograph?'

'Artist's imp-pression. Emphasis on the "imp". Don't ask.'

'Looks like a bit of a bruiser,' Reeves said.

'He has killed over a thousand men mercilessly and without a thought,' Kylah said from behind Matt.

'His son, Gauinebald Le Liare, is his only heir,' Matt continued. 'And yes, it is pronounced "goin' bald". Erthu despises him because Gauinebald's birth also caused the death of Erthu's wife. Gauinebald has been indulged by everyone else and has grown into a vain, self-absorbed bully and psychopath. Chief weapons tester is the job he was born to do. It was either that or chairman of a local council.'

Kylah added, 'The people know him as the Ogre.'

'Do you know what ogres do, Reeves?'

Reeves shrugged. 'They are creatures of legend.'

'They are flesh-eating creatures of legend.'

Reeves looked as if he might object to that, but kept his mouth shut.

Kylah continued. 'Gauinebald is caught in the trap of wanting his father's respect and a desperation to be the ruling baron.'

The second card showed a boy of twenty or so, full of figure with curling hair cascading around a fresh-looking chubby face. It was only the eyes that gave any hint of the swirling, untethered and craven madness beneath.

Reeves peered at the card. 'Is this a trick, or are his eyes really following me?'

'They'll not only follow you; they'll string you up and skin you alive if you let them. Look away,' Kylah said.

Reeves obeyed. It was only then that he realised he'd begun to sweat profusely.

'Gauinebald is aided and protected in his feral escapades by the baron's trusted lieutenant, Turgiss de Wyville. A man who has risen through the ranks thanks to his unremitting brutality. He is the one who carries out Gauinebald's will and does so without compunction. Infanticide, murder, mutilation, they are all on his CV.'

De Wyville's card showed a square-jawed man, ten years older than Gauinebald, with a mop of red hair over his forehead and a stocky body.

'If anything, de Wyville is worse because he has a choice,' Matt added grimly.

'And there is one more Le Liare you need to know about.' Kylah took the final card in the pile and turned it over. It showed a raven-haired woman in a dark green dress. She looked out from a face that would have been flawless had it not been for the paint on her cheeks and encircling those glaring eyes.

'Alienor Le Liare,' Matt said, as if he was describing some deadly virus. 'Erthu's daughter.'

'Don't be fooled by her beauty,' Kylah said. 'She is a killer, a torturer and a dabbler in the darkest kind of black magic.'

'They sound delightful,' Reeves said. 'No black sheep?'

'You'd be hard pressed to find even a grey one.'

Matt continued. 'The person you need to find is a boy named Targan Shadowsmith. He lives in the slums of Gogny Payn where the Le Liares have their stronghold.'

Reeves ran the cards through his fingers. 'I don't have much time for peers and barons. From what I recall of medieval history lessons, it all comes down to some invader favouring his followers in a land grab.'

'That's pretty much it. The indigenous population are more than a bit fed up, too. But they need a spark.' Matt reached into the box and took out a tied leather bag, which he proceeded to undo. From within, he removed a leather thong on the end of which hung an ornate jewel. The top half was metal and resembled a four-tentacled squid whose arms spread out over a heart-shaped stone in brilliant turquoise. 'This is an amulet. The Seren Sea Stone. It has hidden powers that, so our seers think, Targan Shadowsmith can unlock. This is not wand lore; this is a much older power. Targan's family, the Shadowsmiths, once owned it. Get it to him in Candin Lane.'

'Okay, will do.'

Matt pressed something on the back of the stone and it changed shape into a simple, and very ugly-looking brown-and-cream whelk shell. 'This way it's sentimental value only. Hold it at the apices and place your finger in the aperture. There's a small button that's charmed to retransform.'

Kylah handed him a map. 'We intend to drop you at a point some fifty miles from Gogny Payn.'

'Why fifty miles?'

Matt glanced at Kylah. 'Because our intelligence comes from sources that we cannot trust entirely. Our agents are all animorphs. They don't draw very well, either.' Matt unfolded the map and smoothed it out on the canvas bed. A trail was marked in red ink.

'Okay,' Reeves said and folded the map back up.

'No questions?'

'None.'

Matt smiled. 'Good. Nice to see you've bought in to the

project. Of course, if I was cynical, I might believe that you've accepted this mission on the basis that you'll jump under the first cart you see and kill yourself.'

Reeves said nothing.

'Which is why we included a memory charm in the pill you just swallowed.'

Reeves hand shot out and clamped around Matt's shirt. 'What does that mean?'

'It means that all memory of your previous existence, your motivation, anxieties, troubles, will fade into nothing but a recurring dream. You won't forget it completely, but your new identity will be the stronger. At least to start with.'

'You bastard,' growled Reeves. But his expression, twisted with rage, suddenly cleared and he looked down at the hand still clutching Matt's shirt and let it go. 'What's happening to—'

'Disorientation is not uncommon at this stage,' Kylah said. 'There are some clothes under the bed. I suggest you change immediately.'

'Change…yeah…'

'Then when you're ready, exit through the wooden door at the end.'

'Wooden door, right.' Reeves picked up the clothes with not much enthusiasm.

Matt hung the amulet around Reeves' neck. 'Don't worry, your new identity is on the way. It just needs to file away the old stuff temporarily. You will still be Reeves. Your core beliefs, the essence of who you are, will be exactly the same.'

Kylah wrinkled her nose.

Matt grinned. 'Yeah, sorry, the kit's a bit smelly but best to be authentic right? They do bathe in Rathkoorne. Every April. And don't forget to limp with your right foot. That's the one that got damaged in the Scarpment wars. Okay, now you look the part. So, Sergeant Reeves, war veteran, you're all set…except for your eye patch. It actually has a magnifying lens in the middle of it to help you read and see things close up. Under this flap, see? Neat, huh?'

They left him to it. A little later, they returned and Reeves, still woozy from memory charm, got up from the bed dressed in his 'new' clothes, and walked unsteadily towards the wooden door. 'Don't like the eye patch. And I can't promise to remember the limp,' he muttered as he exited.

Matt frowned. 'I worked hard on that.'

'Best of luck,' Kylah called after him, but Reeves barely heard her as he opened the door and the midday heat hit him. Hers was just a voice in the market crowd as he stepped through to the welcome shadow of a saddler's tent. He was hungry now. He hadn't eaten since breakfast the morning before, and that was only some stolen bread. He needed meat. He'd try the butcher near the wine vendor, since he was a lazy sod who could be easily distracted by anything with a bosom. He took one step forward and felt his legs swept from under him. He hit the ground with a jarring crack and heard a voice.

'Get out the way, beggar. You're stinking up my stall.'

CHAPTER TEN

RATHKOORNE, THE FAE WORLD

REEVES LOOKED up into the scrawny face of the man that had shoved him, and at the wooden club in his hand. He knew he could have disarmed the man and beaten him with his own weapon with ease. Part of him wanted to do exactly that, but that wasn't why he was here.

Instead, he put his arm up in a feeble protective gesture and shuffled off into the shadows, mewling pathetically. He knew this place as Lindmouth, a market town on the edge of the Wetwood. Twice weekly the stall holders came with their wagons to ply their wares. He stared about at the people, listening to the hawkers' shouts, all so familiar and yet so strange. He knew this place, knew its layout and yet he had the strangest conviction that he had never been here before. How could that be? Perhaps he was thirstier and hungrier than he thought.

He eyed the long corridor of stalls. The baker had one of the busiest. It stood about a third of the way down a selling lane of some two hundred feet, next to a small concession with a board on which were drawn ornate depictions of people with warts and worse, and embellished with flowery promises of cures and tonics.

An apothecary. That, too, was a busy stall.

He waited for an appropriate gap and crossed the lane. He knew he smelled bad by the way people's noses wrinkled and they drew back to let him pass. So be it. He slid into the gap and made his way along the rear of the stalls amidst the discarded rotten vegetables and flotsam. No one paid him much notice apart from a couple of dogs who approached warily, took one sniff and walked away, happy to find something that smelled worse than they did. He hovered behind the baker's stall in its shadow, as much to keep out of the sun as to plot his approach. He had no money and so this needed to be done carefully because Lindmouth was not a prosperous place and money, like everywhere in Rathkoorne, was hard to come by. The people of Rathkoorne had little tolerance for petty theft. If he got caught, he'd be in serious trouble. Definitely out on a limb, possibly end up losing one.

But there was always a way if you waited long enough for a distraction.

This one came stumbling out of the tavern fifteen minutes later. Reeves had seen the horses tethered outside the Weary Shepherd and noted the colours on the saddle blankets: black with the silver crowned boar. Three of Baron de Courcy'smen returning to the north. To be avoided, if at all possible.

Today, one of them looked a little pale and was massaging his ample belly. Dressed in brown from head to foot with a rusting iron chain belt and two silver coins worn as earrings either side of a face scarred from duelling, the man oozed malevolence. Reeves could almost hear the collective intake of breath as vendors and buyers alike saw the small eyes squint in their direction, noting how his body swayed as he spat in the dirt before setting out unsteadily. The crowds parted, many of the women pulling their children to them and hurrying away. Others pressed themselves to the side to give the man passage.

Reeves watched it all from the safety of the shadows, sensing violence.

The soldier, his wand sheathed on the right of his belt, meandered down the aisle, pausing to peer at the stalls, taking an apple from one, which he bit into, before spitting it out and tossing the fruit with a grimace. He paused momentarily at the bakery but his attention didn't linger on the bread and pies. Instead, he grimaced, rubbed his belly once more and turned to the apothecary stall.

Reeves took his chance. Keeping low, he loped across the gap to the rear of the stall. The baker and every single shopper had eyes only for the soldier. Careful to stay below their eyeline, Reeves reached up and managed to grab a pie and a small loaf, which he stuffed into his shirt. He was about to slip away when the soldier's voice rose to a shout.

'Stomach. Stomach! I need something to settle it, you cretin.'

Reeves inched forward to peer around the edge of the stall into the aisle. The apothecary, an elderly man in a tattered grey robe, fumbled with some bottles. A difficult trick given that he was being held roughly by his shirt front. Behind him, a girl, somewhere in her teens but, like everyone in the market, small and thin, knelt in the corner, trembling, eyes averted. The soldier saw her, let his drunken eyes linger on her, belched and then squeezed his eyes shut.

'I have camomile and fennel,' said the apothecary. 'It will calm—'

'Don't want it calmed. Want it gone. My alchemist just waves a bleedin' stone over it and it's gone. You got no stones?'

'All our cures are natural remedies.'

The soldier frowned. 'Natural?' He snatched the small bottle out of the apothecary's hand. 'I'm supposed to drink this, am I?'

'Yes,' said the apothecary. 'Drink it. There is a little ginger and raspberry to add sweetness, as well as the herbs.'

Swaying, eyes blinking slowly in that way the very drunk do, the soldier unstoppered the bottle and drank.

'Tastes like flowers,' he said with distaste, before planting both hands on his waist and standing, or rather swaying. After ten seconds, he looked up at the apothecary. 'Nothin's happenin'.'

'It might take a few minutes,' said the apothecary.

'I don' wannit to take a few bleedin' minutes. That's drinkin' time wasted, that is. This is rubbish. You're a bleedin' quack. Nothin' but a bleedin' quack.' His eyes turned again to the girl. 'Maybe the girlie there can make me forget my gut rot.'

The soldier stepped forward, bumping into the wooden stall front and leaning over the array of bottles, sending several toppling and tinkling. He lunged for the girl.

'No!' yelled the apothecary. 'Not this time.' From behind his counter he produced a large iron pan and aimed a blow at the soldier. It struck his shoulder but he did not fall.

'You little shit,' roared the solider, and in one fluid movement his wand was in his hand and aimed at the apothecary. 'Scum,' said the soldier and sent a jet of power into the old man's chest. Instantly, the man convulsed and fell forwards onto his counter, the bottles scattering.

Reeves saw the soldier's eyes dart towards the crying girl.

Cursing, Reeves kicked out at the corner post supporting the awning above the apothecary's stall. It gave and the canvas fell forwards, engulfing the soldier and half a dozen white-faced onlookers.

Panic ensued. People began screaming and running. Many of them pausing only to help themselves with a grab at the wares on display. The people of Lindmouth were poor but not stupid. The baker reached for his club.

Reeves was already moving. He'd spied the leather purse that had fallen from the soldier's belt to within arm's grasp and pocketed it. Then he reached in for the girl.

'Come on,' he urged her. 'Get out of here. Once that idiot is free, he'll be looking for you.'

'But Molk,' she wailed.

Reeves lifted up the canopy and ducked in. He felt the old man's throat. His pulse was faint and fading fast. The old man grasped Reeves' wrist and opened his mouth to speak.

'Look after Milda,' he croaked.

'I'll get her away—'

'Please. I feel your touch…You are…good man.'

'Not so—'

'Charm…around my…neck.'

Reeves frowned. He did not want to take anything from this dying man. There wasn't time, though the soldier was making a pig's ear out of trying to extricate himself. But more importantly, Reeves had a task to complete and could do without complications. He started to pull away but the man's grip was iron.

'Charm,' he insisted. 'Please.'

Behind him, Milda was sobbing. Reeves reached for the charm. It was silver and delicate, made with craftsmanship.

'My gift,' breathed the old man.

'This isn't the time nor—'

'Take it…please…open it…when it is…safe.'

A crowd was gathering. Reeves yanked the chain from the apothecary's throat. With it, he heard a rattling final breath and his grip relaxed.

'Molk,' wailed the girl again.

'Is dead,' Reeves said. 'And if you don't want to join him, or maybe end up wishing you had, we leave. Now.'

Whimpering, the girl stood and, keeping hold of her wrist, Reeves retraced his steps into the shadows. There he slumped again with the refuse while chaos ensued just yards away, the girl crouching next to him. 'We can't stay here. The noise will alert the soldier's friends. We need to get out of this town.'

'But Molk, he's…,' pleaded the girl.

'I saw it, too. I'm sorry. But no matter how hard it is, you need to put it from your mind. They've seen you. You need to hide.'

The girl wailed again.

'I know it's horrible and there will be time to grieve. But it's not here and it's not now.'

She looked up at him. 'You're a beggar,' she said. 'And you stink.'

'Correct on both counts. But I am also your best bet to get out of here. You need to follow me and do it now.'

She nodded.

'What's your name?'

'Milda. Milda Bickle.'

'How old are you, Milda Bickle?'

'Fourteen.'

'Right. Well, keep low, Milda, and follow me,' Reeves said. 'And don't look back.'

'But you are a beggar, aren't you?' Milda asked.

Reeves tore off the patch from his eye and tossed it aside. 'Not always. Now please shut up and move.'

CHAPTER ELEVEN

Reeves led them out through one of the side gates, which was normally used to throw all the discarded food waste into the midden. You could follow the way with your nose. Luckily, Reeves' smell was just as pungent.

The Wetwood was well named.

They took a path next to a stream and were soon in a green universe beneath a dense canopy of ancient trees. Despite the brightness of the day, it was cool and dark and the ground beneath was a carpet of leaf fall and dried, and sometimes not so dried, mud. They followed the stream past the midden, the sun a shining ball glimpsed only rarely along their passage, obscured by leaf cover from huge hemlock, oak and, further from the streams, larch and pine as tall as a craned neck would allow the eye to follow. The cool air was heavy with moisture and smelled of wood and toadstools now that they were far enough away from the stronghold. Everywhere they looked grew orchids and anemones, wood-sorrel and ramsons, yellow archangel and the lords-and-ladies. Ferns arched tall near the stream, and where boughs had fallen and begun to rot, toadstools sprouted against the background of moss furring almost every surface.

A botanist's dream though it might have been, it was a

nightmare for Reeves and Milda, and made the fleeing fugitives' progress painfully slow.

After Reeves lost sight of his foot in another ankle-deep patch of mud, he'd had enough.

'Okay, so this deep in the woods may not have been the best idea,' he conceded. 'We need to find somewhere with firmer ground.'

Milda nodded, but said nothing. Still in shock, Reeves concluded.

He ducked to avoid a dragonfly as big as his hand and waited while a squadron of butterflies drifted past. It was then that he heard the chirruping above him. It took a while to find the source but there, twitching its tail on the branch of a willow, was an animated red squirrel. As Reeves made eye contact, the squirrel leapt away onto a low branch of an adjacent tree and then turned and scampered back, its tone changing from the chirrup to a squeaking bark now that it had Reeves' attention.

Milda too was staring at it. 'Why is that squirrel so angry?'

'It isn't angry. It's signalling. And about time, too. Come on, we follow.'

They climbed a bank, following the squirrel's signal through the trees until they came to higher ground and what looked like a bridle path. There Reeves called a halt. He retrieved the pie and broke it in half. Milda took it and they sat in the shade and ate.

Milda's shock had given way to confusion. She stared at the squirrel, who seemed to be acting as a sentinel above them, darting back and forth on the higher branches, and then at Reeves. 'You are more than you seem, beggar.'

'Reeves is the name.'

'You have the beastongue?'

'No, I don't. But I do have some friends in this forest.'

'Then you do not speak to it?'

'I can't. But it is more than it appears.'

Best to remain woolly on the detail, thought Reeves. Mainly because he was woolly himself. In fact, his brain felt like it was crammed full of the fluffy stuff. He knew he was here and he needed to get to Gogny Payn and deliver a package. He knew he'd been a soldier and had fought many men. He knew that if he was caught, he would likely be tortured and killed.

But other things were far less distinct. A childhood somewhere cold with constantly bruised skies and snow and ice for four months of the year. A fishing community, a war, soldiering, campaigns in hostile environments and then a different kind of war. One fought not with armies but with surgical incision, where he was the scalpel smuggled into enemy lands. And though all of this was there and available, he could not recall places nor names other than his own. He was surprised by how little this worried him. Yet the task was clear, like a road map in his head.

'Like you,' Milda said softly, bringing Reeves back to the present.

'Do you have any family you could go to?'

Milda shook her head. 'My mother was taken when I was four. Father told me she went to work in the kitchens of Blackston's keep, but I think she was taken as a slave. No one who works for the Striklin, the barony I'm from, gets paid. If the baron liked her, he may have kept her for a while. Once he lost interest, she would have been thrown to the wolves that make up his guard. They are renowned for being the worst in the whole of Rathkoorne. The same happened to my aunts. My brother died young from the stridor. My father died of the pestilence, Molk helped me. He knew my father. He took me in, he taught me the healing. Molk…' Milda gulped; fresh tears came.

'I'm sorry. No one should die like that.'

Milda shook her head. Tears fell like rain from her downturned face. 'People die like that all the time. The Zatrank—'

'Zatrank?'

'That's what we call them. What they like to be called. The barons and their families and men. The Zatrank use us like cattle. I told Molk not to come here, but we needed money. We have travelled in the lowlands, the fairs and markets. But last year's harvest was poor and the people have no money. So we came here and now…now…'

Tears fell again.

Reeves sighed. 'I can take you to the next town, but there you will have to fend for yourself. I suggest you get away from this manor, though the man who killed Molk is from the north. With luck he will leave us alone and bugger off back to where he came from. I would suggest you go south. Try and get across the border into Fitsot.'

Milda shook her head. 'Many try, few succeed.'

'It's your best hope.'

'They say that Fitsot men sell Rathkoorne girls to trolls for sport.'

'Really? Who told you that?'

'The overseer in my village.'

'What else did he tell you?'

'That smiling too often called to demons and that laughing out loud made all your hair drop out. That too much food made you slovenly and that riding a bicycle was too adventurous for young girls and invited lascivious thoughts.'

Reeves, for several seconds, was lost for words. 'What about Molk? What did he think?'

'Molk had travelled far, sometimes to the border in the south before they clamped down. He said that healers in Fitsot could make a living selling hangover cures to the rich.'

Reeves nodded. 'There's always money in hangover cures. Did he see any trolls?'

Milda shook her head.

'Exactly.' He put the last of the pie in his mouth and chewed. He'd tasted better. But beggars could not be choosers, even where they weren't really beggars and there wasn't any choice. 'Come on. Let's move.'

The squirrel led them the rest of that day and Reeves felt confident that they would be alerted of any danger. They took it slowly, reasoning that either the three Zatrank in Lind-mouth would get even more drunk and forget the girl or would set off in search. Either way, they were safe in the dense woods.

For now.

Milda, still tearful but fortified by the food, began, slowly to open up as they trudged through the rest of the day, and Reeves was happy to listen. Her experience of life in Rathkoorne was as incredible as it was harrowing. Yet, the more he could learn, the better informed he would be because, as he listened to her speak, he became increasingly aware of how ill-prepared he was for being in this godforsaken land.

CHAPTER TWELVE

RATHKOORNE

Milda looked away briefly, as if debating whether to trust Reeves. 'You swear you're not an informer? Blood swear?' she asked quietly.

Reeves shook his head solemnly. 'I blood swear it. Whatever that is. You've nothing to fear from me.'

She took a shaky breath and began cautiously. 'Molk despised the Le Liares. He used to tell me stories—terrible, haunting stories. Things I never fully understood until now.'

'Go on,' Reeves said gently, sensing how fragile her composure was. As she spoke, he felt something inside him stir; memories half-buried by his handlers, which was how he thought of Matt and Kylah, slowly emerging. It felt like peeling back layers of his own history, each revelation grimmer than the last.

'It all began during the troll wars,' Milda continued, voice barely above a whisper. 'Twenty-five years ago, Karssinad's royal household was massacred by trolls. Liare—just a remote corner known mostly for making wands—armed its militia to survive. With the warlocks and war-mages already slaughtered, the militia turned to ancient magic. It was meant as a desperate act of survival.'

'And it worked,' Reeves said slowly, feeling the pieces align in his mind.

'Yes, it worked too well,' Milda said bitterly. 'They called themselves Zatrank—from the old word meaning magic potion—and their victory was overwhelming. They pushed the trolls back to the northern mountains, but victory corrupted them. Molk said it was like getting a drunken tattoo: a good idea at first, disastrous later.'

Reeves winced slightly. 'Absolute power corrupts absolutely.'

She nodded grimly. 'When the troll threat ended, the Zatrank filled the power vacuum, claiming Karssinad as their own, renaming it Rathkoorne. And when the loremasters—the very ones who granted them their magic—tried to restore balance, the Zatrank murdered them.'

'Erthu Le Liare and his cronies,' Reeves said quietly. 'I was briefed…I know about him, but not well enough from what you're saying.'

Milda's voice hardened. 'They built hex-walls, Reeves. Hex-walls to trap us inside and to keep outsiders at bay. They spread lies, calling the neighbouring nations monsters and savages. Rathkoorne became a fortress ruled by ignorance and cruelty. Allegiance to Erthu became everything. Not showing enough enthusiasm at his name could cost you a limb. Everything is regimented. From haircuts to music. Religion is banned, poetry punishable by death. They even made us sing songs praising that monster.'

She paused, swallowed painfully, then murmured with a shaky voice, 'I can still remember every word of "Erthu, My Erthu, You are My Inspiration." They make children sing that song.'

Reeves felt bile rise in his throat at the thought. 'And the trolls?'

'Scapegoats, mostly,' she said bitterly. 'Every murder, every disappearance blamed on them, while in reality, the

Zatrank guards pushed dissenters off cliffs to stage troll attacks. They needed fear to maintain their power.'

'And your people accepted this?' Reeves asked, disbelief creeping into his tone.

'We had no choice. They forced obedience through starvation, informants, violence. Anyone who questioned them disappeared. Life became endless toil just to survive, let alone resist.'

Reeves exhaled slowly. 'Molk must have been incredibly brave—or incredibly reckless—to speak of this openly.'

'He was both,' she said softly, eyes glistening. 'And they killed him for it.'

Reeves felt the silence grow between them, heavy and sharp. 'I'm sorry, Milda. Truly.'

She gave a fragile nod. 'The Le Liares rule through fear and ignorance. They've abused magic, corrupted minds, and broken countless lives. And now they're hungry for more power, expanding their cruelty wherever they can.' She met Reeves' gaze with sudden intensity. 'But even tyrants must be careful. Molk used to say, "Beware the sleeping tiger, especially if you poke it."'

Reeves felt something cold and certain settle deep inside him, an uncanny familiarity stirring within. 'Molk was right,' he said slowly. 'All we need to do is find the tiger.'

CHAPTER THIRTEEN

PICT

THE DOF AGENTS met with Rimsplitter in adjacent Pict on a cold, crisp morning.

Matt frowned. 'You've, erm, got something on your beak.'

'Ah,' Rimsplitter said, removing the offending fur-covered strip of flesh delicately with a talon. 'S'wot's left of breakfast. You've heard of Welsh rarebit? Well, this was Pict harebit. Fast little buggers, too. I have to work for me dinner, and me breakfast and me tea.'

'You love it,' Matt said.

Rimsplitter nodded. He might even have been chuckling. 'Anyway, I've been asked to provide a progress report on that tee, Reeves.'

'Tea Reeves? Is that some form of divination?' Bobby asked. She was still behind the curve in Rimsplitter speak.

'The tee could stand for anything. Could be "tit" or "twit" with an "a" where there should be an "I",' Kylah explained.

Bobby nodded. But the frown remained.

'F3, that's the squirrel in old money, made contact yesterday. Seems old Reeves has hooked up with a girl.'

'Really?' Matt asked.

'Yeah, but keep your dirty thoughts to yourself, bee. This one is young. Lost her protector in a market fracas. Anyway, Reeves has taken her under his wing and she's providin' local knowledge. Fair effin' exchange, if you ask me. He's staying well away from them Zatrank bees, so it's all good so far.'

'So, he hasn't tried to do anything…stupid?' Kylah asked.

'Apart from hookin' up with your lot, you mean?' Rimsplitter guffawed.

'I mean, he seems…stable?'

'F3 said he was good. They're headin' in the right direction. With a bit of luck, we'll get him to that ess-hole Gogny Payn yet. But wot you hintin' at, Cap? You worried about his oriental 'ealth?'

'Oriental?' whispered Bobby.

Matt supplied the answer in an equivalent whisper. 'Chicken oriental. Slang for mental. Rimsplitter here is working on improving his vocabulary.'

'Improving?' Bobby sounded sceptical.

'We had some concerns, yes.' Kylah ignored the asides.

'Oh, that's great, that is. Now you tell me he's a bit Patrick Swayze. Or is he out and out Saddam--?'

'Whoa there, horsey,' Matt said. 'We don't use those kinds of terms anymore. It's considered…offensive.'

That earned Matt some very old-fashioned looks from the others. Rimsplitter was hardly the epitome of nuanced language at the best of times.

'Saddam?' Bobby asked.

'Even worse rhyming slang, I think,' Asher said.

'Oh, excuse me for breathin'. Sorry for any offence,' Rimsplitter squared his shoulders

'Yes, it looks like you mean that,' Bobby said. 'Not.'

'How about off his effin' rocker, then,' Rimsplitter interjected. 'I mean, that's all we bleedin' need, that is. Wot's he likely to do, then? Howl at the moon? Eat dog muck because he thinks it's cake? Wot degree of…outlandishness are we talking about here?'

Kylah bristled. 'We really shouldn't be "talking" at all,

since his fitness for the job, physically and/or mentally, has nothing to do with you.'

'No? Whose boys are in there, watching his back? Mine. We need to know this stuff in case he does something out of the ordinary. If he is a bit radio—'

'Psycholgically fragile,' whispered Matt quickly.

'—then we don't need to worry if he starts waving his Brighton rock on top of a grassy mound in the moonlight like he's conducting an orchestra. If he isn't, doing something like that could mean that he's been wanded, know wot I mean?'

No one spoke, all of them a little stunned by the thought of anyone conducting an orchestra, imaginary or otherwise, with his Brighton rock on top of a grassy mound in the moonlight.

'He has had his troubles in the past. And who hasn't,' Matt said after an elongated pause. 'Just keep an eye on things and let us know.'

'Oh, I will, sonny Jim, I will. Fancy some breakfast? I'm sure I got some jugged hare hangin' about somewhere.'

No one took up the offer.

CHAPTER FOURTEEN

RATHKOORNE

Reeves and Milda saw no one the rest of the day and kept to the old bridle path as they travelled west. Towards dusk, they spotted a shepherd's hut on the far side of a meadow. The squirrel finally left them and Reeves made Milda hang back while he reconnoitred.

It was empty.

'Probably used in the spring for lambing,' Reeves said, surprising himself with this unearthed nugget of knowledge.

They made beds out of gathered fern and branches but it was warm enough not to light a fire. Reeves shared out the loaf he still carried and they found water in a clear stream.

'Let's get some rest and get going as soon as it's light,' he suggested.

Milda said nothing. She looked exhausted and unhappy.

'What will they do when they catch us?' she asked later when they were both lying on their makeshift beds in the gloom of the hut.

'I have no intention of letting that happen,' Reeves said.

'I heard tell of a girl who was caught stealing a turnip,' said Milda, her voice small. 'They sent her to a garrison on the eastern border as a serving wench for the troops. Many of the men there had not been away from their outpost for years...' She didn't elaborate. The hanging sentence somehow made it worse.

'Hush now. Get some sleep.'

'But we cannot hide forever.'

'No one said anything about hiding forever.'

Reeves lay back and listened to the sounds of the forest at night. A hoot of owl, the bleat of a goat.

Haven't they got any homes to go to?

As he turned over, something poked his side. He reached into his pocket and pulled out the charm that Molk had insisted on giving him. Sitting up, he moved to a patch of moonlight and examined it. The delicate silver charm, shaped like a crescent moon, hung from a slender chain, its surface etched with faint runes that shimmered subtly. Perhaps it was the poor light, but they seemed to be moving, rearranging themselves into something legible. Reeves peered closer, trying to make them out, whispering the words as they appeared to him.

'Concus...concussion? No, concusto...con custard? Stupid. Concustio...dio. Hmm. New one on me. Concustiodio.'

It happened immediately he spoke the word. The charm glowed bright, the letters darkening and lifting off. Reeves was so shocked that before he could even drop the thing, the letters had flown up and into his open mouth. He tasted dust for a fraction of a second, spluttered as something dry hit his throat and then was on his feet, staring at the charm that had already returned to a dull metal. He got a stick and poked at it for a second or two before lifting it again. But the letters had gone. In his head he saw words burning as if they were branding themselves on his visual cortex.

POWER THROUGH FEAR IS A CITADEL BUILT ON SAND.

BEWARE THE RAIN THAT FALLS AND DOES NOT CEASE.

'This bloody place,' he muttered. 'Now I'm swallowing words.'

But he didn't feel ill or strange and so there was nothing for it other than to lie down again, the charm replaced once more in his pocket.

Great. All he needed now was to be poisoned by some old alchemist. It kept him awake for a while. But the noises of the forest crept back in. Rustling, hooting. Somewhere far away, a dog, barked. They lulled him into unconsciousness. But once there, his dreams were anything but reassuring.

He did not dream of the wars he'd been involved in.

He did not dream of his role as an 'envoy', with special emphasis on the quotation marks.

He did not dream of the Zatrank.

He dreamt, instead, of a man in a strange world where buildings were tall and roads were black and smooth and vehicles rolled along, horseless and speedy. He dreamt he walked amongst people dressed in clothes of strange material and bright in colour. He dreamt of a dark-eyed woman with a cruel mouth. He dreamt of men, pierced by metal on their faces, their skins adorned with tattoos. Violent men with whom he was acquainted and whom he did not fear. Men who, for some reason, obeyed him. He dreamt of climbing a tall building, of standing on a parapet. He dreamt of falling, but though he fell, he never reached the ground. He dreamt of watching from the edge of a beach a girl standing on the rocks as a huge black wave erupted from the sea like a gigantic hand reaching up and forwards.

Reeves jerked awake, sweating, his breathing ragged, disorientated in the blackness, waiting for memory to come back. And though it was little consolation, his and Milda's predicament was infinitely more acceptable than the horror of his nightmare.

He slept no more that night and when the grey light was bright enough for him to make out the shapes of trees through the tiny crack in the door, he got up and roused Milda.

The weather stayed dry and they made good progress. Two hours after setting off, with the sun already warm on their faces, they emerged into a more open landscape of gorse and hazelnut trees. They heard the goats long before they came into sight, their bells echoing across an open valley. They were a large breed, with those unsettling eyes that Reeves knew he would never get used to. Horizontal slits as pupils went beyond the exotic and bordered on the downright bizarre. The goatherd was young and male, his face and hands nut brown from the sun. He wore a conical hat and a smock and held a long crook in his right hand. Though not chewing on a stalk of grass, Reeves would have put good money on betting he probably did when not in polite company. He stood on the path as Reeves and Milda negotiated the herd, eyeing them suspiciously.

'Good afternoon, young man,' Reeves said.

'Awright?' said the boy, his wary expression unflinching.

'Is this the road to Gogny Payn?'

'Might be.' He was looking at Milda as he spoke. Girls, it seemed, were a bit of a novelty.

'Do you have a name?' Reeves asked.

'I do, but I daren't give it to you in case you're a wight.'

'A wight?' Reeves asked.

The boy nodded; his lugubrious expression unchanging. 'Loads of wights round 'ere, there are.'

'But wights live underground and have pale limbs and long straggly hair.'

The boy nodded.

'Okay,' said Reeves. 'How about I give you my name, then? Will that help?'

The boy considered this. 'A name given is a name lost.'

Reeves shook his head. 'Milda, can you help here?'

The boy's eyes narrowed. 'Milda? That 'er name then, is it?'

'Yes, it is. And mine is Reeves. So how about you give us yours.'

Again, the boy hesitated.

'Okay, let's forget the name. Is this the way to Gogny Payn?'

The boy nodded. 'The long way round. There is a road,' he pointed his crook to the left, 'that way.'

'But this takes us there eventually, right?'

The boy nodded. It was then Reeves noted his satchel. 'Do you have food?'

The boy nodded again.

'Can you spare us some? We'll pay.'

'With what?'

Reeves reached inside his loose-fitting coat and removed a leather purse. He threw it up on his palm and it jingled.

The boy's eyes widened. 'Kift,' he said. 'Name's Kift. And that's real money, is it?'

Reeves took out a couple of tarnished coins and let them rest on his palm. Kift stared at them as if they were rare jewels.

'What have you got in that satchel, Kift?'

'Two apples and a pasty.'

'I'll give you a copper thistlehead for the apples.'

The boy's eyes lit up. 'You can 'ave the lot for two.'

'Won't you get hungry?'

'Goat's milk.' He nodded at the herd. 'Plenty of it.'

Kift emptied his satchel and Reeves inspected the goods. The apples were dull russets, but firm and untarnished. The pasty smelled of swede, the pastry thin and pale. But it looked edible. He gave the food to Milda to carry.

'You don't want to give that to a girl,' said Kift.

'And why not?'

'Bears. There's bears in these woods. They go for girls. Smell 'em, they do.'

Reeves thought about this for a moment. If there were bears, they'd do well to eat the food now. He told Milda this and she sat and they ate while Kift watched. 'Know much about girls then, do you, Kift?'

'No,' said the boy. 'Not supposed to. I'm not nineteen for another four years. I'll find out about 'em then soon enough.'

'Don't you have any sisters?'

'Yeah,' Kift said in a defiantly teenage way. 'But they're kept in the women's house.'

'A mother?'

''Course. What you take me for?'

'So hasn't she explained to you why it might be that it isn't safe for women and girls to go into the woods at certain times of the, uh, month?'

'When the moon is full, you mean?'

Behind him, Reeves heard Milda cough. It might have been a stray pasty crumb. Then again, it might have been suppressed laughter.

'No, that's not what I mean. So, you're kept away from girls until you're nineteen? Then what happens?'

'You marry one.'

'Any particular one?'

'Yeah, the one your parents pick out for you. What are you like?' A rare smile broke across Kift's face. The kind triggered by an encounter with a slightly odd stranger. One so ignorant as to be laughable.

'And you like being a goatherd, do you, Kift?'

''S'alright. S'not what I'm goin' to do, of course. Once I'm twenty, I'm trying straight for a job in the baron's stable. Lookin' after the horses, an' that.'

Reeves chewed reflectively. 'You'll be married then, though. Will you take your wife with you?'

'No!' the word escaped as a truncated guffaw. 'She'll be at home, lookin' after the kid, I expect.'

'Right. Being a stable boy is your life's ambition, is it?'

'It is. Likes horses, I do. And you get to pick stray oats off the floor after the horse has eaten. You can keep 'em, too. At the end of the month, they say there's enough for a bowl of porridge.'

'And that's a good thing, is it?'

'Porridge is lovely. I smelled a bowl once. And if I work in the stables maybe the baron will see me.'

'As in pick you out?'

'No, see me as in see me. You're funny, you are.'

'So I've been told,' said Reeves. 'But I can't wait to find out why it is that you want the baron to see you.'

''Cos if he sees you, right, they say it's worth three years' protection from the lurkers.'

'Of course it is.' Reeves nodded. 'The lurkers.'

'A kind of bad luck demon,' said Milda from behind.

'Sods, they are. My cousin was struck down by a lurker. Poisoned, he was, from eatin' rancid butter.'

'Didn't he know it was rancid from the smell?'

'Yeah, but he was hungry. So he had no choice. Lurkers got him.'

'I see we shall have to look out for these lurkers,' said Reeves, while his mind was silently screaming: *What sort of a place is this? What sort of a city state starves their population to the point of them eating decaying food and blaming imaginary demons called lurkers when they die of food poisoning? What sort of mindset keeps the young people apart so that they're pig ignorant of each other? What possible purpose could that have? And let us not forget killing vendors because you don't like their stuff. There's backwards and there's*—'Rath bloody koorne.'

The words escaped his lips. He could feel the blood rising in his face. Not good. Bad things tended to happen when the blood rose in his face. Still, it wasn't this simple boy's fault.

'Well, Kift, the best of luck to you.' Reeves had already finished his apple and was two bites into the unpromising pasty. It did not disappoint on the flavour score, being full of root vegetables boiled to the point of nutritional neutrality and no meat. He looked at the last crusty piece and handed it back to the boy. 'Go on, you look as if you need it.'

Kift took it gratefully and put the piece back into his satchel.

'Is there any habitation on the way?' Reeves pointed to the path.

'There's the Wheel Askew eight miles ahead. This path takes you to it an' the road.'

'Excellent. Kift, it was nice meeting you. An education, some would say.'

Kift nodded. 'I wouldn't go into them woods with a girl if you paid me.'

'Ah well. We won't, then. Pay you, I mean. And we'll take

our chances.' Reeves threw the apple cores well off the path and beckoned to Milda. In a low voice he asked, 'You aren't…are you?'

'No, I'm not, thanks for asking.'

Over his shoulder, Reeves yelled, 'I'm not scared of bears, Kift.'

They heard a couple of bleats and the goats' bell in reply. The herd, it seemed, was speeding up.

Reeves sighed. 'We'd better hurry. News of this encounter will not doubt spread like a nettle rash. Are all the boys in Rathkoorne like him?'

'No,' Milda said. 'Some of them are just plain ignorant.'

Reeves toyed with responding but decided against it. After all, what was there to be said that had not already been spoken.

CHAPTER FIFTEEN

T̲he̲ p̲ath̲ m̲eandered̲ through groves and open pasture. Some clouds arrived to take the edge off the sun's heat. Under different circumstances, it might have made for bloody good walk. The type with wild moorland where nothing but the keening whistle of a red kite accompanied you through a breathtaking landscape of emptiness and peace. But Reeves was in no mood for any of that poetic stuff. He was still troubled by the utter strangeness of his dreams. Their sheer vividness had stayed with him and he could recall effortlessly those outlandish scenes with astonishing clarity. And that was remarkable for all the wrong reasons because dreams, in his experience, were often the most difficult of the mind's little japes to recall with any accuracy.

With Reeves thus preoccupied by his subconscious, they walked and saw no one. They saw no bears either. After another hour and a half, they crested a hill with the way stretching down in front of them. At the bottom, the path joined a dirt road at a crossroads. The junction was empty in all four directions, but Reeves suggested they be prepared to dive for cover if they saw anyone approach. One odd feature drew his attention as they descended. A tall, thick pole at the top of which was an iron cage.

'A gibbet?' said Reeves. 'They still use them here?'

Milda nodded. 'Be thankful that this one is empty. I have seen some dreadful sights. Men, women. Even children sometimes. The baron sees everyone with the same eyes.'

'Sounds like a wonderful chap. Makes you wonder why someone like Kift would bother.'

'Starvation is a great motivator, Reeves.'

They headed west, the sun leading them on through the afternoon until, like a mirage, a building appeared at the top of a gentle rise, its position commanding a view of the surrounding moorland in every direction.

'The Wheel Askew,' said Reeves, indicating a substantial inn with stables and a two-storey building with lodging for those in need.

They left the road half a mile before and approached the building from the rear. Reeves told Milda to make herself scarce. If there was anyone watching, they'd be less worried by a male traveller on his own than a girl and a man.

'Hide by the edge of the stables while I talk to the innkeeper,' he told her.

With Milda out of sight, Reeves entered the building and found it empty except for a couple of barmaids scrubbing the tables, a dwarf behind a curtain of yellow smoke puffing on a pipe in the corner, and a red-faced innkeeper carrying barrels to the cellar.

Reeves soon purchased a bucket of hot water, some soap and permission to wash in the empty stables, as well as some crusty bread and cheese. He joined Milda and gave the girl some space while he did the same in an adjacent stall. He threw off his rags, scrubbed himself with the soap and put on a simple shirt and breeches from the bundle he had around his waist. Lighter and cleaner, he waited for Milda in the stable.

'Said I'd return the bucket,' he said, taking it from her. 'Hang on here and we'll be on our way. It's a good thirty miles to Gogny Payn.'

Milda nodded, her eyes slitted. 'You don't look like a wounded soldier anymore.' She lifted her nose. 'Nor do you smell like one.'

'Time I became a merchant, I think.'

Milda nodded. 'It is definitely an improvement.' A tiny smile lifted the corner of her mouth and bunched the little muscles under her eyes. It was noteworthy as being the first time Reeves had seen her do anything of the kind.

Doesn't say much, does this one, he thought. *But she's tough. Maybe I can get her over the border once I've done what I came to do.*

The idea brought Reeves up short. He hadn't planned that far ahead. There was usually someone to pave the way for his extraction, though he generally had some inkling as to who it was. But this time he didn't. Judging from the total repression he'd seen so far, it might be that they hadn't entrusted him with a name. Best he finish the job and wait for whoever it was to contact him. It had happened before…

Had it?

Reeves carried the empty bucket back, rounding the corner of the stable block, still wondering at his own vagueness and caught up in the memory of his dreams. Glancing up, he caught sight of three horses tied up in the yard where there had been none before. He froze and let his eyes fall to the saddle-blankets. The crest there was black with a silver crowned boar.

De Courcy's sigil.

Coincidence was a dirty word in Reeves' world.

Shouts erupted from the rear entrance of the inn. Reeves stepped back under the cover of a barn entrance and saw a small figure come flying through the air to land with an uncomfortable-sounding thud on the hard packed floor. The dwarf coughed twice and rolled over with a groan. Behind him, a much larger and by now familiar figure swaggered out. Same brown attire, same rusting chain belt and same silver earrings as he'd worn in the market at Lindmouth.

'I don't like dwarfs,' said the soldier. 'Specially ones who try to sell me weed that's half horseshit.'

The dwarf got to his feet. 'I didn't sell you any, I gave it to you. And I did tell you that it was different. We smoke a lot of kale and kelp where I come from. It's medicinal.'

'Kake and kilt?'

'Kale and kelp. Kak for short.'

'You got that right. S'made my throat burn, you tosser.'

The dwarf shrugged. 'I'm sorry, I really am. But I did warn you. Definitely not for the amateur, is kak.'

The soldier bristled and walked down the steps, removing his wand as he did so. Reeves realised that it was probably his default response.

'You trying to poke fun at me, short house?' snarled the Zatrank.

'Hang on, I've said I'm sorry,' said the dwarf, alarmed and doing the backwards quickstep.

The soldier kept on walking, circling now, very much the apex carnivore enjoying himself. Reeves was half expecting his mates to appear but realised with a growing sense of horror that they probably wouldn't bother. They'd seen this play out too many times before for it to have any entertainment value. That in itself spoke volumes as to how this was going to end.

'I'll give you a choice. Slow and horrible death or quick and easy?' the Zatrank drawled, as if he was discussing the dwarf's choice of dessert.

The brute had his back to the barn now. From his hiding place, Reeves could see the dwarf's expression clearly. Far from breaking down and begging for mercy, which he guessed was the Zatrank's aim, the dwarf stood his ground.

'I have no argument with you and I did warn you about the weed. As I said, kak isn't for the uninitiated.'

'Slow and agonising it is, then. Ever heard of the unravelling curse? My speciality. Slits your guts open and makes your innards uncoil in front of your eyes. I've seen people last an hour trying to stuff 'em back in. Never fails to make me laugh.'

'Sounds like you need another hobby,' said the dwarf.

The soldier nodded and let out a gruff laugh. 'Funny little man. What was your name again? Raymounde. Well, Raymounde, you're about to get a lot funnier.' He pointed his right hand, wand flexed. But instead of the curse, what emerged from his mouth was a grunt to the thudding accompaniment of a heavy wooden bucket making contact with his skull. The soldier fell; the wand flew forwards onto the ground at the dwarf's feet.

'Pick it up,' said Reeves, still holding the bucket.

Raymounde looked from Reeves to the wand, his eyebrows, dark and bushy as they were, a mere millimetre from his hairline in an expression of horrified surprise. 'Wha—'

'I've seen this idiot in action. He was not bluffing. Pick it up.'

'But it's a wand.'

'Oh, for god's sake, it won't bite.' Reeves hurried over and picked up the wand himself. It felt warm and thrummed gently in his hand.

'You've disarmed a Zatrank,' whispered the dwarf.

'So?'

'So that's a—'

'Capital offence,' growled the soldier.

Reeves pivoted.

The brute was up on one elbow, massaging his head. He looked pale and unhappy, but still capable of issuing threats. 'Give me the wand back now and I'll make it quick. You have my word.'

'Make what quick?' asked Reeves.

'Your execution. That way no one will need know about the…incident.'

Reeves smiled. 'The incident whereby I disarmed you, you mean? Oh, I'm sure your mates inside would love to hear all about that.'

The soldier glowered, pushed himself upright and stood on shaky legs. 'Give it back, now.'

'Why? So that you can unravel us? How exactly do you do this stuff? Do you say it out loud? Think it?'

'That is something you will never know, worm.'

'Can't be that hard. I mean, what if I pointed it at you and said explode?'

The soldier laughed gruffly and shook his head. 'I am so going to enjoy turning you into jam.'

'Is this how it goes?' Reeves pointed the wand.

Despite his bravado, the soldier frowned in a way that said that this was a totally new experience for him. Having a wand pointed at him was a worry. Having it pointed by one of the 'ordinary' people was something he clearly thought he'd never experience. But he recovered quickly. 'Go on, then. Try, little worm. Try and see why it is that everyone in this world fears us.'

'To be clear, you're giving me permission to use your wand?'

'Use away, you piece of dog turd.'

Reeves shrugged, pointed the wand and said, 'Explode.'

There was no bang as such. More a sploshy pop, followed by about fourteen stone of bone and gore flying in every direction to land, with several liquid sploshes, on the floor, walls of the barn, horse trough and roof of the Wheel Askew. Somehow, it all missed Reeves and the dwarf.

'Okay,' said Reeves. 'I wasn't expecting that.'

CHAPTER SIXTEEN

Raymounde looked like he wanted to say something, too, but his mouth could only open and close like a door in the wind as he pointed with a slightly weak finger towards Reeves and then the crimson mess everywhere else. Finally, he found his voice, though it didn't seem to be of much practical use to him.

'You…you…you just…you.'

'I think we'll leave the bucket here,' said Reeves as he placed it gingerly on the ground. 'Now, what to do with the wand?'

The dwarf reacted quickly. He grabbed the wand from Reeves and stared at the ground until he found a pinkish-looking thing with a couple of fingers still attached.

'Backfire. Known to happen,' said Raymounde as he undid a scarf from around his neck and trod it into a purplish mess nearby that might have been the soldier's lights—though if they were, they'd well and truly gone out. 'Hopefully, they'll believe that half of this "jam" is me. We need to go.'

'Agreed.' Reeves strode back towards the stables, where he found Milda staring at them. 'Sorry you had to see that,' he said when he was close enough.

But Milda didn't look horrified, or even worried. Instead,

there was a certain glint in her eyes that had not been there before. 'I am glad,' she said.

Raymounde groaned dramatically, as though auditioning for a tragedy. 'Great. Just my luck to end up with a pair of bloody psychopaths.'

Reeves tilted his head, feigning surprise. 'No one's asking you to come with us, you know. Feel free to stay and knit more decoy scarves.'

Raymounde straightened his shoulders, affronted. 'We're all dead if I stay. Hopefully, my scarf will throw them off the scent. Knitted for me by my sister, that was. Family heirloom.'

'Are you saying,' Reeves said, a leery glint in his eye, 'that it's my fault you lost your scarf?'

The dwarf sniffed. 'Well, it wasn't me who decided to kill the Zatrank, was it?'

Reeves frowned thoughtfully. 'Did I misread the situation there? Because from where I was standing, you were about to be disembowelled.'

'Really?' Raymounde squinted up at him. 'I thought I had the situation well in hand.'

Reeves waited, eyebrows raised, for some sign the dwarf was joking. None appeared. He exchanged a glance with Milda, who looked like she was suppressing laughter. 'Are they all as belligerent and ungrateful as you are in…wherever it is you're from?'

Raymounde drew himself up with great dignity. 'Now, that's nasty. That's just plain dwarfist.'

Reeves smirked. 'I'd say more…belligerentist.'

The dwarf scowled but said nothing. His silence lasted an impressive thirty seconds before he began chatting again.

———

THEY HEADED SOUTH at a brisk trot, the Wheel Askew disappearing behind a dip in the landscape. The distant line of trees offered some hope of cover and so there wasn't much time for talk. But in what little there was, the dwarf was more than happy to take the lead. Reeves learned that his name was Raymounde Bloodbower and that he was on the way to Gogny Payn to see whether Baron Le Liare might be interested in setting up a trade deal.

'And what, pray tell, are you intent on trading?' Reeves eventually asked when Raymounde stopped talking long enough to breathe.

'Precious gems,' Raymounde announced, puffing out his chest. 'That's our trade in the Neverlands. Dig holes, find gems, repeat. Oh yes.'

'Is the Neverlands in Rathkoorne?' Reeves asked.

'No. Strictly speaking, it's under Rathkoorne. We claim sovereign rights to the caves. Ancient law.'

'Have you dealt with Baron Le Liare before?'

'Oh, sure. We send envoys every few years.'

'And…they return, I assume?' Reeves asked, though the answer already seemed depressingly clear.

Raymounde scratched his beard. 'Funny thing, that. We've never heard back from any of them.'

Milda snorted.

Reeves stopped walking. 'You've sent envoys before and never heard from them?'

'Probably too busy negotiating. These things take time, you know.'

'Probably too busy trying to stuff their entrails back inside themselves,' Reeves muttered. He stared at the dwarf. 'Were you chosen for this task or did you volunteer?'

Raymounde puffed out his chest. 'I was chosen. Perfect timing, too. I'd just left my last job.'

'And why's that?'

'The supervisor at the mine and I didn't see eye to eye.'

'He wasn't a dwarf, then?' Reeves asked innocently.

'There you go again! Yes, he was a dwarf. It was metaphorical. I just had…suggestions.'

'Suggestions?'

Raymounde nodded sagely. 'Parrots instead of canaries. I told them parrots could shout warnings instead of just keeling over. And a pop-up restaurant underground for variety. You know, bring in the odd celebrity chef. It's morale-boosting.'

'And they didn't think that was a good idea?' Reeves asked, his face a mask of polite disbelief.

'Old-fashioned, that's what they are.' Raymounde sighed. 'The minister for mining himself called me in. Said I had a… special way with people.'

'Copy that,' Reeves muttered under his breath.

'So here I am, sweet-talking the baron into a lucrative deal.'

'Sweet-talking? That's what you call what you did back there with his henchman?' Reeves asked.

'Just a misunderstanding,' Raymounde said breezily. 'These things happen. Besides, it's my destiny.'

Reeves caught Milda's eye. She shook her head and mouthed, *'He's an idiot.'*

Reeves coughed to cover a laugh. 'Destiny, you say?'

'Oh yes,' Raymounde continued, oblivious. 'I've always been different. Even in school, I was a bit of a loner—'

'*Friendless,*' Milda mouthed silently.

'And the usual life of nine-to-five in the mines, wife and kids, never appealed to me—'

'Hopeless with girls,' Milda muttered.

'No. Adventure and a quest!' Raymounde declared grandly. 'That's what was written in my stars.'

Reeves smirked. 'Are you sure you read them the right way up?'

'You'll see,' Raymounde said, smiling cryptically.

'I'm sure the baron will be delighted to give you a hearing,' Reeves said dryly. He managed not to add, *Even if it's destined to be an extremely short one.*

CHAPTER SEVENTEEN

THE UNLIKELY TRIO made good progress as the afternoon wore on. Twice they stopped and hid when they heard horses. But the riders were a long way off; too far to detect three specks hidden in the bushes. Soon the moor gave way to rolling countryside and they were forced to divert away from the road that they had kept in view since leaving the coaching inn. Deep valleys made their travels more difficult so they stayed on the higher ground, using the sun to navigate a broadly westerly path.

It was well past noon when Milda called a halt and held up a hand, signalling for the others to stop. The land fell away to the east and it was from that direction that the breeze carried to them a noise. They heard shouts, laughter and the whinnying of horses.

Reeves signalled for them to stay low. They descended quickly through trees until they could look out from a rocky viewpoint onto a lake below and a strange and unsettling scene.

Less than fifty yards away on the far edge of the lake, a company of horsemen had dismounted. The twisted pines around them creaked in the wind, their branches gnarled and bare on one side from years of mountain storms. Jagged boulders thrust up through the earth like broken teeth, dusted with the same pale green lichen that covered the stones hiding Milda, Reeves and Raymounde. The terrain dropped away sharply below their position, creating natural stone steps down to the lakeside. A carpet of rust-coloured needles muffled their footsteps as they crept forward for a better view, the resinous scent of sap heavy in the air.

Banners fluttered from a troop of Zantrak some distance away, their riders watching the spectacle of the three people involved in some sort of chicanery at the water's edge. One was almost as broad as he was tall, powerful-looking with hair as red as the sunset. Of the other two, one stood subdued, silent almost as if in contemplation, dressed in a long cloak with a pointed hat. The third was probably the strangest being Reeves had ever seen. He was dressed as a soldier with a tunic and chain mail but he did not behave like a soldier. Instead, he ran up and down the shore—well, waddled quickly or as much as his chubby frame would allow—as excited as a child, his voice high and wild and gleeful for no apparent reason. But then the cloaked figure raised his wand, and a jet of power shot from its tip into the centre of the lake. The very air shimmered and seemed to reset itself. It was also the signal for the capering soldier to stop and step forward, staring into the water in anticipation.

'What is this?' Reeves whispered to Raymounde and Milda.

The girl shook her head but Raymounde spoke. 'I have heard tell of this thing. A monstrous piece of black magic that the Ogre indulges in.'

'The Ogre?'

'The jester you see dancing like a baboon is one Gauinebald Le Liare, the baron's son. As cruel as he is unhinged.'

'What sort of black magic?'

But Raymounde had no time to answer because the water in the centre of the lake began to bulge, as from it an immense dark bubble rose into the air, never quite separating from the water. It hovered, unearthly and terrible and within it, Reeves saw movement.

At first, he wasn't sure what it was he was seeing, but then the image cleared and he could make out people, a desert landscape, the walls of a great city. But these were not the same people he'd seen in Rathkoorne. Their skin had a different hue and the buildings were of a style he had never seen, with oddly bulbous turrets and angular minarets. And from the lake and its strange bubble the heat and smell of a strange and arid place drifted up to Reeves' nostrils and he marvelled.

At the top of a citadel in the walls of the great city, a flag flew. A banner with images arcane and unrecognisable by anyone on that rocky viewpoint. On the parapet of the citadel stood a man and a woman, waving to the crowd that had gathered in the great square beneath. But it was only when Milda nudged Reeves that he forced his attention back to the lake edge. The mage still had his wand pointing at the dark bubble, but Gauinebald, too, was now hopping from foot to foot as he gazed into the great image until he stopped and pointed his wand as if taking aim. Another jet of light flew forward, this time into the bubble. It struck the mighty pillars of the citadel above where the two people were standing.

The walls exploded, raining down blocks of stone the size of carts. The couple on the parapet stood no more chance than the screaming people below. A catastrophic scene unfolded before Reeves. Devastation, destruction, death.

And all the while, above the screams and cries, there was laughter as Gauinebald watched with glee, examining the results of his murderous handiwork with rapt attention. For ten minutes he watched the mayhem, his laughter gradually subsiding until either disgust or more likely boredom made him turn to the cloaked figure and yell. Instantly, the figure's wand arm fell and the bubble descended back into the water with its desperate scenes still playing out.

Gauinebald turned to his large companion and spoke. He in turn spoke to the cloaked figure who nodded and fell to his knees. The squat man pulled him roughly upright and spoke to him once more, none too gently it sounded like, though the details of what passed between them were unintelligible. The cloaked figure nodded and returned to his contemplation once again. Gauinebald, meanwhile, began skimming stones into the water.

'Who are the others?' Reeves asked.

'I know that the big man is Turgiss de Wyville. Baron Le Liare's loyal lieutenant. He accompanies Gauinebald as his minder.'

'And the cloaked figure?'

'Some poor mage, I expect.'

'You seem to know an awful lot about this?'

Raymounde bristled. 'As an envoy, I have been briefed. It is my job to know.'

Reeves nodded. 'So tell me what I have just witnessed?'

Raymounde spoke quietly. 'It is said that the madness that rides with Gauinebald is never satiated. What you see before you is the Le Liares' weapon. The mages have learned to conjure windows into other places. Some say into other worlds. The Ogre takes pleasure in wreaking destruction. The victims never see their tormentor. They simply accept the fickle anger of their gods. A mad god.'

'Their mage doesn't look so happy.'

'This is dark magic. It takes a great toll on the user. The mages suffer greatly. I dread to think what hold the Le Liares have on this poor soul.'

Below, Gauinebald had tired of his game and had started chattering again. In fact, as Reeves watched and listened, the chattering turned into a strange and simple song.

If a raven plucks out my eye in the cage,
And a wolf tears my arm in the night,
With my liver weighed out and my guts on a stage,
I could still gut your heart in a fight.

'Charming,' said Milda as Gauinebald sang out to his heart's content while the mage slowly got to his feet.

Once more the wand was deployed, this time with a trembling hand, and another huge black bubble eased out of the water. This time the images were much stranger. A teeming city, strange metal carriages without horses speeding along dark and metalled roads. Streets of stone houses many storeys high, a huge river crossed by arched bridges. Reeves caught his breath. This was a different world, but one that he was not entirely unfamiliar with.

Was this…the world of his dreams?

Gauinebald peered into the city, his eyes watching in fascination, much longer than last time. But his dark and sinister intent remained the same. Finally, with a whoop of delight, he swept his wand along the river. A tsunami of water rose up, engulfing a bridge, spilling out onto the roads and adjacent streets, washing vehicles and people away and back into the river. It was a harrowing sight made all the more disturbing for Reeves because of his half-remembered dream and the jarring, raucous delight of Gauinebald Le Liare.

Again and again, the monster churned the water up and over the embankments, the people of the city helpless to escape its power, their screams mingling with the stench of silt and mud. A bridge was swept away, ships and boats hurled onto the land.

Reeves watched until he could stand no more. He pushed back from the edge, kicking at the ground until he'd loosed some hefty stones. When he rejoined the others, he made no attempt at hiding. Instead, he threw three stones in quick succession high into the air. The first fell short, but the second found its target and splashed into the water on the near side of the lake. The distraction was enough to break the mage's concentration.

Immediately, the image in the black bubble faded as the mage's wand hand dropped. The lake water bubbled and frothed and Gauinebald cried out in frustration. But there was nothing the mage could do. He fell to his knees just as Gauinebald ran over and aimed a kick into the man's chest and then another at his head. Curling up into a ball, the mage lay on the ground as the angry Zatrank stood over him, screaming out insults punctuated by blows and more kicks.

De Wyville signalled and the soldiers on horseback rode around. By the time they arrived, Gauinebald's anger was spent. The mage remained unmoving. De Wyville mounted his horse and waited for the baron's son to do the same. He did, finally, but as he rode away with his men, he pointed his wand back almost lazily and slowly the mage began to slide into the waters of the lake.

'The Ogre is not human,' muttered Milda.

'Come on,' said Reeves and began to hurry down the stony slope.

By the time they got around to the far side of the lake, the riders had gone but the mage was almost totally submerged. Reeves plunged into the water and dragged the man out. He seemed petrified, unable to move a muscle. But his terrified eyes confirmed that he still lived, though his injuries from the beating were severe.

'What is your name?' Reeves asked.

'Baraman.' The whisper was very faint.

'What can we do to ease your suffering, Baraman?'

'Wand. Wand.'

Reeves found the wand in a sodden pocket. He tried to place it in the mage's hand, but his arms were broken and useless.

'Forehead,' whispered Baraman. 'Forehead.'

Frowning, Reeves looked around at Raymounde and Milda but they both shook their heads. Reeves took the wand and touched it to the mage's forehead. Nothing happened.

'Hand,' said the mage. 'My hand.'

Slowly, agonisingly, Reeves moved the mage's fractured arm up so that it held the other end of the wand, every inch causing him immense pain. Finally, weak fingers grasped the wood.

'Thank you,' said Baraman.

The wand tip glowed blue and the mage's form became limp once again. This time, there was no eye movement.

'He's gone,' said Reeves.

'You did him a great kindness,' said Milda.

'And you got his wand,' said Raymounde.

Reeves glared at him, picked up the wand and hurled it into the lake.

Raymounde's face turned purple and his voice went up an

octave. 'Wha…you idiot! What did you do that for? Those things are worth a fortune to certain…people.'

'I can just imagine,' said Reeves. 'Seems to me that wands cause an awful lot of trouble. Best we get shot of it. Baraman certainly doesn't need it anymore.'

They turned away from the lake. Milda and Reeves walked together. Raymounde, too shocked and upset by the loss of the wand to speak, took up the rear.

After a quarter of a mile, Milda said, 'Those people in the lake, do you think they were real?'

'I do. I think that the Le Liares are using this lake, or the mage's ability to open a door through the lake, as a testing ground. Those people were real. They could not have any idea of what just hit them. It must have been terrifying.'

Milda nodded. 'I am glad you threw the wand away.'

A few steps behind them, Raymounde snorted.

CHAPTER EIGHTEEN

PICT

'You are not going to believe wot that berk Reeves has done.' Rimsplitter paced back and forth outside a shepherd's hut on the slopes of Pict. The others, Matt, Kylah, Asher and Bobby, were clutching mugs of hot tea and sitting around an open fire. It was early in the morning and they had been summoned.

'Berk as in Berkeley' whispered Bobby to Asher.

Asher nodded. 'Hunt. Yes, this has been explained to me by Matt.'

'We're all ears,' said Kylah. 'All early ears since it's not yet five in the morning in civilisation.'

'Civilisation!' Rimsplitter squawked. 'Lucky you still got any, that's all I can say. F3 is out of commission 'cos some cee tried to clobber 'im with a club to make squirrel stew. Only just got away, did Nutty. They will eat anything over there, bees. And as for them Zatrank, they ought to be shot, the lot of 'em. And then, and then, Reeves only goes and clocks one of the Zatrank cavalry with a bucket, whips away his wand and goes and curses the double-you in a very permanent fashion.'

'What?' Matt sat forward. 'He's killed someone?'

'That's wot F4 said. He was on aerial recon. Almost got hit by the fallout, there was that much effin' gore. They were at this pub and this Zatrank, he was not best pleased with this dwarf, and then Reeves sticks his nose in and before you can say abra-bleedin'-cadabra, the soldier's brown bread, and Reeves, the girl and the dwarf are leggin' it before his mates find out he's been turned into Zatrank effin' jam.'

'Brown bread and jam?' Asher asked.

'I'll explain the slang later,' Matt said. 'I am shocked, though. I didn't think Reeves had it in him.'

'In 'im, on 'im, and all over 'im. And there's more. Lots effin' more.'

'I'd better throw another log or two on the fire, then.' Asher proceeded to fetch some wood.

'Bring the tea, Ash,' Matt called after him. 'This sounds like we'll need at least one more mug of brew.'

'Is the squirrel badly hurt?' Bobby asked.

'He's not a squirrel anymore, now that he's back with us. But he's in the hospital with severe concussion and a broken bacon.'

'Bacon?' Bobby asked.

'Bacon and egg. Leg,' muttered Matt.

'Oh dear,' Kylah said, her lovely face crumpling.

'Yeah, "Oh dear" is exactly what Nutty said when it happened,' Rimsplitter said. 'Not.'

Asher returned and added fuel to the fire while Matt replenished everyone's mugs from a large teapot.

'Okay,' said Kylah to an impatient-looking Rimsplitter, 'what else happened?'

'Did you tell Reeves to try and stick his fireman's into every effin' place he could find trouble?'

'Fireman's?' asked Asher.

'Fireman's hose. Nose,' Matt explained. 'Not really. His task was very specific.'

'Well, not only has he blown apart a Zatrank soldier, which makes him the most wanted bee in the country, he's also spied on that cee, Gauinebald. F4 was there, hiding in a convenient tree. He saw the whole thing. And I can tell you that some place in the universe is now a lot of worse off, thanks to 'im. He's a caution, that Gauinebald. Or something beginning with a cee, anyway. He's perfecting some kind of weapon and F4 says he caused this massive earthquake somewhere where they all wore sandals and drove chariots. Nowhere near us, but somewhere.'

Asher nodded. 'That explains it.'

'Explains what?' Kylah asked.

'The owls Duana got this morning.'

'Owls?' Rimsplitter asked.

'Owls deliver messages at night, pigeons during the day,' Asher said patiently.

'What owls?' Kylah demanded.

'Addressed to some very disgruntled historians. You will know that New Ron University remains on a ten-week delay due to a temporal displacement experiment gone wrong?'

'Yes?' Kylah's answer was a prolonged, pensive and upwardly inflected affirmation.

'One of them happened to be in correspondence with a colleague in the sister university in Bogof, and they had an argument. According to the Bogof historians, the once great empire of Egglip collapsed in 875 because of a huge earthquake that killed the royal family and most of the court. Whereas, according to our chap here in New Thameswick at the New Ron, the empire lasted another two hundred years. It was all very confusing, but now it makes sense. If Gauinebald caused an earthquake in Egglip, it would have changed history. Whereas according to our bod at the New Ron, their books and research still show what history was like ten weeks ago.'

'Now I'm confused,' Bobby admitted.

'Well, you've no right to be, not after what happened to us and Arthur Pendragon,' Kylah reminded her.

Bobby grimaced. How could she forget the fact that she and Kylah were in King Arthur's court only last year, due to some Krudian slip.

'See,' said Rimsplitter, 'Gauinebald was a complete Kate Mosser.'

Not even Asher needed that one explained.

'But Reeves was there and he saw it all and then he goes and helps this mage that Gauinebald had used to cause all the mayhem. Uses them up like effin' batteries, he does. Anyway, Reeves finds this mage and he could have got hold of his wand then but the tee throws the thing back into the lake. I ask you. What a Richard.'

'Richard?' asked Asher.

Bobby explained this time. 'As in Richard the Third rhymes with—'

'Nice to see you're gettin' the hang of it.' Rimsplitter tilted his crowned head from side to side.

'At least he's not trying to get himself killed,' said Matt.

''S'only a matter of time.' Rimsplitter harrumphed. 'Bee miracle it hasn't happened yet.'

Kylah and Matt exchanged glances. Rimsplitter caught them at it.

'Woss that about, that meaningful look? He isn't trying to get wanded, is he?'

'Doesn't sound like it,' Matt said, but his tone was less than convincing.

'Stone me, is there no end to Reeves' baggage?' Rimsplitter spluttered.

'But he didn't, did he?'

'Didn't what?'

'"Get wanded", as you put it?' Kylah stared the eagle down.

The stare was returned with interest, but though there may have been creatures in the universe who could stare down Captain Kylah Porter, Rimsplitter was not amongst them. He did a semi-unfurl of his wings instead, and looked away. 'No, he didn't but, strewth, if he carries on like this, it's only a matter of bleedin' time. I just wish he'd hurry up instead of gettin' sidetracked. Oh, and I got a new joke for you.'

'Oh, is that the time?' Kylah stood.

'You ain't finished your tea yet, Cap,' Rimsplitter observed.

'Oh, no, silly me,' Kylah replied with a look that almost set Matt's hair on fire. 'We still have our third mug of tea to finish.'

'You'll love it. It's a good one.'

'Like all the others were?' Asher said with a rictus grin.

'Exactly,' said Rimsplitter, demonstrating that his feathers were in fact armour-plated. 'Me girlfriend has started dressin' like a nun when we go to bed. She says it turns her on but it does nothin' for me.'

They waited.

'Now I just can't seem to get her out of the 'abit.' Rimsplitter paused and then convulsed into eagle laughter.

'Shall we leave the tea?' Matt asked.

'Good idea,' Kylah replied and followed him and the others quickly back towards the portway.

CHAPTER NINETEEN

ASABONE, RATHKOORNE

THEY SMELLED the woodsmoke before they saw the village. The little bread that Reeves had left had gone stale and they'd found only stagnant water on their travels. Though Reeves retained a healthy wariness, the village looked harmless and there was certain to be a well.

There was always a well.

They were met by the stares of curious oxen and a corral of goats. The single and dusty street seemed deserted. As expected, the well was in the centre of the straggly collection of huts and houses. There was no one to ask and so Reeves helped himself, after first Milda and then Raymounde had filled their flagons. It was as he was refilling his, having thirstily emptied it once, that he heard a shout.

'Oy! What you…doing there?' The voice belonged to a wheezing, bent-over man shambling down the street at a rate of inches. A man so wizened he looked like a crumpled paper bag on legs.

Reeves held up both hands. 'We can pay for the water—'

The man paused to get in a few extra wheezes, leaning

against a convenient post as he did so. 'Pay? For…water? What are…you talking…about?'

'Umm,' said Reeves.

'Well…don't just…stand there…give me a hand…or we'll all…miss the…hanging.'

'Hanging?' Raymounde echoed.

The old man squinted. 'My, you're a…hairy child…aren't you?'

'This hanging?' Reeves said before Raymounde could explode.

'Is happening…in five…minutes…It's taken me…twenty to…get…this far.'

'Where exactly is it?'

'You journalists…all the…same…Turn up…Big on splash…thin on…detail…In front of…the statue…of course…Any chance…of a lift?'

'Lift?' Reeves asked.

'Yes, lift. Same way as…you'd carry…a billy or…a nanny.'

'Who's Billy?' asked Raymounde.

'He means goats. Male and female goats.' Milda rolled her eyes.

'How do you carry a billy or a nanny?' Raymounde asked.

'On your back,' Milda said.

'You mean a piggyback?' said Reeves.

'Hush,' said the old man. 'We talk…not of…the flat-snouted…ones.'

'So, a goatyback,' said Reeves.

'Never heard of it,' said Raymounde.

'Only kidding,' said Reeves.

Raymounde groaned.

Reeves shrugged and gave him a pointed look. 'Journalistic licence. So, Mr, um…'

'Ockham…Ockham Frond.'

'So, Mr Frond.' Reeves knelt and let Mr Frond climb onto his back. 'Tell us about the accused.'

Rejuvenated by the water, Reeves carried the still-wheezing and startlingly light Mr Frond the length of the street, learning in the process all about the justice system—for want of a better word, or even several, if you threw 'non-existent' into the mix—as it applied to rural Rathkoorne.

The accused, it appeared, was one Omeolegamundi, a native of Rathkoorne and a member of the tribes that occupied the land long before Mr Frond's lot pitched up and therefore an eon before the Zatrank claimed sovereignty. The words Mr Frond used was, 'them Naris.'

This particular Resonari was accused of stealing a chicken.

'Known to be…partial to…chickens…Naris are.'

'He was caught red-handed, then?' Raymounde asked.

'Yes…we lost a…chicken…and then…we saw…him.'

Reeves was about to question the obvious flaw in the chain of evidence when they rounded the corner at the end of the street. They immediately found themselves facing a crowd of around fifty people—men, women, and children— all craning their necks to get a glimpse of a rickety, makeshift gallows constructed from a rope and pulley system positioned just above the stable's first-floor hatch.

Standing beneath the gallows, a noose already looped around his neck, was a surprisingly calm, bearded Omeolegamundi. His skin was coffee coloured, and his hair, spiked upright, held in place by what appeared to be reddish mud. Beneath a broad forehead, a pair of hazel eyes stared out calmly. He wore a loose, sleeveless waistcoat over his bare chest, accompanied by equally loose and comfortable-looking trousers. Were his skin was bare, it had been decorated with white and red lines and dots across his arms and torso. These markings twisted and curled in such a way that, if one stared too intently, they seemed to ripple with an unsettling illusion of movement.

A huge bronze statue of a man, caped and facing the wind, provided a backdrop, a look of intelligence and wisdom on his fatherly face. One hand rested on a sheathed sword hilt; the other was outstretched and holding a wand.

'Who's that?' asked Reeves.

'The father of the land. Erthu Le Liare,' whispered Milda, faintly irritated and with a look that implied Reeves must be some kind of imbecile.

The crowd buzzed excitedly. Reeves concluded that this level of entertainment didn't happen all that often this far off the beaten track.

Someone at the front with a shiny chain around his neck started speaking. 'So, Omeolegamundi, before we hang you by the neck until you are dead for rendering missing a chicken from the communal chicken shed, I, Pilt Angst, mayor of Asabone, must deliver your last rites. Do you have anything you would like to say?'

'The chicken may be less of a chicken, but the fox is hungry no more.' Omeolegamundi stood unmoving, his hands tied behind his back, seemingly untroubled by his predicament.

'Do you have anything to say that we can understand?'

'Voice without truth is thunder without rain,' said Omeolegamundi and then he looked at Reeves and added, 'trust the voice within; it knows the song you have forgotten.'

'Very nice, I'm sure,' Angst said, ' But all those words do is give me a headache. Will you admit to taking the chicken?'

'That chicken is no more.'

'If that means it's dead, then of course it is,' said Mayor Angst. 'Say hello to it for me, then. When you join it.' He looked up and addressed the crowd. 'The chicken went missing yesterday morning and shortly afterwards, this Nari was seen walking across the highland to the south of the village with a feather between his lips. Pretty strong evidence, I think we all agree. The elders certainly do. And so, unless anyone offers up a sensible objection that doesn't involve airy words or some song nonsense, we will proceed with the punishment.'

Reeves slid Ockham Frond off his back. None of this was his business. He had other sardines to grill.

And yet he was irked. *This is not justice* argued a thought somewhere deep in the soup that was his subconscious. This place was getting under his skin. Random killing of just about anyone, but in particular the innocent and unarmed, by both the ruling class and now some jumped-up official, was becoming monotonous. Reeves felt an itch inside his skull demanding to be scratched.

'Yes, I have a question.' Reeves pushed his way forwards. The throng parted to make a path.

Pilt Angst followed his progress with a wary expression. 'And who might you be?'

'Mardock's the name. A Merchant, passing through.'

'So, someone who can spread the word of what we have to offer.' Angst's eyes lit up.

Reeves looked around at the few animals and the odd stall. 'Spread the word? Right. Just a couple of things I wanted to clear up then. So I understand it.'

Angst stuck out his chest. 'Of course. We here in Asabone pride ourselves on judicial transparency.'

'So I've heard. And you caught this … Ari is it?'

'They go by Resonari. We call them Nari. Sly sods at the best of times.'

'Right. Caught him red-handed, holding the chicken?'

'Holding a chicken feather,' said Angst. He opened a muslin cloth to reveal a bedraggled-looking white feather.

'But not the chicken?'

'No. Not the chicken. That particular chicken cannot be found.'

'And what has the accused said about being in possession of the, ah, feather?'

Angst frowned. 'Haven't asked him. Finding someone with the remains of a chicken on his lips seemed pretty conclusive to us.'

'Have you lost many chickens?'

'One every couple of weeks.'

Reeves turned to Omeolegamundi. 'Why did you have a chicken feather in your mouth?'

'My family all walk with the water-bird feather lizard skin ancestor. The feather breathes in the wind. You can hear it if your listen. He helps me find the echopath with no rocks.' Omeolegamundi smiled. An open, beautiful, guileless smile.

'Was there any blood on his hands?' Reeves turned to Angst, who responded instinctively.

'No, but he did have a chicken feather—'

Reeves felt a warm breeze stir up the dry earth. He reached up and plucked something from the air. When he opened his hand, he was holding a feather. 'They seem to be all over the place, these chicken feathers.'

Angst blinked.

Reeves studied his surroundings and settled on a fenced off area to one side of the stables. A dozen chickens were rooting around in the dusty ground. The majority were brown or black. 'Do you have many white chickens?'

'We had several,' said Angst pointedly.

From the assembled crowd, someone said. 'You're wrong there, Pilt. Haven't had whites for a couple of months. Not since that wild dog—'

'Shut up, Tibben.' Angst rounded on the man.

'You have trouble with wild dogs?'

'Part of my election manifesto was a promise to control chicken theft by dogs and...' Angst turned to glare at Omeolegamundi, 'other thieves.'

'Plague of wild dogs in these parts,' said Tibben, a man clearly as stubborn as he was weathered.

'So,' said Reeves to Angst. 'You're about to hang a man who denies stealing a chicken based on him having, in his possession, what is clearly a seagull's feather.'

Angst turned his back on the crowd and spoke in an urgent whisper behind a hand held up over his face in an attempt at directing the words purely towards Reeves. 'What sort of merchant are you?'

'One who will cheerfully pass on to all and sundry that a miscarriage of justice has been avoided thanks to the clear thinking and compassion of Asabone's mayor towards the indigenous population. If you let this man go, that is.'

Angst, whose demeanour had become increasingly sour, frowned. Behind his eyes there appeared to be a lot going on, albeit at a pace unlikely to threaten the speed of light, sound or even geological change. 'But a crime has been committed.

And, more to the point, there is a bounty on every Nari's head. A silver lupin for each one…' He paused and then added in a whisper, 'And you'd say that? In those words?'

'Under the watchful eye of The Father of the Village, blah-de-blah. Plus, I have money. I'm sure that there's more than one silver lupin in my purse. And we will be wanting food.'

That, it seemed, was the clincher. Angst turned around and addressed the crowd. 'We in Asabone pride ourselves on our open and friendly approach to tourism.'

There were a few nods but many more confused looks at this sudden change of tack.

'Not that we get many visitors,' Angst continued. 'But we wish to assure those that do come that they will find a welcoming and honest hamlet.'

This time, there was a smattering of applause.

'Therefore, I have to report that in view of the new evidence that has come to light, there will be no hanging.'

Disgruntled moaning oozed up from the crowd.

'You will know that, as the arm and hand of justice for the region, I have pledged to leave no stone unturned, or feather unexamined. As such, a more careful analysis of this feather shows it to be from a seagull, not from a chicken.'

The moans turned into gasps of surprise at this astonishing bit of deductive reasoning.

Angst waved his hands to quieten them. 'But the good news is that our visitors are here with money.'

The gasps became instant cheers.

'I think that a communal traditional brown-grass dance demonstration might well be in order.'

The crowd evaporated. To Reeves' surprise and bafflement, every person who walked past the statue of Erthu Le Liare bowed their head in a gesture of reverence. Depressingly, he realised that this was an automatic response.

Seeing his bewilderment, Milda explained, 'Worshiping the Le Liares is a requirement.'

Angst cleared his throat. Reeves turned and realised that Omeolegamundi remained under the block and tackle with the noose around his neck. Reeves climbed atop the rickety arrangement and took off the rope.

'You're free to go.'

Omeolegamundi grinned. 'Uncle said you'd come.'

'Me?' said Reeves. 'Do I know your uncle?'

'Maybe. He's been gone for twenty years but he watches over me. They call me Ome.' He held out a hand and Reeves shook it.

Angst, having dismissed the charges, was keen to move on. 'Now, about this money you have. How much exactly?'

Reeves walked off towards the small hostelry that served as a saloon to join Milda and Raymounde. When he looked back, Ome was walking off into the distance holding a long tube up to his lips.

'What is that thing?' Reeves asked.

'It's a combination of a musical instrument and deadly blow pipe that uses darts. Called a thiswilldoo,' Raymounde said with authority.

'What happens if you're hit with a dart?'

'You go songlinewalking on the echopaths,' said Milda.

'And when you wake up?'

'You generally thiswilldon't,' said Raymounde.

CHAPTER TWENTY

As Ome disappeared over the horizon and the tiny band began warming up in the nearby hostelry, a little girl in the dispersing crowd let go of her mother's hand and ran across to a low building standing on its own.

'I want to see Chasy,' she wailed. 'I want to see him.'

In hot pursuit, her mother grabbed the little girl's arm and chastised her. 'You know you can't see Chaise. He's not well. He has to stay in the torium for now.'

'But I want to see him. Chasy! Chasy!' Her cries rang out before she was swept up into her mother's arms and quickly taken away.

Before Reeves could say anything, Milda stepped across and stopped the woman. They spoke, but they were too far away for Reeves to hear. Yet it was obvious that the little girl's outburst had upset the woman. She broke down and sobbed as Milda tried to comfort her. When she finally hurried away, Milda stood on the dusty square, her face troubled, staring at the long low building the woman had referred to as the torium.

Mayor Angst emerged from the hostelry, full of the bonhomie induced by the prospect of real money and with a glass in his hand for Reeves. 'We'll just be a few minutes,' he said, wiping the sweat from his brow. 'It's a hot one. Care for some rice wine?'

Reeves waved away the drink.

'I'll have it if he doesn't want it,' Raymounde said and took the glass.

'It's much cooler inside,' said Angst.

'What's that?' asked Reeves, pointing at the torium.

'Oh, it's nothing for you to concern yourself with,' said Angst.

'I'm not concerned, merely curious.'

'It is a place where the sick and injured can rest while they recover,' said Angst. 'Now, about this food you want, we have some excellent choices including goat curry with shiny rice, nettle soup with shiny rice and yoghurt, and shiny rice pudding on a stick.'

'Is it frozen?' asked Raymounde.

'No, more lukewarm and cheesy hard, I'd say.'

Before Raymounde could respond, Milda came striding towards them. 'I'd like to see inside the torium, please.'

Angst let out a dismissive laugh. 'Strictly off limits, I'm afraid. Especially for girls. The people in there are in quarantine.'

'Why?'

'Something that's going around. We call it the blue lurgi. Quite a few children have come down with it. Best we let them, um, get over it in the cool and the dark.'

'I'd like to see,' said Milda, firmly.

'I really don't think that's wise. The blue lurgi is a nasty thing—'

'She's a healer,' said Reeves. 'Maybe she can help.'

'But the band—'

'Can wait,' Reeves said in a way that brooked no argument from the mayor.

Milda's eyes shone with a cold and brittle light. The mayor had seen it too and was frowning in that way most belligerent people do when stoking up for a urinating contest.

'It would also be useful for us to report on the good work

you're doing for the sick and injured,' Reeves schmoozed, thickening the plot with a little flattery in the process.

Angst swallowed, considered this new carrot and made his mind up. What he said next was delivered half apologetically as his gaze strayed to the huge effigy overlooking them all. 'We follow the instructions of the Great Wandmaster and Guiding Star to the letter, you know. We have, of course, informed Gogny Payn of the lurgi.'

'Then our visit should be enlightening,' said Reeves with a smile absent of sincerity.

Angst bowed slightly, though his own smile morphed into something fixed and sickly. They followed him across the square, under the watchful glare of Erthu's statue. There was no door at the front of the low building. Instead, they walked around the side to the rear. Here windows were open, covered by muslin curtains that wafted in the breeze. A man with a large club stood guard. Angst waved him aside and stood back.

'Feel free, Mardock', said the mayor, who showed no desire to enter the building himself. 'There are masks inside.'

Milda pulled the door open and Reeves and Raymounde followed her in, the latter with a most unhappy look on his face.

It was dark. Children were moaning and crying. The room consisted of two rows of low cots, every one of them occupied by a small body. Most were under blankets; some, those whose limbs were continually convulsing, were not. Apparitions hurried along the wide central aisle and between the cots, bringing water or damp rags to soothe and succour. They seemed to float rather than walk. But when Reeves' eyes adjusted to the gloom, he saw that every one of them wore voluminous gowns from neck to foot and, bizarrely, each one had the head of a long-beaked bird.

The air smelled sickly and sweet, redolent of vomit and worse. It was unpleasantly hot. Reeves felt a hand on his arm. Raymounde was holding something up for him and he recoiled immediately. It looked like a petrified bird's head until he realised that these were the masks that Angst had told them about.

Plague masks.

Reeves took one but before he could fit it, Milda had walked into the room, mask-less. Several of the nurses—because Reeves now realised that this is what the weird bird-masked creatures must be—rushed towards her. But Milda was having none of it. Instead, she walked the length of the room, staring down at the children. Stopping occasionally to get closer and peer and examine. She held up limp arms, steadied a flailing leg. Some of the children were moaning, but the noise they made was muted and pathetic. Some had grotesquely swollen limbs. All were struggling to breathe, their skins waxy and pale, some blue from lack of oxygen as their lungs failed them.

Reeves joined Milda, who had stopped halfway down to look at a boy of around four years old. Barely moving, his chest heaving, his eyes were crossed from pain or some quirk of the disease.

It was a harrowing sight.

'Milda, we can't stay here,' said Reeves. 'This lurgi is obviously dangerous. You're not even wearing a mask.'

'We do not need masks,' said Milda. Or rather, spat Milda.

Reeves had expected her to be upset, but not, now that he close enough to really see, this trembling, barely constrained fury.

'We need to talk to Angst,' Milda said, not waiting for an answer. She stood abruptly and stormed from the building.

Angst was outside and living up to his name. 'As you will see, we have, as per the Wandmaster's instructions, built this splendid, modern facility to house the sick—'

'What do you eat?' demanded Milda.

Angst blinked. 'What?'

'What do you eat?'

'Ah, that is yet another munificent example of the wonders of modern Rathkoorne. Over the last three years we have established a trade cooperative. In exchange for our wonderful goat's milk products, we now have access to rice. Ever tasted rice? Wonderful stuff. Especially shiny rice. Our children have benefited hugely. Why, over the last two years the average height of a ten-year-old has increased by three quarters of an inch. And—'

'What is shiny rice?' Milda stopped him mid-flow.

'An investment we in Asabone made into our futures. We take milk and yoghurt to market and trade it for dirty rice. Awful stuff. Brown and chewy. But then our Most Worthy Baron sent out his chief food management officer and allowed us to invest in a rice mill. Wonderful device. Changes dirty rice into shiny white rice and it only takes one mule. Of course, we have to pay for this technology, but in thirty years' time, the village will own the mill and half the mule. We saw it as a very worthwhile investme—'

Milda screamed.

It took everyone by surprise, largely because the scream was accompanied by her waving both fists at the sky. It went on for a long time. When she'd finished, her face was contorted with anger. 'You have sunflowers at the edge of that field,' she said, pointing to the edge of the village.

'Yes,' Angst said, relieved that Milda's attention had drifted in a horticultural direction. 'Damned nuisance. Popping up all over the place. We usually cut them down and burn the lot.'

'Get someone to collect as many as you can. The flowers only. We need the seeds.'

Angst frowned. 'But we're about to have some dancing.'

'If you want to see those children live, you'll collect the seeds.'

Angst swallowed loudly. He turned again to Reeves. 'Is she a witch?'

Reeves shook his head. 'Possibly. But even if she isn't, I wouldn't test her at this moment. I don't think she'd need any witchcraft to do some serious damage. She looks like someone who has seen this before.'

'I have. Get the seeds,' Milda repeated through teeth not so much gritted as clamped together, alligator-style.

Angst called to the man with the club and issued some orders. The man responded by laughing and slapping his knee. But when Angst repeated the order and cuffed the man around the ear, he hurried away towards the flowers.

'Show me this mill,' Milda demanded. She turned to Raymounde and whispered something.

The dwarf's eyebrows lifted a quarter of an inch. He finished his wine, gave the empty glass to a bystander and wandered off towards the stables.

Angst, still smiling like the good politician he was, nodded and headed for a side street. 'Of course. The mill. Delighted. My great aunt was a witch, you know. Fought in the troll wars, she did. She got a medal, too. Well, the bits they sent home in the cigar box did.'

Milda remained tight-lipped as she followed Angst, who was now elaborating on how the official from Gogny Payn had come with two carts to set up the rice mill.

'It was a great day. They taught us how to clean the rice. Mill it, make it shiny for the children. Oh, and how to make rice wine.'

'All for a price?' Reeves asked.

'Investing in the future of the people of Rathkoorne and eliminating poverty, that's what the man said. We even had an extra hour of singing songs of praise to Erthu, our Great and Munificent Father.' Angst beamed. 'It was truly a wondrous day.'

At the end of the street, an open building revealed a mule yoked at right angles to a wheel that followed a bumpy route around a stone circle. Attached to the wheel was a large wooden beam, on the end of which was a thick pestle. Each time the wheel went around, the pestle went up and down and thumped into a bowl full of rice inside the stone circle.

'Marvellous piece of kit,' said Angst. 'Beats all the husk off the rice. We wash it and then mix it with delicious things like grasshopper or mealy bug. Ever tasted ying-yang-hop? Basically, fried rice with a hopper of your own choice.'

Raymounde appeared at Milda's side. 'Here you are,' he said, and handed her a sledgehammer.

Milda took it, walked forwards calmly and brought the sledgehammer down on the stone wheel. It shattered on the third blow. Not completely, but enough to startle the mule into a braying panic, which ended in it cantering off, yolk dangling and pestle flailing.

Angst's mouth worked silently as he stared at the ruined mill, his dreams of shiny rice and financial independence reduced to rubble. When he finally found his voice, it emerged as a strangled squeak. 'But...but the payments... thirty years...the mule...'

CHAPTER TWENTY-ONE

Angst waved his arms just as Milda was gearing up for another smash.

'Stop! Stop! Are you mad?' he screamed, trying to grapple the sledgehammer away from her.

'No, I am not,' Milda protested. 'In fact, I think I am the only sane person here except for Reev—Mardock. I am reserving judgement on Raymounde. But I am also saving the lives of your villagers.'

The commotion brought people streaming out from the hostelry and from the decrepit houses nearby. They took one look at the mill, the hammer and Milda, and turned ugly. Or uglier because the hard life of Asabone had not left many of them with a complete set of teeth, an unlined face or many straight limbs.

Raymounde shook his head. 'I didn't sign up for this.'

'You provided the weapon,' Reeves reminded him.

'Yeah, but I didn't know I was giving it to a card-carrying bloody lunatic.'

The crowd shouted and gesticulated as Milda swung the hammer away from Angst's grasping hands..

Reeves placed himself between Milda and the angry mob. 'If you've got something to say,' he yelled over his shoulder at the girl, 'now would be a good time.'

Milda, out of breath from fighting with Angst, looked out at the crowd who, disappointed from missing out on a hanging, looked likely to segue into a lynch mob without passing go. 'I am a healer,' she bellowed. 'I have travelled all over Rathkoorne and I have seen the blue lurgi more than once.'

They stopped shouting.

'I have watched Molk make potions and seen them all fail. Until we went to the Hightops. There we saw two villages, separated by a river. It was a twenty-mile trip to cross the bridge between them. Like you, they were benefiting from the rice harvest and were able to trade. But, in one of the villages, we found many children with the blue lurgi. In the other, we found none. It took Molk a long time to work out why there was such a difference. Some thought it was the river gods cursing one village and blessing the other. But we realised that the Zatrank had not crossed the river to the furthest village. It had not received the offer of a mill. It still had to eat "dirty" rice.'

The crowd made collective 'ugh' noises.

Milda shook her head. 'You don't understand. It was the village that ate the dirty rice that had no blue lurgi. Something in the husk prevents it.'

'But our children love the shiny rice,' said a petulant voice.

Milda nodded. 'And it is the shiny rice that is killing them.'

'But that's ridiculous,' said Angst. 'Why would his Highest General of the Wand Army want to do us harm?'

Milda's mouth contorted. It could almost have been a smile. Reeves had seen smiles like that before on the faces of some of his clients. The ones who thought nothing of walking into a crowded bar at midnight in deliberate search of violence.

'Erthu is interested only in profit,' she said. She might as well have been wearing a T-shirt emblazoned with the word *Blasphemy*. 'He doesn't care about the effect his rice deal is having. Perhaps, I might even be prepared to admit that he, or his instruments, could be ignorant of it. But you are no longer ignorant. You must stop this milling. Learn to eat the whole rice.'

Angst was probably not a bad man. He was just a man stuffed full of bad ideas who was not used to having them questioned. And Milda, in his eyes, was nothing but a meddling little girl. 'Nonsense. You don't know what you're talking about. Shiny rice is what feeds us. Besides, it tastes much better that the dirty stuff.'

Milda's smile didn't shift. 'Tell that to your children in the torium.'

'I've heard enough.' Angst moved forward.

Milda raised the sledgehammer in warning.

Angst was having none of it. 'Give me that hammer.'

Milda didn't move but her eyelids did. They dropped a couple of millimetres as if in response to a decision made. 'Certainly.' She opened her hand and let gravity take over. The heavy hammer fell…right on Angst's open-toed sandal.

The crowd winced collectively.

Angst made a noise like a screeching bird and began hopping madly until he lost his balance, fell into the donkey's stable and lay there, whimpering.

No one laughed. Most of the crowd also wore open-toed sandals and empathy can be a powerful thing.

'Why should we believe you?' barked a voice from the crowd.

Milda turned to address him. 'Because I have seen this with my own eyes.'

The man with the club appeared with a wheelbarrow full of sunflower heads and negotiated his way to the front

Milda pushed Reeves aside to stand defiantly alone. 'And I can prove to you that this is not a disease and that it isn't contagious. It is a deficiency. With your help, we can make all of those sufferers better.'

'With magic?'

'With these.' Milda picked up a sunflower.

'She's mad,' said a voice.

'No. She isn't,' said the mother of the little girl who had

called for Chasy. 'Britta doesn't like the shiny rice. She chews on the dirty rice. She has never had the blue lurgi.'

The crowd turned to stare at her and the bright-eyed, healthy-looking girl clutching on to her skirts.

'It isn't because she has a birthmark in the shape of a turtle on her ankle, then?'

Milda's eyes went skywards and she shook her head.

'No, it's because she's too stubborn to do as everyone else does,' wailed the woman and clutched Britta to her as if she were a precious piece of porcelain.

A large man in the crowd stepped forward. 'Both my children are in the torium. Tell me what to do with the flowers.'

Milda took out the seeds from a sunflower, threw them into the mill and used the sledgehammer to crush the shell. Then she threw the mix into a bucket of water. The empty shells floated to the surface and she scooped them out before plunging in her hand and pulling out the seeds.

'These will help. Mash them, make then into a porridge with honey and feed it to your children.'

'Seeds?' said Angst.

'Salvation,' said Milda.

There was a long moment when everything stood in the balance. Then Britta's mother stepped forward. 'I will do it if it helps my Chaise,' she said, and grabbed a handful of sunflower heads. Another half dozen women followed and then the large man. With his involvement, the crowd's hostility evaporated like early morning mist.

Reeves knew then that Milda had won them over. Several people ran to harvest more sunflowers and others set to work fetching water. Milda supervised and, once the porridge was made, helped the women with the feeding. Many of the suffers were too ill to feed themselves, but by darkness, all had been given the 'cure'.

Fires were lit so that work could continue with the sunflower processing. In the flickering light, Reeves watched Milda as she talked to the women about other restoratives to aid recovery. They all listened avidly.

'She's a one, isn't she,' Raymounde said.

The dwarf confused Reeves. Despite an ego the size of a small shire horse, he'd spent the best part of the afternoon helping Milda with no further questions asked.

'She's passionate,' Reeves replied. 'And she's good at communication. Always a potent combination in my book.'

'Ah yes, your book.' Raymounde stretched and yawned. 'Still a lot of empty pages in there, right?'

'Why? Does it bother you?'

'No. But I can't work you out. You're a ship without a rudder. All we had to do was call in here for some water and now here we are running a torium.'

'It's Milda that's running the torium.'

'Yes, but it's you that's facilitated that.'

'How?'

'By not slapping her down. By not letting Angst have his way.' Raymounde handed Reeves a hunk of bread but narrowed his eyes before passing it over. 'Ever since you walked into the Wheel Askew, my life has become a lot more interesting. You sure you're who you say you are?'

'Have I said who I am?'

'Not really.'

'Then let's keep it that way.'

Raymounde shrugged, a faint smile playing on his lips. It irritated Reeves, mainly because he recognised the truth in it —he doubted his own identity, even in his private thoughts.

'Did you try one of their shiny rice puddings on a stick?' Raymounde asked.

Reeves shook his head.

'It's actually not bad. You should try it; it's part of their culture.'

'It's worry over what sort of culture a piece of tepid cheese and warm rice is harbouring that is precisely my reason for not eating it.'

'Nah, there weren't many furry bits.'

'Even one furry bit is a furry bit too many in my book. We have a long way to go. I do not want to spend it searching for dock leaves.'

'Why dock leaves?'

'They are big and gentle on the…' Reeves looked down at the hard bread in his hand. 'I'll just stick to bread for now, thanks.'

CHAPTER TWENTY-TWO

REEVES SHARED a room with Raymounde who, for someone not possessing the biggest of statures, made an awful lot of noise when he slept. The snoring was bad enough, but the rhythmic snorts and whistles were interspersed by high-pitched expulsions of air much like someone at the very start of learning to play the trumpet. And though the bits of vibrating anatomy involved were different, if not poles apart, if success could be measured in terms of length of note, Raymounde deserved a gold star. Reeves, meanwhile, would have done anything for a nose-peg and thanked the gods there were no canaries in the room.

Or parrots.

But he was prepared to excuse the dwarf since his efforts at helping dose the sick with sunflower porridge had been heroic. Size was not something you discussed with Raymounde. Any suggestion of heightism was met with a stony stare and an almost visible elevation of neck hair, a bit like an angry miniature terrier. But his smaller size seemed to appeal to the children in the torium and, combined with his gruff manner, proved a useful tool with some of the more recalcitrant patients. Raymounde was willing to use convoluted argument and explanation, referencing his own far-off country with its bizarre and often quirky ways, in order to cajole. He was persistent and patient beyond measure.

'What happened to the crabby, unpleasant rodent we picked up in the Wheel Askew?' Milda asked Reeves in a quiet moment earlier that evening.

'Gone into hibernation, it appears,' Reeves replied, watching Raymounde fly a mouthful of porridge into a four-year-old's mouth by pretending it was an albatross diving through the 'arched sea caves on the edge of the lumpy sea'.

Now, as he lay on a narrow but surprisingly comfortable straw bed, Reeves brought his mind back to his task. Though he did not regret the circumstances, their stopover in Asabone was an unplanned delay. He fingered the brown-and-cream whelk shell amulet around his neck. The Seren Sea Stone, Matt had called it. An ugly keepsake that might be the match that lit a flame. He did not underestimate its importance. Tomorrow, if Milda wanted to stay to tend to the sick, he would go on to Gogny Payn alone. Or perhaps with Raymounde the back seat trumpeter, if he wanted to tag along. But for now, he was grateful for the bed.

He was less grateful for his dreams.

———

HE WAS BACK in the loud chaotic world of the shiny horseless carriage, standing at the edge of a roadway, watching vehicles speed past. In his hand was a smooth flat stone, its surface polished and mirror-like. Suddenly, the stone vibrated and an apparition appeared on the mirrored surface. A woman's face distorted by paint, her ears and neck adorned with gewgaws, her hair streaked in many colours. She spoke.

'I couldn't sleep.'

Reeves stared at the face. It was familiar, but though he was unsure why, something told him her presence was unwelcome.

'Go away.' Someone spoke. It was him. His voice.

'Have you signed all the papers?'

Reeves shook his head. 'Go away, witch.'

'Do you miss me, Trevor?' The woman laughed.

'Begone.'

'Never. You will never be free of me, Reeves. I will always haunt your dreams.'

Reeves stepped off the pavement. He knew the apparition's name but did not know how he knew.

Demelza.

The rushing traffic screeched to a halt. Everything stopped. They stood like great beasts, their hearts thrumming under the metallic bonnets, impatient to roar again. Yet they stopped for him and made a safe passage for him to cross.

The woman, the witch Demelza, was nonsensical now. She used words he did not understand yet her tone was full of mocking. He crossed the great black roadway and stood looking up at a tall building with slatted windows. He peered through and saw the space inside for the shiny metal vehicles. A lair where the beasts slept.

Still the witch jabbered. He tried to rid himself of the stone, but he could not. It was stuck to his hand. He walked in front of the building and found a great entrance with a ramp spiralling upwards. He stopped. Despite having cleared the road, the vehicles no longer moved. It was as if they were waiting. And then, behind him, he heard the baying of a huge hound. He turned and looked back across the way he had come. Beyond the road was a desolate moorland. A barren landscape dotted with gnarled trees and hillocks bathed in a sickly yellow moonlight.

A thing, half female human, half dog, crested a hill and sat, its snout pointed upwards. It opened its mouth and howled. Within that unearthly ululation, Reeves somehow heard his own name.

He started to run, knowing somehow that the beast on the moor had his scent. He could hear his feet slapping on the black road as he climbed the ramps from floor to floor, each stacked full of sleeping metallic vehicles until, at last, he emerged into the cold air. The wind buffeted him and he stood peering up the moon and stars. Below he heard the hound's cry echoing.

Ever louder. Ever nearer.

He began to run again. In his hand, the witch cursed his name.

'Reeves, Reeves, you can never outrun me.'

'I will never pay,' he said, knowing that this would goad the beast.

She screamed.

He reached the far end of the roof and climbed a parapet. There he stopped, surveying the world, a world that seemed to end in blackness a hundred metres from where he stood.

The witch screamed his name.

The hound bayed.

Reeves looked back as the hound emerged, its huge jaws slavering, a hellish light in its wild eyes.

'Never,' he said, and jumped.

CHAPTER TWENTY-THREE

R‌EEVES AWOKE WITH A GASP, an echo of the dreadful falling sensation still in his stomach. He opened his eyes. Daylight.

Quiet.

No Raymounde.

Reeves got up and splashed water onto his face. Outside, he could find no trace of anyone but he could hear noises… was that laughter?

Dressing quickly, he left the small stable annex and made his way along the already warm and dusty street.

Outside the torium, Raymounde was playing catch with a child that could not have been more than four years old. She was pale and weak looking but threw the knitted ball back to Raymounde enthusiastically. He, in turn, missed the ball and let it fall on his head. The resulting 'knock' sent him sprawling in mock agony, much to the giggling delight of the little girl.

There were others outside in the daylight, too. Children and adults enjoying the early morning sun, being helped to walk, ministered to by the 'nurses', who were all thankfully now devoid of those dreadful plague masks. Reeves spotted Milda supervising some women sorting through fresh clothing. She looked tired, but the light had not dimmed from her eyes.

'What's happening?' Reeves asked.

A nearby woman turned to him, smiling. 'It is the cure for the lurgi.'

He beamed at Milda. 'Is this all down to your sunflower seeds?

Milda nodded. 'Some have recovered quickly. Others will take much longer.' One of the items of clothing she was unfolding dropped to the floor. She bent to reach for it, but one of the women stopped her and reached for it instead. Milda sighed. 'They want me to go and rest.'

'Probably not a bad idea.'

Milda shook her head. 'They are calling me the white witch.'

'Could be worse.'

'But I am not a witch. Yet, I agree, this is magic of a kind. A natural magic. A magic locked into the plants and the rivers and streams that they should all know about. How are we ever going to get the people to understand?'

It was a forlorn plea from a tired heart. Reeves looked around. The results of Milda's natural magic were everywhere to be seen. But a small group of three men with grave expressions stood on the far side of the square, watching.

'Not everyone seems enamoured,' Reeves said.

'They are scared. What we are doing is new. It has not been written down by the Zatrank. It makes some people nervous not to have such things sanctioned by wand lore and its enforcers.'

'Does everything have to be written down by the Zatrank?'

'Welcome to Rathkoorne,' Milda said.

'Surely, they'll see the wisdom of not polishing the rice or making sunflower seed porridge if it makes the blue lurgi go away?'

'I would like to think so,' Milda said, 'but what if the father Wandmaster disapproves?'

Reeves frowned. 'You're doing a great job. Let them believe you're a witch for now. Once everyone is cured, then put forward your theory of natural magic.'

'Perhaps you are correct, Reeves.'

Raymounde joined them, the little girl padding after him.

'Didn't know you were into sports,' Reeves said.

'We have annual games in the Neverlands. I am a throwball champion. Watch.' Raymounde threw the ball. Or rather, he threw the ball but let it go early so that it travelled no more than a yard despite his best grunting effort. The girl screamed with laughter, as did the three other little ones that Raymounde had gathered as his audience. They scrambled for the ball to the accompanying peals of delight.

'You're good at this,' Milda said.

'I have half a dozen brothers and sisters. I'm the oldest,' Raymounde explained. 'These children…they have lost much. Many have been orphaned because of this cursed lurgi. How could these people let it get so bad?'

'Ask Erthu Le Liare,' Milda said, darkly.

Reeves shrugged. 'If I ever get the chance, I'll make a point of doing exactly that. In the meantime, I'm afraid I can't stay any longer. I have a job to do. I'm leaving for Gogny Payn as soon as I can.'

Milda and Raymounde stared at him.

Reeves smiled. 'Why don't you both stay here and carry on this work? They obviously need your help. I'll call back once I'm done.'

'But you haven't told us what it is you need to do?'

'Deliver something, that's all.'

Neither of them looked happy. Milda spoke first. 'If you had not challenged Angst over the hanging, we would not have found these people.'

'Yeah,' Raymounde said, albeit with grudging admiration. 'I thought you were mad, but I'm beginning to see a little method there.'

'Don't be too hasty,' Reeves warned them with a lopsided grin. 'And perhaps I can do a bit more to help, but not here.'

Milda threw her arms around his neck. 'Thank you,' she said in a muffled voice. 'For everything.'

When she had disengaged, Raymounde shook Reeves' hand. 'Well met, Reeves. I still owe you a drink. I will make sure that I fulfil that promise in Gogny Payn.'

'Make it a large one.' Reeves grinned.

Raymounde's eyes flashed a warning.

Reeves held up both hands in entreaty. 'Sorry, it's just an idiom.'

'You're the idiom,' said Raymounde as a swarm of small children, most of whom were about his height, began pulling at his sleeve and holding out the knitted ball. He took it and threw it up into the air to catch it in his mouth.

The children cheered and shouted, 'Again, again.'

Milda smiled. 'You must not mind Raymounde, he says these things without rancour.'

'Be careful he doesn't hear you use that word either,' said Reeves.

Milda frowned.

Reeves sighed. 'Oh, what it is to be innocent.'

———

HE BREAKFASTED on rice and meat and, within the hour, had made his way along a well-walked path leading up to a ridge where, he was assured, an old drover's road led all the way to Gogny Payn. Though his task didn't allow for sentimentality, he did spare a thought for his companions. He meant what he'd said. If he could, he would go back and help.

Milda, like a lot of people in this godforsaken country, had become a victim of a totalitarian regime bent on self-destruction, if the way they treated the common people was any measure. But he could not afford to let his concern for her get in the way. Besides, she had Raymounde with her. Despite his shortcomings, particularly when it came to charm, the dwarf had displayed a surprising degree of heart towards the sick and the infirm. He also had the added advantage of not being from Rathkoorne—not officially—which meant that he was not paralysed by a mindset that believed their national leader to be some kind of mystical being whose wandword was law.

He'd walked for almost an hour before he reached the high ground and a linear path leading south. It looked wide enough to have once been a cart track, but judging from the grass that now grew upon it, it was also rarely used. Reeves rested at a trig point and drank some water. From where he stood, he had a panoramic view. Several miles to the east he could just make out the road, and between it and him, Asabone sat in a dusty bowl.

Indeed, it was rising dust that triggered the first tiny twinge of concern. A thin pall arose between road and village. A plume rising up in the still air, as if from the horses of a troop of soldiers. He was too far away to see any detail. But he stood, nevertheless, looking and wondering. But when the dust became smoke, grey initially and then thick and black, concern became alarm. Instinct told him something was amiss. He started to run back down the slope he'd clambered up.

Back towards Asabone.

Reeves was no more than a mile away when he began to make out the screams. He did not try to hide his presence. He knew his efforts would be fruitless against the troop of mounted Zatrank he'd seen, but he also knew he could not abandon these people.

Asabone was alight. Every building burned, black smoke curling up into the uncaring blue sky. He could see horsemen sitting tall in a ring around the village. Sitting and watching. But there were no villagers in sight.

Where were all the villagers?

And then Reeves knew. His stomach lurched and twisted in a swoop of rising horror. At the same time, one of the horsemen turned to look at him. He'd seen this man cavorting at the side of a lake, brutalising a mage in conjuring a portal to another world so that he could cause destruction in the most heinous and cowardly way.

Gauinebald had a plump figure and a face as soft as a child's, but his sharp, restless eyes showed a mind driven by chaos. Behind the mask of a cheerful imp was a man whose dark imagination turned devastation into an art form.

The guards on either side of Gauinebald each had a body

tied across a mule. One was much shorter than the other. Both were alive and struggled against their bonds.

Reeves was beyond caring. Fury boiled inside him. Red hot and volatile. He picked up a rock and threw it at the horsemen. He picked up a dozen more, walking towards them, hurling abuse with every stone. 'Bastards! Filthy murdering bastards!'

A horse broke ranks and cantered towards him, followed by Gauinebald.

The leading horseman kept coming. Reeves kept throwing rocks. One of them hit a rider causing him to swerve.

Behind him, Gauinebald laughed. 'He finds his mark, Turgiss. He finds his mark. Careful, or he'll have you unseated.' He unsheathed a wand and watched as Reeves' rocks fell short.

'Why?' Reeves screamed.

'You cauterise infection, fool,' Turgiss de Wyville replied.

'They are not infected. What they had was a simple deficiency.'

Turgiss' horse was massive and Reeves was now almost under its hooves. He had to dodge to avoid being trampled.

'Then we burn them because we like the sound of their screams,' said Gauinebald. 'And the smell.' He giggled and dropped his voice. 'Is it not a mouth-watering aroma?'

Reeves had two good-sized rocks left. He feinted left and darted right. The horse was too ungainly to follow. Reeves wanted to get close enough to be within range of the grinning Gauinebald. He threw the rock. It was on target. Gauinebald watched its arc until it was within ten yards and then pointed his wand.

The rock exploded.

Gauinebald grinned. 'Your aim is true.'

'The girl and the dwarf, they are my friends. At least let them go.'

'But they spout seditious lies. We need to interrogate them.' Gauinebald's grin seemed painted on his face.

'The gods will never forgive you,' said Reeves.

'Blasphemer,' yelled Gauinebald. 'We are the gods.'

'On your knees, tramp.' Turgiss' boot met with Reeves' shoulder and sent him stumbling. But only as far as one knee. He felt for a knife inside his jerkin, rolled with the fall, and came up and threw the knife at the same time. It was deflected by Gauinebald's armoured saddle but grazed the monster's thigh. Gauinebald screamed.

'The next one will be in your heart,' said Reeves.

'We eliminate infection. Vermin we exterminate,' Gauinebald hissed.

Reeves saw the wand swing towards him, reached for his other knife and then felt something hit his chest. Pain exploded around him, white hot and icy at the same time. It seared his eyes and flew into his mouth. He could not breathe; he could not move. It lasted for a second or two only, but somewhere, he heard someone laughing.

Darkness followed. Complete and utter, it swallowed him whole.

CHAPTER TWENTY-FOUR

HE BECAME aware of light before anything else through filtered eyelids. For some strange reason, he didn't want to open his eyes for fear of seeing something blue. Why was he worried about blue? Surely, being a student of popular culture, he should be anxious about opening his eyes and seeing someone carrying a scythe, possible on a white horse, probably talking in capitals…

His thoughts were weird and jumbled and formless in the darkness. He supposed he could be dead. He supposed in that case, there would be no harm in opening his eyes.

Seeing was the trigger that brought all the other sensations, previously in hibernation mode, back online.

First came cold. Bone-numbing and harsh.

Second came smell. Rotten meat and something metallic.

Third came dizziness. He was high. Suspended? Levitating?

Fourth came discomfort, quickly followed by pain.

He sucked in air. Cold dawn air. And that was when his chest exploded in a bout of dry, wracking coughs, each one like someone driving a spike into his breastbone.

His brain did a quick analysis. Pain and breath meant he was alive. A fact confirmed by the absence of the bloke with the scythe. He was dizzy because a glance told him he was up high, thirty feet or more. The ground below consisted of a dirt road; no, two dirt roads, meeting at a crossroads. The smell? Was it him? No, it was the bits of decrepit flesh clinging to the cage that surrounded him like an iron exoskeleton.

And then there was the noise.

A croaking 'kraa' from above. He couldn't move his head, but he could move his eyes. A raven, sleek and black and large, sat on a beam jutting out at right angles to a pole from which he was being suspended.

And then he knew.

He was alive but should not have been.

The raven cawed again.

Reeves yelled at it. 'Bugger off.'

It fled, flapping wildly and cawing an alarm as it flew.

Probably disappointed at missing breakfast.

But Reeves al fresco was off the menu. For now, at least. He took stock. He wasn't levitating. It was more dangling in an iron cage shaped roughly like a body: arms held out perpendicularly, legs in iron trousers. He could not turn around, but he could breathe. They'd hung him up here for his bones to be picked clean by the crows. They hung him up because they—and for they, read Gauinebald—had assumed he was already dead.

He remembered the pain and the darkness from the curse that he'd been hit with.

It had felt like death.

But he wasn't dead.

Every agonising breath reminded him of that fact. He was also thirsty and about to get thirstier, judging from the cloudless dawn sky and the orange-yellow light that was stretching his shadow like a giant's finger over the ground. To the east, the sun poked its fiery head over the horizon in mock greeting.

He looked up. Another bird was approaching. He saw its shape against the sun. Big enough to be a crow. But when it landed on the crosspiece above his head, it chattered.

'Great,' Reeves said. 'Now the bloody magpies have arrived. Go on, you bugger off, too. No bottle tops here.'

The magpie chattered some more.

'Get lost,' Reeves said and rattled his own cage.

The magpie took off, leaving Reeves once again alone.

Thirsty, angry and alone.

Then he remembered the disguised Seren Sea Stone around his neck. He couldn't lower his chin but by straining hard and driving his eyes downwards he could glimpse his chest between gaps in his ripped cloth shirt. The leather thong was there, and below it, if he wiggled, he could feel the light touch of the shell.

Not even worth stealing.

But what good was it around his neck when he was trussed up like a rat in a cage waiting for the sun to bake him and the wind to scorch his scratchy eyes?

Think, Reeves. Think.

There was a chance that someone might happen along, in which case…But then he thought about how likely it was that one of Rathkoorne's brainwashed citizens would help someone strapped in a gibbet. A criminal left hanging as an example for other would-be miscreants would not be someone to pity.

He turned his attention to the iron cage. It looked as if it was in two parts with him sandwiched between. A simple bolt secured the central belt, locking both halves together. It wasn't locked, but since his hands and arms were a good two feet away from that bolt and held rigid in an iron framework, it might just as well have been welded shut.

His thoughts turned to Milda and Raymounde at the mercy of Gauinebald and he groaned in frustration. This wasn't in the plan.

His thoughts stuttered. What plan? Had there ever been a plan other than for him to get the shell delivered to Gogny Payn? This damned plan seemed the most nebulous of all the missions he'd been on.

More mental stuttering. What missions? He knew he'd

been on missions but for the life of him, he could not remember even one.

Great.

Had Gauinebald's curse affected his brain?

And what about that curse? How come he was still alive to even be thinking about it? He remembered everything about Milda and Raymounde and the Wheel Askew and Asabone—how could he forget Asabone—but before that, nothing. Nothing except his dreams of falling and being pursued by a witch with her face on a slab of black polished stone.

The sun was up now and it was already taking some of the chill out of the air. Reeves knew he was in a tight spot, literally and figuratively. But he knew that panic would not help and so distracted himself with self-analysis. Of course, getting hit by a curse was bound to cause a degree of brain-addling but the more he tried to concentrate, the more his thoughts turned back to his dreams.

His work, the plan, his mission, call it what you like, stemmed from a background in the army. Yes, he could recall that fact. But he could not recall where or when. As for life before the army, that was a black hole.

And yet he could recall his dreams with stark and vivid clarity.

Demelza the vicious witch. Metal horseless vehicles. Falling from a great height. They all felt much more real to him than his army past and his work as a…what? A spy? Part of him wanted to believe that this was concussion or the dehydration cutting in, but another part began to wonder what was dream and what was reality.

The morning wore on slowly and inexorably. The sun, by mid-morning, was a fireball branding Reeves' trapped face and neck. He tried to put thoughts of water on the naughty step, out of sight, but it kept creeping in like an old dog until it was a slavering beast. His lips felt cracked, his tongue huge. At midday, with the sun at its highest point, he saw someone approach. A trundling horse and cart laden with goods. They would have water, too.

'Hey,' he croaked. 'Hey, up here.'

His voice was a thin, rasping ghost of its former self and for a while Reeves wondered if they would hear him. But when the wagon was within thirty yards it halted.

He yelled again. 'Up here. I'm up here. Not dangerous. All a mistake.'

The wagon remained where it was. Reeves could see movement. There was a driver and some smaller shapes. Children, probably. They seemed to be clambering into the rear.

'Hey!' yelled Reeves.

The cart started moving, gathering pace, accelerating until it was within a few yards. The driver had a scarf over his or her mouth. In the rear, some lumpy shapes under old sacks moved and wriggled. Reeves watched the cart rattle underneath him, speeding through the crossroads, the driver not looking up, keen to get away from this terrible place and the horrors it contained.

In other words, him.

He rattled, he screamed, he berated, but it was no use. He stopped when they were thirty yards past and let himself imagine, for one second, being the driver of that cart, taking his family to market and seeing the terrible sight of an occupied gibbet and the maniac within. It was the stuff of nightmares. No wonder the children had hidden.

The sun was excruciating by now. The dehydration a howling dog on the threshold of his consciousness. He was going to die up there in this damned cage. Exhaustion overtook him. If he gave in and fell asleep, he would probably never wake up and Rathkoorne would continue to be a lost world with an oppressive regime so horrifying in its totality it hurt to even think about it. He tried singing but couldn't think of any songs. He tried reciting poetry but couldn't remember any verses. What was wrong with him?

He even tried to remember Demelza. Pretty, devilish Demelza and her harpy voice. Come to think of it, her voice sounded a lot like the crow had sounded. Perhaps they were one and the same. But not the magpie. That had sounded more like a warning.

Thanks for that, magpie.

Squinting through lids swollen from the heat, Reeves saw a speck on the horizon. An animal of some sort, far in the distance. He wondered if jackals could climb poles. It could probably smell him being slowly barbecued. By the time it got to him he'd be a nice medium rare.

Reeves shut his eyes against the dusty wind and thought again of Demelza. At least that way he knew he wouldn't sleep. When he opened them again, the speck was bigger. Taller, upright, not a jackal. Something on two legs.

A man.

He was drifting in and out of consciousness now. Unable to swallow. Maybe this was the Zatrank inspector, coming to check that he was cooked enough for the vultures and crows. One thing was certain: the speed at which the man was approaching could not be described as quick.

Reeves shut his eyes. He opened them again when he heard a voice.

'What you doin' up there?'

Reeves looked down. His vision had blurred, the dryness now sucking fluid from his own lenses, making the world a hazy yellow place and the man a darkish blur holding a big stick. But he knew the voice.

'Ome,' he wheezed.

'You hang on there. We'll get you down.' Omeolegamundi raised the stick to his lips.

Reeves shut his eyes again. All he could hear was a deep, resonant droning. It was an oddly restful sound and in his hallucinating mind, it sent Demelza the witch running with her hands over her ears.

CHAPTER TWENTY-FIVE

PICT

Meanwhile, Rimsplitter was holding another briefing with the DOF agents. No matter how dire the report, he'd decided to start every one by beta testing a joke or two. This time, the head of the Bureau of Demonology, Prof Duana Lewin, chaired the meeting. Once again, they stood in the meadow, a wind warm in their faces, Rimsplitter stalking up and down in front of them.

'Everyone here?'

They all nodded.

'Good. Got one for you.' He chuckled. 'This'll effin' slay you, I promise. So, I was makin' an offerin' in the temple the other day and this bloke stands up and starts reelin' off passages from the holy book. From memory. Bit weird 'cos he was dressed as a chicken. No one minded 'cos he was well impressive.'

'And he was dressed as a chicken?' asked Asher.

'Yeah. That's 'cos he was a lay preacher.'

As before, Rimsplitter erupted in laughter at his own joke despite the stony faces in front of him. He continued to convulse for another minute, referencing the punchline in a way that suggested his audience must be either deaf or mad not to have found the joke hysterical.

'Lay preacher, come on. *Lay effin' preacher.*'

'Highly amusing,' said Duana with a face devoid of emotion.

'You bees are a tough audience,' Rimsplitter said, finally.

'Maybe we're not in the mood,' Kylah said.

'You are no fun, did you know that?'

'What news of Reeves?' Asher persisted.

''E's a proper enigma, your Mr Reeves, ain't he? F4 spots 'im at a bleedin' crossroads trussed up like wossname in them films, you know, flies about and has a battery for a heart.'

'Flies about and has a battery for a heart?' Kylah repeated with incredulity.

'Yeah. Bloke with a balbo.'

'What is a balbo?' Asher asked.

'You bees know nothin' when it comes to facial hair. Whereas me, 'cos I can't effin' grow any, know it all. A balbo's a style of beard, you double-you.'

'I find conversation with you somewhat circuitous,' Duana said with a frown.

'Tony Stark, *Iron Man,*' Matt said.

'That's 'im.' Rimsplitter nodded.

'So F4 found Reeves dressed up like Iron Man?' Kylah asked.

'Yeah. Only this suit he had on couldn't fly and was stuck on top of a pole.'

'A gibbet?' Kylah's voice rose in alarm.

'Exactly. How he got himself stuck up there is anyone's guess. He is such a Kuwaiti tanker.'

Asher mouthed 'Kuwaiti tanker' to himself, looking bewildered.

'Was he alive?' Bobby demanded.

'Yeah. Alive enough to tell F4 and F1 to eff off. Bit of a cock-up in that they both spotted him on independent reconnaissance flights and both went to the nodal point to report. By the time the bees got back to the gibbet, he'd done a Houdini on us.'

'He's gone?'

'Exactly. Done a runner.'

'Someone must have got him down from the gibbet. Do you think the Zatrank removed him?' Asher pierced Rimsplitter with one of his intense looks.

'Unlikely. Them ay-aitches like to let a corpse go good and pen and inky before they clean out the cage.'

'Pen and inky?' Asher looked lost.

'Stinky,' Bobby obliged. 'I am definitely getting the hang of Rimsplitter lingo.'

'Ergo, someone else has helped him,' persisted Duana.

'Looks that way. We'll keep an eye out. We've found the bee once, I'm sure the boys'll do the business. Now, did I ever tell you about my mate Kev who got into trouble 'cos he kept phonin' the RAC?'

'No?' Asher said with untrammelled innocence.

'Yeah, the doctors thought he was havin' a breakdown.'

Kylah shook her head. Matt exhaled.

Asher said, 'Why would contacting the Resonant Arcanum Collective imply a mental condition?'

Rimsplitter's next sentence contained more bees and cees than a butterball carapace.

The others got up to leave, but Rimsplitter hadn't finished.

'I haven't told you the best bit yet. F1, the raven, was targeted by a mob of hostile crows. It may have been a territorial thing, who the eff knows. Suffice to say, F1 only just managed to escape. My theory is that them crows have been wanded to act as sentinels, bees. Now it ain't safe for F1 to go anywhere near. He's been grounded.'

'Who does that leave as our eyes and ears?'

'F4, the magpie and F2, old Marshy,' Rimsplitter said. 'He's carrying a couple of tracer gnats. If anything happens to him, they'll report back. Trouble is, you only get basic intel from your gnat. Stuff like, good, bad, dead or alive. Reeves needs to pull his bleedin' finger out.'

'Keep us informed,' Kylah said.

'And how is your squirrel?' Asher asked.

'Still in the hospital, thanks for askin'. Keeps on about how bad the food is and the nurses don't speak his lingo and the bed is too hard.'

'Really?' Bobby said before Matt could stop her.

Rimsplitter took his opportunity with deadly speed. 'Yeah, doctors say he's critical.'

They left the eagle trying to punch the air with his wing.

CHAPTER TWENTY-SIX

RESONARI ENCAMPMENT, RATHKOORNE

WHEN THE DRONING STOPPED, Reeves woke up to find himself no longer upright. He was lying on some sort of rustling material.

Straw.

A breeze wafted over his face, but unlike the baking wind slowly dry roasting him in the gibbet, this one was cooling and blissful. He opened his eyes. It took a while since they felt like they'd been sandpapered and pasted shut with bits of mucoid string. He rubbed them clear of grit and gunk, looked around and saw that he was in a clearing under a rough awning. On the floor next to him was a metal jug and a wooden cup. He struggled up onto an elbow, filled the cup and drank it. It might have been swamp water for all he knew, but if it was, it was the best damned swamp water in the bloody world. Except that it wasn't swamp water. Not really. This was clear, crisp water that must have come from a well deep underground where the temperatures was just about perfect. He drank the whole jug and could have drunk another.

His eyes took in his surroundings and squinted with the

effort. Outside his resting place was a camp, or, if someone was feeling generous in a let's-not-worry-about-the-rubbish-scattered-everywhere sort of way, a village. Of sorts. Though whoever was meant to do the sorting had decided to leave it for another day, or maybe even decade. There seemed to be no semblance of organisation. A variety of buildings, if the hammered-together bits of spare wood, mud and rusting metal could qualify as buildings, dotted the space. Most had cloth awnings like the one Reeves was lying under as shelter from the sun. Under these awnings sat, or lay, people. That they were ethnically related was obvious. Reeves chided himself for that thought, but there was no denying the broad foreheads, the curious hair arrangement, and, of course, the squiggly body paint.

This was a Resonari place.

As if on cue, a dark figure appeared, silhouetted against the bright sun in the entrance to the bivouac. He stepped inside and Reeves immediately recognised a grinning Omeolegamundi.

'How you feelin, Trev?'

'A lot better than when I was up in that gibbet. And who is Trev?'

'You were pretty croaked when we got you down. But you told us your name okay.'

'How did you get me down?'

'The birds did it. They can sing when they want to.'

Reeves nodded, wondering what singing had to do with anything, and took another sip of the cool water. 'I don't know how much longer I could have lasted. Lucky you were passing.'

'No luck, Trev. I knew you'd be there. Uncle told me.'

Reeves wanted to laugh but there was nothing remotely funny in Ome's delivery. 'Are you serious?'

'Yeah.'

'But how could your uncle kno—' Reeves stopped himself. 'This is your dead uncle, right?'

'Yeah. I'll get Auntie to get you some edibles. You'll feel better.'

Ome disappeared with a grin, leaving Reeves to ponder. And ponder he did, now that he realised he'd been given a gibbet reprieve. Ten minutes later a small woman in a colourful dress brought in a plate full of leaves, nuts and berries. On the side were what looked like orange-brown curled fingers.

'Fried wizardy grub. Good for aches',' said Auntie.

It was, indeed, good eatin'. The wizardy grubs tasted like fried eggs and pistachios. Reeves ate them all. After he'd finished, he felt a lot better. When Ome returned, Reeves was on his feet to greet him.

'See, told you.' Ome grinned. 'Got something to show you.'

Reeves followed the Resonari through the heaps of rubbish and abandoned carts, past tail-wagging dogs and wide-eyed children playing half naked in the dirt.

Ome kept turning to look at him with a smile.

'Thanks for the food,' said Reeves, and conscious of the fact that these people were dirt poor, said desperately, 'I can pay.'

Ome roared with laughter.

'What?' Reeves asked.

'Our camouflage is working.' Ome was still grinning. Reeves failed to see the joke as they approached a jumble of big red rocks and began skirting the base. Halfway around was a deep crack.

'Come on in,' said Ome.

It was only a short passage. The air inside was warm and smelled musty. Within a few steps it was pitch black. Reeves felt rather than saw Ome stop. 'There's a big rock in front of you. You need to feel your way around it.'

'Can't we get a torch?'

'No. Doesn't work here. Nothing works here. You'll be okayTrev. Follow me.'

The rock was cylindrical and as big as a man. At first Reeves felt nothing but solid sandstone, but as his fingers groped, he felt the curve to his left open up and he was able to squeeze through. Immediately he did, he could see a thin slash of light ahead and the familiar figure of Ome moving towards it.

Reeves followed with the light growing brighter with every step until the last one brought him out into full sunlight. There, blinking against the sun while his eyes adjusted, Reeves stood and stared. Before him was a green vale, lush with vegetation, full of tidy parcels of fenced-off land growing produce of all sorts. At the far end sat a circular array of well-built huts with solid wooden walls and thatched frond roofs. The paths and roads were spick, the verges span.

'Wha…' Reeves said.

'This is the other side, mate. Where my family's really from. Not everyone can come through the space to this place. But Uncle said you would. Fancy a tour?'

Reeves did. Ome took the long route on the perimeter of the vale close to the rocks that completely ringed the settlement. People smiled or said hello before getting back to their tasks of tending to the crops or feeding the chickens, mending fences, gathering bugs. Halfway around, Reeves couldn't stop himself.

'Okay, okay, I get it. You're efficient market gardeners, self-sufficient by all accounts, so why the hell do you have the other place?'

Ome grinned. 'So's the Zatrank leave us alone. They think we're like animals. But animals a lot cleverer than they are. Even the tuckeraloo is, and he's as thick as pigtoot.'

'Okay, so why then did you expose yourself to the people of Asabone, who seemed to require bugger all excuse to lynch you?'

'Ah,' said Ome dismissively. 'To meet you, Trev.'

'Meet me? But how could you possibly have known I'd be there?'

'I didn't,' said Ome. 'Uncle did.'

'Uncle? Who is this mystical Uncle? And whop the hell is Trev?'

They were standing in front of a small grove of trees at the centre of which a red rock protruded.

'Ask him yourself,' said Ome and pointed into the groves.

The rock had been carved by the elements to look like two people sitting on top of it.

'That's Uncle. He's solid.' Ome pointed to one of the figures. 'Go on over. He wants to see you.' He gave Reeves a nudge.

The figure on the rock may once have been flesh but was now nothing but petrified stone. Even so, given what Reeves had already been through, he approached warily, half expecting the stone figure to sit up.

'Hello Uncle,' said Reeves.

Ome let out a huge laugh. 'He can't hear you.'

'I thought he spoke to you,' Reeves said.

'Only when I'm singing on the echopaths. But he'll be glad you called by.'

They continued walking, but Reeves was becoming restless. Memories of the gibbet and Ome's vague explanations were being pushed to one side by fragmented recollections of how he got there in the first place. Especially being struck by Gauinebald's curse. 'How come I'm still alive,' he asked Ome. 'Does Uncle know?'

'Oh yeah, he knows. My uncle, he's a Voxari, A teacher and a guide, he sings us all the old songs and channels the Lumia. That's our power. The thing that makes all this,' he waved a hand vaguely. 'He reckons your being alive has got something to do with that shell around your neck.'

Reeves hand went automatically to his chest. The shell was still there. 'Really? It's a message.'

'It's more than that,' Ome said.

Reeves waited for the qualifier; it never came.

'Come on, Uncle says you better see this.'

Reeves followed Ome past the rocks and down into the heart of the vale. There was more greenery here and Reeves assumed there would be water. It wasn't until they pushed through some eucalyptus that he saw the building. It wasn't like anything else he'd seen. This was cut stone. A flat impregnable building. Ome walked to one end and an open doorway. Inside it was dark, but Ome did something with a flint and suddenly the whole place lit up with oily torches flickering into life.

Inside, it was bigger that Reeves had thought. Bigger and full of shelves. And on each of the shelves were wands. Reeves moved to the closest one. It lay flat on a piece of parchment, on which was drawn some sort of arcane symbol. A quick glance to either side told him that the symbols were all different.

'What is this place?' whispered Reeves.

'A wand house. This is what was left after Le Liare and his lot took what they could from the druids. But there were other wands. The druids brought them to us.'

'But…'

Ome grinned. 'You're going to yarn that there are enough here for all of Rathkoorne, right?'

'Exactly. You could fuel a revolution.'

The grin never left Ome's face. 'But we know what happens if you give people wand power, right? It's too rubbish. So, these wands have no power.' Ome picked on up and tossed it into the air before catching it. 'Try if you like.'

Reeves picked up a wand and pointed it at the roof and imagined a light. Instantly, a mini sun started to glow.

'Wow,' Ome exclaimed. 'You can drive one of these things, can you?'

Reeves dropped the wand. 'Apparently. What does that mean? What did I do?'

'I reckon it's that dandy shell around your neck. Maybe you can turn them on and off with it.'

They walked the length of a long aisle. At the end was a small amphitheatre and a chair right in the centre. 'What's this?'

'It's a curse player. Lets you see who's cursed you and what happened. Like if someone was trying to curse you on the sly, give you humbug. You'd catch them out with this, alright. Give it a go, if you like.'

CHAPTER TWENTY-SEVEN

REEVES WALKED to the stone chair and sat. Instantly, a representation of what took place on the outskirts of Asabone started…playing. It was the only way Reeves could explain it given his own buried context of watching TV and films. Something, a shimmering crackle in the air solidified into some kind of imagery. He watched as Gauinebald's curse sent him into paroxysms of agony and what appeared to be a very definitive death. The scene faded and was then replaced by the stable yard in the Wheel Askew. The drunk soldier and the inadvertent curse by which Reeves had turned the bloke into chum. Obviously, the scenes were being played in reverse order with the most recent first.

Reeves watched, fascinated, as the images played out in front of him and the drunken soldier got decimated. He was halfway up out of the chair when the stage crackled once more with power.

'What's this?'

'Someone else got you, Trev mate.'

A third curse? But he had not been cursed three times. At least, not to his knowledge. 'No, there hasn't been a—'

Reeves never finished. Another image appeared. A very strange image. Something dredged up from his weirdest dreams. The sea and a landscape with buildings the like of which he had not seen in Rathkoorne. Whitewashed cottage-shard, black roads. He could see himself, or at least a younger version of himself, and he could see a girl.

The strength drained from Reeves' legs and he fell back onto the chair. The girl was out on the rocks, smiling and waving. The day was bright but wild with wind. The kind of day one would want to capture, if at all possible, because the girl with her infectious smile and the day with its golden light and cloudless sky combined to form something natural and rare and precious. She was out on the shoreline and he was higher up on the dunes, holding in front of hie eyes a flat stone. Reeves could feel his heart swelling. Somehow, he was sharing, not only the imagery, but the youthful joy at seeing such a wonderful sight.

And then it happened. The sea rose up. Or rather a huge hand of water rose up from nowhere. One second a calm gentle swell, the next a wave in the shape of a hand so huge that it fell with a crushing weight on the girl. If the blow didn't kill her, then the surge of water that dragged her away into oblivion surely would.

But Reeves knew the truth of it. Ome, or his uncle, had revealed it to him. It was as if someone had stabbed him in the brain with a stiletto. He knew that they would find her body in two weeks, washed up on a beach twenty miles away, already a sad and picked-at buffet for a thousand sea creatures.

And, like the tons of water that had fallen on the girl, memory now came plummeting down onto Reeves. He even knew her name. Rhiannon. He knew the cove where it had all happened: Abereiddy on the far western reaches of Wales. Knew he wasn't a sergeant in the army, nor a spy, but a suicidal idiot who'd let himself be tricked into some wild ride that was worse than the weirdest computer game ever invented. Worse because it was so bloody real. And yet worse, too, because it patently could not be.

Could it?

Without warning, Reeves needed to heave. He got up

from the seat and ducked to the side, losing the wizardy grubs in the process in a spattering mess.

'You okay' asked Ome after a while.

'No,' moaned Reeves. 'I am bloody well not. I need some fresh air.' He staggered past Ome and out into the sunlight, anger and confusion trumping the nausea.

Reeves, Trevor Reeves.

That's who he was.

A sad man trapped in a cruel marriage, the consequence of the worst of the many, many poor decisions he'd made during a wasted life. And he remembered the blue room, and Danmor and Porter and the jump off the multistorey and Miss Fenella Whitney and Kwantum whatever it was. He knew he should not have remembered, but he did. Seeing Rhiannon so cruelly crushed had given him a severe mental jolt and somehow jump-started the part of his brain that should have been in hibernation.

Yet the anger and confusion that were coursing through him were not aimed at the DOF and their offer of death or salvation. It stemmed from the sudden, horrifying, despicable realisation that what had happened on that beach all those years ago was not some freak accident of nature.

What had happened was the result of a curse.

He heard the word echo around the inside of his skull. A bloody curse? It sounded arcane. Like something from a kid's story. Definitely not a part of Reeves' reality.

But somehow, horribly, it fitted the narrative perfectly because no one else, no meteorologist, or sympathetic coast-guard, or old sea dog who'd lived on or around that coastline had given him any sort of satisfactory answer.

And then, hot on the heels of Reeves' reluctant accep-tance came the question.

Why?

Why would anyone want to curse him or the girl he had loved?

It was at this point that his mind might have stalled on its fast track to the truth. For years, he had replayed his memory of events. Tortured himself with a battering ram of what-ifs, and found the capriciousness of nature an impenetrable and implacable brick wall. But now all that had changed.

Because suddenly and sickeningly he knew why. And that nauseating realisation crept over him like a stench-filled marsh fog.

He knew because he had seen.

He had witnessed at first hand on the shores of that dark and terrible lake the random and wanton destruction wreaked by the Ogre, Gauinebald. His destructor curse chose victims at random in places where they would be clueless as to the cause. And who was to say in this mad world he had been catapulted into that unbalanced wand-bearing sadists could not transgress time as well as dimensional space?

Ome emerged from the wand house, took one look at the trembling Reeves and said, 'Take the songline to the echopath by the stream there, Trev. It's peaceful down there. You'll feel better.' He pointed toward a path.

Stumbling, Reeves took it, glad of a chance to be alone. The path meandered down through a grove. He heard a magpie chatter and looked up. The same bird that had visited him on the gibbet. Probably one of the spies Danmor had mentioned. Reeves let out a thin laugh. How could he know that? All magpies looked the same to him.

He kept walking because he didn't want to stand still.

Reeves had never been to a psychiatrist. Never had counselling for his grief following Rhiannon's death. He knew without ever having had it explained that he'd suffered post-traumatic stress disorder or whatever other post-modern slant was currently being given to a human's inability to accept and process scenes of horror. He knew that you didn't ever recover from anything like that. Not in his world where there weren't any wands that could wipe your mind clear of memory. There was not a day that went by that he would not see that image of the water hanging over her. The way her smile faltered at hearing him shout the warning. The way her hair caught in the wind as she turned to look…

But now he had seen it again, and in truth it was worse

the second time. Reliving it had been harrowing and despicable. Then why did he feel better?

For years, Reeves had agonised, torturing himself for letting her clamber alone onto the rocks. A part of him knew that it was ridiculous to punish himself like that, but somehow it had helped. Just as it had helped when he finally made the decision to end it all.

Or was it to join Rhiannon?

He'd used Demelza's poison as an excuse, but the truth was that the kernel of that idea had grown inside him since Rhiannon's death. The same idea, he now realised, that made him a willing participant in the DOF's espionage.

The stream he was following emerged from a rocky outcrop, meandered for a hundred yards and then disappeared again. More than an oasis, it was a cool, shady Eden. Reeves walked along the path, crossed a small wooden bridge and came to a second bridge. It was no more than a quarter of a mile circuit, but he kept on walking. And as he did, he could feel the change inside him begin.

Admittedly, there was something attractive in being the mindless sergeant bent on delivering his package; the false narrative they'd implanted inside him. It didn't take a genius to figure out that in that guise he'd been ignorant of his previous life and spared the horrific memory of the beach. But it wasn't real, that existence. And he'd been more troubled by his lack of memory than by some nebulous motivation to get the job done, hadn't he?

But the real Trevor Reeves had history. Real history.

For the first time since that fateful day, he could examine the situation coldly, see it for what it really was. And though he could still frame a tortuous argument around the fact that he had let Rhiannon walk out onto those rocks, it was spurious. And blaming nature in all its cruel, capricious glory, was equally ludicrous. Nature had played no part in what had happened. The event was as unnatural as it was possible to be. And now, with malice aforethought added to the mix, blaming himself was doubly nonsensical.

The truth was that the dark hand of a very bad actor had

played its part in Rhiannon's death. A brief and monstrous moment of malevolent whimsy that made it all the more evil.

The Zatrank hold over their people stemmed from a great power. But with such power came immense responsibility. Or, in the case of a reckless, malicious fool like Gauinebald, an even greater irresponsibility. Much had been written and said about the most powerful men in history. The consensus was that they tended to end up with worse natures than they had to begin with.

Nor was it uniquely the fate of dictators and emperors. Many people acquired power, fame, or wealth without ever bothering to read the instruction manual—knowledge essential for handling such privileges wisely. Sadly, it was all too tempting to flex one's egotistical muscles by humiliating those on the lowest rung, and to revel shamelessly in that cruelty. Gauinebauld was a prime and especially vicious example of this tendency. So, Reeves now faced choices. He could talk to a magpie or a bloody squirrel and let them know that his mental cover was blown. That way, he might be extracted from the situation and face his life, or death, back in Manchester.

Or, knowing what he now knew, he could continue to tread the path he'd been following before Danmor and Porter had interfered, but forget the Manchester multistorey and do it all here. Assuming the shell offered control: without it he'd be vulnerable and another encounter with some wand-happy Zatrank could easily end it all.

Or he could continue playing the game, knowing that he had around his neck a weapon that gave him the same power that the Zatrank wielded so mercilessly. There was also a weapons cache within a stone's throw of where he stood. He could mobilise an army if he wanted to.

Reeves paused on the second bridge. It was the third time he'd crossed it. Memory of his last encounter with Gauinebald made him clench his hands on the rail. Not because of the pain. Not because of the leer in the madman's eye. Reeves was remembering the mules and the bodies tied across them.

He needed to think. Frustration boiled and he turned his face up to the sun and roared. No words, just a wild and necessary guttural appeal to the gods. The magpie took off in fright.

He walked the echopath circuit one final time, having decided that Ome's songline meant a direction and the broader way the echopath, and stopped once more on the footbridge and looked at the stream, his thoughts now settling into a decision.

'Do you think I'm mad?' he said to the water.

The voice that answered was inside his head. 'As a box of frogs.'

It had Uncle written all over it.

CHAPTER TWENTY-EIGHT

In the end, it was a porcupine that settled things. Or at least that was the descriptive word that popped into Reeves' head as he rounded a corner on the echopath and saw what was sitting on the verge. It had a crest of black-and-white hair on its head and a vicious array of sharp-looking quills beginning halfway along its body pointing backwards into a semblance of a tail.

It looked like it was waiting for him.

Reeves' first instinct was to backtrack and try and find a way around it. But when he turned, the porcupine whined and clicked its teeth. Reeves turned back, staring at the large rodent.

'No, you can't be serious.'

The porcupine clicked again.

'You're DOF?'

The porcupine inclined its head.

'Wait, okay. If you are a DOF agent, turn around in a circle.'

The porcupine got up from its sitting position and turned a full, slow circle.

'Great. A pirouetting porcupine. Did they send you to find me?'

The porcupine began its slow and laborious turn again.

'Wait,' Reeves said. 'Just nod your head instead.'

The porcupine hesitated in its turn, turned slowly back and nodded once.

'Shake for no, nod for yes, agreed?'

The porcupine nodded.

'Well, I'm still alive.'

Nod.

'But only just.'

Nod.

'This country is a complete craphole run by a bunch of murderous thugs.'

Nod.

'I've still got the stone,' Reeves showed the animal the shell.

Nod.

'They still want me to complete the mission?'

Nod.

'Do I have to?'

Shake.

'But it is the only hope for the people, isn't it?'

Nod.

'Why didn't they tell me about Ome and the wand repository?'

Nothing.

'What else aren't they telling me?'

Nothing.

'They're a bunch of gits.'

Tiniest nod.

'Now, because of me, other people are in trouble.' Reeves sighed and shook his head. 'Oh, and you can tell them that I know. I know everything. I know who I was before they did their voodoo in the blue room. I'm not Sergeant Reeves anymore.'

Nod.

'Bloody DOF.'

Nod.

'Do you have a name?'

Nod.

'Don't tell me. Spiney or Needly Nobby, is it?'

Shake.

'No, it'll be something ironic, won't it?'

Nod.

'Cuddly?'

Shake.

'Squeezy?'

Shake.

Reeves thought hard. The porcupine plucked a low-hanging berry from a bush, placed it on the path and stepped on it repeatedly until it was pulp.

'Squash?'

Shake. The porcupine did a bit more pulping.

'Squish…flatten…pulp?'

More treading in of the berry.

'Grounding? Mashing—'

The porcupine nodded once.

'Mashing?'

Nod and shake.

'Mashing…mash? Nothing very ironic about—'

The porcupine tilted its head and touched one ear with a paw.

'Oh, wait. Sounds like mash?'

Nod.

'And it's ironic…mash…mish…marsh—'

Nod.

'Marsh…marshmallow?'

Nod.

'Bastards,' said Reeves.

The porcupine tilted its head again, turned slowly and waddled off into the undergrowth.

'Not exactly the pony express,' muttered Reeves, 'but I suppose you'll have to do.' He kept on the echopath as it meandered back towards the wandhouse. Eventually, he emerged a few yards from where he'd left Ome sitting on a tree trunk. He was still there, whittling. He looked up as Reeves approached.

'Get what you needed, Trev?'

'No. But then who does?'

Ome grinned. 'That sounds like something Uncle would say.'

'I met a porcupine called Marshmallow.'

Ome nodded, completely unfazed.

'I've sent a message up the line, but who knows how long porcupine mail takes to be delivered. But I need to find out if Milda and Raymounde are okay. That'll mean going to Gogny Payn and delivering this package.' He flicked at the shell hanging around his neck. 'I can't take on the Le Liares. But if there is someone in Gogny who can use this thing, then perhaps he or she can help me get Milda and Raymounde out. That is, if they're still alive.'

'And after that?'

Reeves smiled. 'After that, I'm a free agent. I can finish what I started.'

'Or start what you tried to finish?'

Reeves nodded. 'Now that sounds like something Uncle would have said.'

'I like you, Trev. You're straight up.'

'I might need a bit of help to get to Gogny.'

'No worries. But first we better get you fed since you threw up the wizardy grubs. My auntie's made smoked eel patties. You got time. I mean we all got time. Here especially. The Zatrank think you're in a gibbet.'

Reeves nodded. 'I'm a dead man walking.'

'No mate, that's a different gang. I can introduce you, if you like?'

Reeves had a moment in which to contemplate whether Ome was having him on or not. It was difficult to tell because the constant grin he wore gave no clue as to whether the news was meant to be bad or good or weird or ordinary. Reeves plumped for the safe option. 'No, that's okay. I'll pass on that. Smoked eel patties, eh?'

'Yeah. They're to die for. But only one or two people a year.'

This time Reeves plumped for laughter as a response. Ome joined in, much to Reeves' relief.

Until they'd walked thirty yards and Ome asked, 'Why are we laughing?'

———

UNDER NORMAL CIRCUMSTANCES, a porcupine moves pretty slowly through its habitat, does not see well but has an excellent sense of smell. But they are intelligent. And Marshmallow, or Marshy, as named by his squad leader, Rimsplitter, knew it would take a long time to walk to his den. But the DOF had thought about that and had set up relay stations whereby the agent could send back reports. By necessity these were well disguised, and the one Marshy headed for doubled as a fallen fencepost. Once there, all any porcupine had to do was rest its head against the two little jade nodules hammered into the rotting wood. Even these were well disguised as bits of lichen, but unlike lichen, these charmed connectors were capable of memory extraction. It was easier this way than having translational devices and spells. It meant that Marshy didn't need to understand one word of Reeves' speech, though he clearly did. In effect, the porcupine was a mobile CCTV camera, and all it now needed to do was thaumaturgically upload the information. Though its prime directive, the trouble was that it also had a fair amount of porcupine instincts. And, existing as it did on potassium-rich foliage, old Marshy was quite partial to a bit of sweat-stained wood full of sodium. Which went some way to explain why, mid-way through its mission to report back its encounter with Reeves, it found an abandoned walking stick, which had been handled at least a thousand times.

In the interest, therefore, of metabolic balance and because it tasted delicious, Marshy's report had to wait while he chomped through the stick. He was still chomping when he saw the dog. Or rather heard the dog as it charged towards him. There was a moment of searing pain in Marshy's leg before he was flipped up in a somersault. Mercifully, he landed on all fours and went immediately into defence mode.

Contrary to popular knowledge, a porcupine does not fire

off its quills. But they do stand to attention when the animal is threatened. The dog, hungry and having tasted blood, went in for the attack and came away with a quill in its snout, howling in pain and leaving Marshy to hobble away, knowing that the nice, tasty stick should be left for another day and hoping that the dog didn't have too many friends nearby

CHAPTER TWENTY-NINE

GOGNY PAYN, RATHKOORNE

Erthu Le Liare, the baron of Rathkoorne, stood watching his favourite troop of female singers, the Rathbong Bongadiers, entertaining the crowd. The girls, all hand-picked for their looks and voices, were dressed in daring ankle-length dresses with a slit to the mid-calf at the rear which, since they always faced forwards, was unlikely to drive anyone watching into a sexual frenzy. They were all of the same height and hair colour and harmonised the instantly forgetful melody to perfection. The song they sang was nicely arranged and the accompanying band played their instruments with military precision.

The Gogny Payn crowd listened politely, one eye on Erthu so that whenever he let his gaze drift in their direction, they would instantly begin swaying enthusiastically to the music. When his gaze drifted away, so did their enthusiasm. Not that the band wasn't any good. It was more what they sang than how they did it. The lyrics of this song, catchily entitled 'Dig for Farming Victory', was meant to stir the soul. But once you'd sung along to one chorus of

Dig with your shovel, weed with your heart,

Together we can slay our foes.
Mighty as warriors, stronger as growers,
To the sky we lift our hoes,

a second rendition generally foundered on the rocks of ridicule and self-consciousness. Unless you were a member of the Rathbong Bongadiers who would sing any bloody thing Erthu wanted so long as he left them alone and gave them three square meals a day, thank you very much.

The song ended and the crowd applauded. With a drum roll, they all turned to the main event inside the Keep: the dismemberment of the Advisor on Agricultural Taxes with an extirpating curse. It was done swiftly because it was necessary and the Zatrank were not, contrary to popular opinion outside Rathkoorne, all monsters. The man's sobs ended in a single scream as the executioner's wand made a swift criss-cross movement. The diagonal strokes were like scalpel cuts, slicing the man from shoulder to groin so that his legs fell from under him, then each arm, and finally, face down, what was left of the trunk.

There was no blood.

The watching crowd remained silent. It might have been out of respect or fear, or, more worryingly, that they were inured to such horror. It was impossible to say. Erthu Le Liare contented himself by assuming it was a little of each. Such demonstrations of his willingness to destroy one of his own were always highly effective. He liked to be seen as an equal opportunities dictator.

The advisor's crime was one of disrespect; he had fallen asleep during a feast. Such weakness could not be tolerated. The advisor would not be missed; he was old and was becoming forgetful, but the people did not need to know that. They only needed to understand and witness the baron's swift and merciless retribution.

He waited until the crowd began to disperse before stepping back from the balcony where he'd stood to supervise. Once out of sight, he strode through the Keep's opulent corridors and past the expensive tapestries and paintings towards a stairwell. At the half turn, unseen from above or below, Erthu tapped a stone in the wall. It melted to reveal another staircase leading down to a place where the only lights were flickering torches leaning out from wall sconces and the air was permanently damp and heavy with hopelessness.

He hurried past locked doors until he came to one where thin light oozed beneath. He pointed his wand and the door opened onto a dank space occupied by three people and lit once more by oily torchlight. Two of the figures were huddled in shadow at the far end, as if they were trying to get as far away as possible from the third.

Alienor Le Liare, as pale as milk, face painted garishly, her bare arms alive with inked symbols and writhing shapes, squatted next to a smokeless flame. The room reeked of sulphur and charred bone. She did not look up as Erthu Le Liare entered.

'Well?' he said.

'I have done as you asked, Father. The girl I have left alone. Gauinebald says he wants to play with her. The dwarf and I enjoyed a game or two before he sang.'

'Did he take much persuasion?'

'He has a loud scream for such a small body. He did not like the squeezing vines, nor the scorpion's kiss. Yet it was only when I threatened the girl that he sang.' The woman turned her face up. Her teeth were filed and glittered golden; her alabaster skin was pierced by eyes the colour of a storm at sea. In her braided hair nested the bones of small animals. She looked at the two huddled in the corner and smiled.

'Of what did he sing ?' Erthu asked.

'Of a traveller. A foreigner in Rathkoorne.'

'Impossible,' Erthu protested. 'We have the land and every border hexed.'

'This man is different. Different from us and the... people.' Alienor seemed to struggle with the word as if it was distasteful. 'He has knowledge. He has wand lore.'

Erthu's eyelids fluttered with confusion, as if he was hearing her words in a foreign language. The fluttering extended to his arms and legs. It was the kind of tremor that presaged a most violent act. 'No man can wield power in Rathkoorne except us,' he whispered.

'The dwarf was not lying.' A smile of amusement played over the woman's lips.

'What else did he say?'

'That he wanders in search of a beacon. A child with whom he can forge an alliance and move against you.'

Fury bled the colour from Erthu's face. 'Move against me?' he whispered, deadly calm now. 'Who dares move against us?'

'The dwarf does not know. His meeting with the traveller was fortuitous.'

'You know this to be true?'

Alienor nodded. 'Twice he has defied the Zatrank. One experienced soldier has died at his hands. Reeves was left for dead by Gauinebald in a gibbet. Yet the wind tells me that he is no longer in that gibbet and likely not dead.'

'What of the beacon? What do we know?'

'Nothing. The dwarf is ignorant. The traveller did not share his destiny. But he does remember that the beacon is a boy of apprentice age.'

'Then we will seize all males of between eleven and fifteen years. Let this Reeves meet with ghosts.'

Alienor nodded. 'It may be the safest way.'

Erthu looked down at his daughter's hands. 'Why is it that you refuse to use your wand? This information could have been extracted with minimal effort through a confession charm.'

'I prefer my own methods,' Alienor replied, cocking her head.

Erthu did not press her. She was too dangerous to goad.

'We will, of course, have to make an example of these two interlopers,' Alienor continued. 'A grand gesture. Mass murder perhaps? To entertain the masses. That I will leave to you and my brother.'

The baron nodded and, though it sent a deep and sickening chill through him, laid a hand on the woman's inked arm, like any proud father might.

But when he pulled his hand back, he couldn't help but glance down to ensure that all his fingers were still there. He stepped back through the door and called to some guards. 'Bring the dwarf to the throne room. I feel in need of some entertainment.'

CHAPTER THIRTY

RESONARI ENCAMPMENT

The smoked eel patties were excellent, and Reeves ate well. Ome's family, a gigantic extended family, were a friendly bunch and made sure that he was stocked up for the journey. But finally, Ome led the way back along the songline and around the big rock until they emerged once again into the rubbish-strewn encampment that acted as the Resonari's' expression of their place in the world of the Zatrank. All in all, Reeves thought it was a bloody good joke. He learned enough to know that the Naris had an oral tradition passed down through chants and songs, exalting their lumia, an energy that linked all living things. Their songlines followed this energy using sound, to the echopaths. Ways safely guided by oral maps. The shapes painted on Ome's skin reflected echo spirals and star traces. Things the Zatrank had no idea about or likely dismissed.

Ome's auntie insisted on performing a chime ceremony in which she tied small beads and pebbles on string to Reeves' hair and sang something called a chronochant Though few, the beads fell against his neck when he tossed his head and made a wonderful melodic noise..

'What do they mean?'

'Reminders of your visit. You'll be like one of us when you need to be. When voices join, the path appears."

Reeves nodded. His visit had been memorable, but perhaps for the wrong reasons. He said nothing to Ome but read understanding in the Nari's eyes.

'If it all seems a bit of a muddle, don't worry. It'll clear.'

They walked on towards the edge of the scruffy camp.

'Okay Trev,' Ome said as a dog urinated nearby. 'Chico says the coast is clear.'

Reeves looked from the dog to Ome, searching for any sign of humour. He found none but felt obliged to comment. 'I have to say that you lot have an elaborate signalling code.'

Ome frowned and then collapsed in a heap of hooting laughter, trying it seemed to point at something on the horizon, but failing each time his eye caught the bemused look on the dog's face. Between gasps for breath, Ome explained, 'Chico…Chico is…he's my cuz…you thought…dog piss… Chico is over on that hill.' Finally, Ome's waving arm veered towards the right direction.

By putting his hand over his eyes, Reeves managed to make out a tiny figure on the horizon.

'You crack me up, Reeves,' Ome said, tears streaming down his face.

'Glad to know I've raised a smile.'

This brought on another fit of Ome giggles with, one arm grasping his stomach and the other around Reeves' shoulders. 'Head for Chico. Then it's the big rock on the left. Just keep going after that and you'll fint it.'

'Head for the rock? Hardly an OS map.'

'Listen out for the noises on the songline. Couple of farms over there if you need some food. Besides, you won't get lost with 'im.' He nodded towards a magpie in a nearby tree who suddenly unfurled its wings. 'He's the fella that told me where you were when you were up in that gibbet.'

Reeves nodded. 'I wonder if he knows Marshmallow?'

'He'll see you okay. I know he will.'

'Well,' Reeves held out a hand and said with feeling, 'thanks for all your help.'

'No trouble. I hope you find what you're looking for, Trev.' Ome stared, clearly bemused, and a grinning Reeves realised that hand shaking was not culturally universal and it had been pretty arrogant of him to assume it was.

He headed for the shimmering horizon. As he passed the tree, the magpie took off and flew on ahead, chattering a magpie noise. The Nari sitting in the shade of their awnings made a low ululating noise in their throats as he passed. It was a strange and oddly soothing sound. Reeves, for some reason, found it both touching and comforting. When he turned back to wave at Ome, the Resonari had already gone.

For a single, panicky moment as he turned back to resume his journey, Reeves found himself directionless. But then the magpie landed some twenty feet from him, chattered an invitation and hopped in a direction that Reeves took to be the correct one.

It was hot. The ground beneath his feet looked parched with the thin grass scorched and lifeless.

'Looks like they could do with a little rain,' he muttered.

The magpie chattered away.

Reeves thought about trying to find out if it had a name, but the heat was unbearable and he was keen to get off this bleached land and find some shade. The magpie kept flying ahead by some thirty yards and then landed either on a bush or on the ground and hopped in the general direction Reeves was to take. Occasionally, it would take off and fly much higher, scoping out the land before landing again. Reeves spotted Ome's big rock on the horizon and an hour later, the land began to climb, the grassland giving way to shrubs and small trees and an altogether greener moorland. He spotted his first building four hours after leaving Ome. Though Reeves could have taken the detour around the buildings, the magpie was taking him the direct route, and that meant passing close to the structures.

Like the Resonari village, these farmhouses were simple and wooden with roofs of branches held together with mud and covered by grass. Reeves recognised the plants in one field as potatoes. In another, some not very tall corn. He spotted a figure in a wide-brimmed hat weeding in another field. It stopped on seeing Reeves approach and called out. Three other figures appeared, rising up from stooped positions. Two were significantly smaller than the others. All wore smocks, their heads protected by hats. All had simple hand-held hoes.

When Reeves was close enough to speak, he called out a 'Hello.'

The farmers stood stock still and did not reply. Reeves noted the youngest—a child of perhaps ten—eyeing the magpie.

'Afternoon,' said Reeves.

The magpie landed on the arms of a nearby scarecrow. The farmers' eyes followed it before they all turned back to look at Reeves.

'Don't see many birds then, do you?'

No one replied.

Reeves blew out air. 'Sorry to bother, but I wondered if you had any water to spare? I'd be happy to—'

He never finished the sentence. The youngest farmer turned and threw something at the magpie. It was a quick and deft movement. Too quick for the magpie, who let out a squawk and fell off its perch. The kid threw off his hat, revealing short hair and boyish features. He plunged towards the fallen bird, a knife already in his hand.

'No! Wait,' yelled Reeves and hurled himself after the boy, tackling him before he could reach the stricken bird. On the ground, Reeves grabbed the boy's smock and yanked him backwards, clambering over him to reach the magpie, who was stamping about, one wing unfurled and looking pretty much the worse for wear.

'Shit,' said Reeves. 'What the hell is wrong with you people?'

'We are hungry,' said a voice behind him.

Reeves looked around.

One of the taller farmers, hatless, stared down at him. 'Meat is valuable wherever we can find it.'

'But this isn't meat. It's a…pet. My pet.'

'We did not know,' said the farmer. He helped the younger boy up and stood in front of him. 'Forgive my son. He is hungry. We are all hungry.'

'That doesn't give you the right to just…attack.'

The man shrugged. 'We are hungry,' he repeated.

'Okay, I get it, you are hungry. We're all flaming hungry. But that doesn't mean you have to kill everything you see.'

'We did not know you were attached to the bird.'

Reeves reached into his bag and took out four wizardy grubs, all still writhing. 'There. Barbecue these.'

The farmer looked at the grubs, his face wide with delight. 'But there is enough here to feed the family for seven days! Such bounty.'

'Really?'

'Yes. My wife will make a stew. You must join us.'

'No thanks.'

'Please, my wife is also good with animals.'

'I bet she is.' Reeves was still angry.

'She will fashion a sling for the bird. You must let us help.'

'What about your trigger-happy son?'

'He will be locked in the cellar as punishment.'

Reeves swung his head around. The boy looked anything but contrite. 'There's no need for that.'

Suddenly and inexplicably, the family all started laughing. 'That was a joke. We do not have a cellar. But we do have an outhouse.'

The boy moaned.

'There's no need for that, either. Can you really help the bird?' Reeves glared at the woman, who had also now removed her hat to reveal a pleasant, sun-browned face.

She nodded.

Carefully, Reeves lifted the magpie into his arms. It flapped its wings impotently. Reeves wondered if it was in pain. The farmers watched, the boy standing well back, his sister clinging on to her mother's tattered clothes. They turned and walked towards the building. Reeves followed, noticing for the first time how poorly fitting their clothes were. There was no doubt that this family had won the battle against obesity hands down. The little girl in particular wore trousers that ended halfway down her calf. Her legs were stick thin.

The worn dirt path led to a battered wooden door. Reeves stood on the threshold, wondering at the wisdom of accepting this family's invitation. They'd just tried to kill the magpie because of near starvation. What was to stop them jumping him? This wasn't Texas and they didn't have anything remotely resembling a chainsaw, but still, it was an isolated property and it would be four against one. Reeves looked at the small woman smiling and motioning him in. She was so thin and frail that if he picked her up, she might break. Her husband and son were not much better.

On balance, Reeves thought he could probably trust them.

Shrugging, he entered.

CHAPTER THIRTY-ONE

THE ROOM HAD a swept earth floor, the walls unadorned with shutters over the windows. Despite the day's warmth, a fire burned in one corner with a scattered array of blackened iron utensils on the hearth. The chairs and table were handmade and devoid of any decorative cushions.

Reeves, in his life as a probation officer, had seen some deprivation and even a touch of overt poverty in his time. But he had never seen anything like this. He turned back to the woman still holding the door open.

'Reeves,' he said, holding out his hand.

She bowed her head and held out a hand. 'Prandy Lathrop,' she said. Her hand in Reeves' felt as leathery as a satchel.

'And I'm Welwyn,' said the man. 'My son, Moga, you have already met. And this,' he beckoned to the little girl who ran to her father, clasping him around the knees, 'is Robyn.'

'Is there anywhere I can put the bird?' Reeves asked.

'The kitchen. There is a table.' Prandy led the way into a room that was equally as stark but at least had a handpump sink and a table as well as a cupboard. Reeves made a mental bet with himself that if he pushed it, the cupboard would rattle with a few cups and dishes.

He put the magpie down and Prandy fetched a basket

containing scraps of material and sewing implements. He watched as she carefully bound the magpie's wing. They put the bird on the windowsill with some water in a saucer.

'We don't see many strangers in these parts,' Welwyn said when all was done. Prandy busied herself with a large cooking pot and some vegetables. Robyn simply watched while Moga went outside to forage.

'I'm on my way to Gogny Payn, but had to take a little detour.'

'Ah, you're off to the city,' Welwyn said in awe.

'You ever been?'

'Me, no. Oh no. It wouldn't be allowed. Farmers stay with the farm.'

'But aren't you curious?'

'Moga is, but me, no. I know my place. The agricultural collectors make sure of that.' Though Welwyn smiled, Reeves detected a flicker of wariness in the man's eyes.

'And what do they do, these collectors?'

'Take what we can produce,' Prandy said, stirring her pot as she dropped in two wizardy grubs.

'Don't you sell it?'

'Sell…no, we do not sell it. We are allowed to live on the land so long as we produce. We have a small vegetable plot for our own use, though the drought this year has taken its toll.'

'Hang on a minute. You're farmers. You grow crops and sell them to make money, don't you?'

Welwyn smiled again. 'We are leading a happy life under the warm love of our leaders.'

'Cut the bullshit. I am not one of your leaders, okay? I'm a traveller whose bird you just attacked because you're starving, yet you live on a farm and, if I am not mistaken, I saw crops out there.' Reeves was still smarting from the attack on the magpie.

Prandy nodded. 'You have provided food for us and now you are our guest. But if you live in Rathkoorne, then you must know that our great and everlasting leaders require that we grow all our food for them. In return, they allow us to live in this generous house and use land to grow our own food.'

'What land?'

Prandy nodded. Her obsequiousness was painful. She opened a door at the rear of the house and beckoned to Reeves, who looked from the bird to the man and held up a warning finger before following the woman. At the rear of the property another path led to fields but a strip of land some thirty feet by twenty contained rows of tightly packed vegetation and some hutches piled on top of one another. Inside the hutches, Reeves spotted some rabbits.

'This?' he asked.

Prandy nodded and smiled. The area was a quarter of the size of the allotment his old dad used to grow marrows on. The fields beyond looked huge.

'Who else works the farm?'

'No one,' Prandy said. 'We work the farm and we have an ox for the ploughing and transport.'

'Pesticides? Fertiliser?'

The look on the woman's face told him these were not words she knew.

'Our great and beneficent leader sometimes sends us help, but we are not allowed to feed them. The last three were too unwell to survive the winter. Our land is unfortunately not the best.'

'And the children? Do they go to school?'

'They are happy to help us on the farm. Moga is a good hunter.'

'So I've noticed. But don't you have ambitions for them?'

Prandy frowned. 'Ambitions? I do not know this word.'

No, of course you don't. Reeves dropped his head. He was doing it again. Applying his world view to this…this…'What does Moga think?'

Prandy shivered. 'It is best that he does not think. People who think tend to disappear. To the copper mines or…other places.'

'Can I talk to him? I promise I am not one of your great leaders and I promise none of it will leave here.'

'Let me discuss it with Welwyn.' She came back a few moments later, grinning. 'You can talk to Moga after supper.'

Over wizardy grub stew and black bread, Reeves said little. But afterwards, he sat outside with Moga while the rest of the family cleared up.

'I am sorry about your bird,' said the boy, eyes fixed on the floor.

'So am I. He was my guide to Gogny Payn.'

Moga looked up. 'I can show you the way. I will draw you a map.'

Reeves smiled a wary smile. 'How do you know the way?'

'Once, I followed the collectors. I got to a place where I could see the city and then came back. I know the way.'

'Don't you fancy going there yourself?'

'I could not leave my family. They depend on me. One day I hope to learn to fight.'

'Become one of the Zatrank?'

Moga shook his head. 'No. Never. I would like to fight them. They are pigs. They took my uncle far away. They say there are places, camps where men are tortured just for what they say or believe. Our neighbours were killed for having a book. A present brought to them by a visitor from across the border. It had pictures of another world. I did not see it. But I did see the Zatrank burn it after they had…' The boy stopped and wiped his face. 'Sometimes, inside I feel something catch fire and I want to run and kill. But then I look at my sister and know that I must stay here. We hide her when the soldiers come. If they found her, they would…' Once more he stopped, but the tears had gone. In their place was defiance. 'I am sorry about your bird.'

'I heard you the first time.'

'You are not like them. You are different. My father says you remind him of the old peacekeepers. My mother says you look like someone who has seen people at their worst and been wounded by it. Why do you want to go to Gogny Payn?'

Reeves pondered Moga's words. There were surprisingly many of them and they were weighty with information. But as always, he answered without giving much away. 'Someone I have to meet. I have something to deliver.'

'They say there are streets with golden doors.'

Reeves shook his head. 'And ermine roofs and diamond windows.'

'Really?' The boy's eyes sparkled.

'No. I doubt it very much. That sort of thing is usually peddled by a certain class of people who want others of a different class to visit wide-eyed so that they can employ them to clean boots or make beds. That's when they realise that the doors are solid wood and need a coat of paint, and the roofs are slate and need to be cleared of leaves in the cold and wet, and the windows need a regular going-over with water and vinegar.'

Reeves did not want to disappoint the boy, but he despised propaganda. It was dangerous stuff when combined with ignorance and servitude and, like all other poisonous creatures, deserving only to be trodden underfoot.

Moga blinked. 'Will you tell them that we helped you if you are tortured?'

'I would rather cut off my own leg.'

Moga considered this before replying. 'I believe you.'

'Good. Perhaps, if you're lucky, you may be able to visit Gogny Payn one day and see it as it should be.'

'Like it was before the Zatrank? With markets and fairs and games?'

'Why not?'

Moga's eyes focussed on a point in the universe that existed only in his imagination. 'That would be nice.'

Moga took a small plate of grubs over to the magpie, who pecked at the food. It was then that Reeves noticed an oblong square on the wall behind where Welwyn sat at the head of the table. It looked like an empty frame but was comment-worthy as it was the only adornment that Reeves had seen in the whole house.

'What is that?' Reeves asked.

Welwyn and Prandy exchanged glances. 'Show Mr Reeves, Robyn.'

The girl stood and, reaching up, lifted the frame away from the wall and turned it so that it faced the other way. What was revealed was a portrait of a man. A smiling man, his head ringed with a golden halo, shone against a sky of lapis lazuli. His hand, raised in benediction, held a slender white wand that swayed as he turned his gaze, serene and radiant. This divine figure filled the upper half of the painting. Below, tiny figures gathered in fervent clusters, their faces uplifted in triumph, brandishing sickles and hammers like offerings to the heavens.

'Every home has one of these,' Prandy explained. 'But you must know that?'

'I don't,' Reeves said.

'It depicts our great and beneficent leader, Erthu Le Liare, his supernatural munificence, the father of his adoring and beloved people.'

Reeves nodded. 'I guess that's why you keep it turned towards the wall?'

'No, Mr Reeves,' her earnest expression well practiced. 'It is so that the sun does not bleach his features or the colourful wonder of the image. Once the sun sets, we always turn it back.'

Reeves looked at the faces of the family all looking at the portrait. Solemn and intense. Was this real? Even after all he'd heard and seen, how could it be that these poor honest folk had been brainwashed so badly? He searched for something to say. For a word of succour, but he drew a blank. He'd thought that perhaps he'd detected a little spark of fight here. Especially in Moga, but even he was staring.

'Turn it back now, Robyn. Protect him that protects us.'

The little girl did as she was asked and they all turned back in unison to look at Reeves, who couldn't help but feel a wave of disappointment wash over him. He'd got these people very wrong.

'I see,' was all he managed to say. 'I had no—'

His words, sympathetic and defeatist, ended abruptly as Welwyn leaned over onto one buttock and let out a very long and very loud fart.

Prandy grinned approvingly. 'That's what we really think. But we can't do that in front of him. The portrait is hexed. He watches all the time.'

There are moments in life when surprise not only pops up out of the cake wearing a silly hat and a grin, but does so holding that shiny bicycle you'd been lusting after in the high street shop throughout the long winter. That single, irreverent, defiant expulsion of air left Reeves shocked and delighted and utterly speechless. He could only blink. Not so much taken aback as removed completely, for one delicious moment, from the desperation these people were suffering. Even in the most harrowing of conditions, their spirit was incorrigibly indomitable. The blinking lasted a good five seconds until Robyn, unable to contain her mirth, dropped her chin to hide the smile that was distorting her lips.

All Reeves could do was grin himself and raise his mug of water. 'I haven't found much to cheer since I got here, Welwyn, but I'll bloody well drink to that.'

CHAPTER THIRTY-TWO

PICT

'Right,' Rimsplitter addressed the assembled Hipposync team. 'I am not even going to start with a joke today, 'cos what I've got to say ain't in the slightest bit effin' funny. We've lost the effin' last of our mincers.'

'Mince pies. Spies,' said Bobby in answer to Asher's frown.

'What?' Kylah said.

'Got a message from Marshy. He's been attacked by a dog and hurt his leg. He managed to get back, just about. He told us Reeves ended up being rescued and taken to a Resonari camp. That's where he met Marshy. And the bad news is your amnesia charm is effed. Reeves remembers everything.'

'Shit,' said Matt.

'The good news is he's still goin' to Gogny. But there's more bad news. We don't have an effin' clue where he is.'

'Double shit,' Matt added.

'Yeah. One of the tracer gnats came back last night. F4 is down, too. Damaged wing. He's with Reeves, but it means we have no idea wot that bee is goin' to do next.'

'This is bad,' said Kylah.

'Bad is one way of putting it,' Rimsplitter said. 'Effin' catastrophic is another. We always knew this was going to be tough, but the boys were up for it. Them Zatrank, they're such a bunch of cees. S'all their fault. Can't blame the people for wanting blackbird pie or squirrel risotto 'cos they're bleedin' starving. But this little fiasco'll do nothing to forward my cause, either. I'm not feeling' sorry for meself, don't get me wrong. But this was a chance for me to prove my worth and I've effin' blown it.'

'It was a tough gig,' Bobby admitted.

'Yeah, but we should have done better. Not blaming the lads, mind you. It's just that our intel was crap.'

'Non-existent,' agreed Asher.

'Meanwhile, Gauinebald can wreak havoc in the universe.' Matt's face was flushed.

Kylah's eyes fell to the floor. 'I had reservations from the start about Reeves.'

And though she didn't actually say it, Matt knew she meant the idea. His idea. No one else seemed to sense the subtext, except Bobby, who sent both Matt and Kylah pained, almost pitying looks.

'Yeah, well,' he said, 'if it all goes to crap then it'll be on me. But I'm here because I have this…thing, whatever the hell it is. An idea pops into my head, a "what if" idea. And more often than not, it works out. Sometimes it doesn't. But that's fate having another laugh and reminding me to keep it real…though it hardly ever is. Not since I started to go out with a demon called Silvy.'

That earned him a sharp look from Kylah.

'My point is that I have no option than to go with my gut. And my gut says Reeves.' He leaned forward. 'We're talking here as if it's over. But I have not heard the famine-resistant female sing yet, have you?'

They all looked at him.

'You need to trust me on this one, Captain Porter.'

Kylah looked like she'd already had this argument with herself in her own head. She threw Bobby a glance. They'd talked about this. The conflict that Kylah faced. The risk in having Matt as part of the DOF. She knew she had trust issues. Bobby knew that too. And she had given Matt free reign here. Now was not the time to backtrack.

He saw the hesitation in her face and doubled down. 'Come on. This is Hipposync we're talking about here. We're not going to let a little shit like Gauinebald hold us to ransom, are we?'

'But—' Kylah began only to be cut off by Rimsplitter.

'That's fightin' talk, that is. Wot you got in mind?'

'There aren't any more troops to send in, right?'

'Perspi-bleedin-cacious as ever.'

'Right, then we'll have to go.'

Rimsplitter made a noise that was something between a screech and a hysterical scream.

'And how do you propose to do that?' Kylah asked. 'It's suicide.'

'Not if we use a transmorph potion. I've seen it on sale in Herod's.'

Asher shook his head. 'Matt, that is a mere fancy-dress party trick. Such potions last only a few hours.'

'Fine, but there must be a way of extending that. Bobby, you're the witch?'

Bobby made a face. 'It's theoretically possible. The transmorph spell within the potions commercially available all have temporal limiters built in. But the root charm doesn't. And some of them are very old.'

'Exactly what the old witches used to turn people into frogs and stuff,' Rimsplitter said.

'Yes.' Bobby nodded.

Asher was frowning. 'And how does that differ from the FF and you, Rimsplitter?'

Matt answered, 'Rimsplitter is a transferred soul. His original corporeal form is dead. He is officially on the transdimensional witness protection programme.'

'And as for the FF, they were TSDs,' Kylah explained. 'Temporary Soul Displacements. In that instance, the occupied body—the animals—need to be recovered for reverse transference to take place. That's why it's so dangerous. If they were killed over in Rathkoorne, there'd be no way to get them back into their original forms. But that's not what Matt is suggesting here.'

'No,' Bobby answered. 'This is a full-blown transmogrification spell. We stay as we are and appear as something else to observers. Also, time limited because at the end of the period, wherever the transformed target is, he or she will transform back. I'm sure we could get a couple of days at a push.'

'It's worth a try, surely?' Matt said.

'But you've heard what Rimsplitter said. The Rathkoornians seem to want to eat and kill anything that moves or flies,' Asher pointed out.

'Perhaps not everything.' Rimsplitter had moved closer to the group and, with head tilted, was staring at Matt. 'What do you have in mind?'

'I had an old-school thought. Flight for ease of travel to start with.'

'So, a bird?' Asher asked.

Matt nodded. 'And what bird never ends up on anyone's table, or in a pie?'

'A hummingbird?' Bobby offered.

'I was thinking something more substantial.'

'A seagull?' Asher suggested.

'Too loud.'

'Cormorant?'

'People in the Hebrides make then into a stew, or stuff them on the end of a stick and burn them as torches.'

'Ugh.' Bobby grimaced.

'No, I was thinking more along the lines of carrion feeders. That usually puts people off,' Matt said, eyebrows arched and gaze fixed on Rimsplitter.

'Now you're talking my kind of effin' language!'

'Have I missed something here?' Kylah asked.

'Vultures,' said Rimsplitter. 'He's talking vulture culture.'

'Oh dear,' said Bobby.

'Exactly,' Matt nodded. 'See, that's precisely the sort of reaction we'd want to get. People look at vultures and immediately think, yuk. And, they always appear as groups. I recall a group of vultures sitting in a tree is called a venue, a flight is called a kettle, and a group feeding is called a wake. It's not unusual to see them in groups, and it means we can go in as a squadron and stick together.'

'Are you serious?' Asher looked to Kylah for her reaction.

The captain was deep in contemplation. 'I hate to admit it, but it might just work. Matt's right. Vultures are usually not bothered by predators, and that includes humans. If we did this, we'd need three days as a minimum. Bobby, can I ask you to liaise with the Le Fey on that?'

Bobby nodded, though her expression was still one reminiscent of someone finding a snail in their porridge—and not having paid a Michelin-starred chef to put it there.

'I'd insist on Rimsplitter leading us,' Kylah continued. You are the only one with aerial experience.'

Rimsplitter puffed up his feathers. 'Yeah, no worries. I'll come. I'm a quarter of a mile up. They can't touch me, cees.'

Kylah turned to the others. 'Of course, none of you would have to come. Strictly voluntary basis.'

'When do we start?' Asher said and got nods from Matt and Bobby.

Rimsplitter chuckled. 'You're going to effin' love it, all of you. There's nothing like soaring on the thermals, spotting some bee who never paid you that fiver you lent them back in the day and launchin' something green and white from a great height.'

Once again, Rimsplitter's ability to silence his audience was awe-inspiring.

The crew turned to leave but Bobby grabbed Kylah's arm. 'Um, as vultures, would we be expected to eat... carrion?'

Rimsplitter overheard her. 'Too bleedin' right, you would. I know for a fact that there's a three-week dead water buffalo near one of the springs to the north. Be nice and ripe by now. Still a load of meat on the ribs. Riper than a council gritter.'

Everyone managed to grasp what rhymed with gritter.

Bobby gagged.

Rimsplitter squawked with delight.

'He's just pulling your leg,' Kylah said. 'We'll take provisions.'

'Yeah,' said Rimsplitter. 'Carry out instead of carrion. Oh, my days, where do I bleedin' get them from.'

CHAPTER THIRTY-THREE

THE NEXT MORNING, at the farm, Moga drew the map on a piece of clean rag using charcoal from the fire. He did it with great care and concentration, marking out landmarks—well, two landmarks—which he carefully explained.

'When you get to the big tree that has two branches crossing the path, you need to take a right fork that will lead to the path towards the eastern gate.' Moga handed over the rag.

Reeves stared at the single line of his path, which bent at the more branching squiggly lines of trees and ended at a squiggly crenelated castle. 'Nice and simple. Right, then. I'd better get going.'

The day was not as hot as the one before, which made it merely stifling. Clouds were building, but Welwyn said there would not be rain for a few days. Reeves surveyed his hosts. He wished he could give them something to help and said so.

Welwyn shook his head. 'We have enjoyed your visit. Though you have not told us the purpose of your quest, we hope you succeed.'

'I haven't told you because I don't exactly know myself.'

'And perhaps because we cannot reveal under duress of that we know not.'

Reeves reflected on Welwyn's words, finding their blend

of philosophy and truth desperately sad. He shook hands with everyone, expressing his gratitude once more.

The magpie rested in a makeshift sling Prandy had fashioned, draped around Reeves' shoulder. The bird was unusually quiet, and though Reeves was no expert, he guessed it was likely both frightened and unhappy.

The Lathrops stood and watched him leave. Reeves turned back once and waved. The next time he looked, they were gone.

'Right, well, I don't know where we should be going to get you sorted,' Reeves said to the bird. 'I doubt there's an animal hospital here, or if there is, it's probably got "abattoir" written in parenthesis after it. But maybe there'll be some kind of witch or wizard who'll know what to do. What we really need is a healer—' Reeves caught himself as thoughts of Milda and Raymounde came crowding in. He didn't even know if they were still alive. Guilt piled in on him and he set his face to the wind. He needed to finish this, whatever this was. Then he could allow himself time to consider his own fate.

A tiny chord of self-pity and irritation sounded a discordant arpeggio somewhere in his consciousness. Why was he bothered about these people? They had nothing to do with him. There were thousands, perhaps even millions, of Mildas and Raymoundes and Lathrops in this joke of a country. All suffering. All victims. And he wasn't here out of choice and they were nothing but midges nipping at his skin and interfering with his vision. There was nothing he could do to save them all. But then the arpeggio changed into a familiar tune. One that Reeves had not heard for a long, long time. It took him a moment to recognise it, but when he did, he let it play in his head because, damn it all, he found it soothing.

What played was the theme tune of his old life. The one he had tried to make sense of after Rhiannon. The injustice of her awful demise had set him on a course of trying to rationalise a cruel and capricious world. A course that led eventually to him becoming a copper. And Reeves had been a very good copper until the politicians placed money and votes above criminal justice. That was when Reeves decided it was time to leave and see if he could try a bit of reverse engineering on the lags who came out of the other end of the system, lost and more criminalised after a spot in the clanger than they had been before.

But the music Reeves almost whistled along to was a simpler tune and came from a time when he'd been happy to catch villains. Watch their features change from smug to horror when they realised their brilliant, why-has-no-one-ever-thought-of-this-before schemes were nothing but last year's sorry ideas. Or face their victims in court and finally understand the cost of their moment of drug and/or alcohol-induced violence. He did not know what this music meant in terms of his here and now, but he listened to it anyway and found it comforting because the melody was uncomplicated and the chorus rousing. And there was nothing grand and orchestral about it. This was an arrangement from when things were a lot clearer and less cluttered.

Reeves had never been a great one for introspection but he knew enough to understand that there had been a time, in the aftermath of Rhiannon's demise, when he'd seen little or no sense in anything. Washing, eating, getting up? All activities for people who actually gave a toss. It would have been easy to slip and slide into a twilight existence of alcohol or some other poison that dulled the senses and smoothed the emotional sharp edges.

But Reeves hadn't done those things because Rhiannon would have hated him for it. So somehow, five months after that day on the beach, Reeves woke up in his bed covered with unchanged sheets and smelling like slightly wet dog, looked in the mirror, shaved off his beard and got on with it.

Because it was what Rhiannon would have wanted.

No, expected.

But she wouldn't have expected him to swan dive off a multistorey, would she?

No. That all came later. After all these bad choices he'd made, with Demelza topping the list by a long, long way.

But he wasn't on that multistorey now. He was in Rathkoorne and here things were very different. For the first time in a long, long while, Reeves could hear the melody of his old life clearly and without interference. And the Rhiannon he had known would expect him to fulfil his side of a bargain.

Okay. He owed her that.

————

AT FIRST, the paths he trod were empty, but gradually, as the miles rolled by, he saw people. Some travellers, but mainly farmers in their fields. Many would stop and watch his progress. Others would look up and then bend to their tasks once more with little heed. Part of the great Rathkoorne machinery. More than once he came across statues, similar to the one in the square in Asabone. Huge and bronze.

Erthu Le Liare the wise and fatherly.

Erthu Le Liare the powerful.

Erthu Le Liare the tyrannical.

Reeves did not pause at any of these great statues, except once, to pass water. He made sure some of it splashed on the statue's base. Puerile it may have been, but it made him feel a lot better after doing it.

The farms gave way to hamlets that gave way to whole villages until, finally, he saw the tree with two branches over-hanging the path. He took the right fork that climbed up over a hill. At the top he paused and looked down on a sprawling collection of houses and cabins that spread out in a 'V' from a magnificent castle dominating the town itself and the lake beyond. Flags flew from the Keep's ramparts: the black iron fist and the silver wand of the house Le Liare.

There were roads into the town and they ran through areas where the houses were well appointed, but from where he stood high up, Reeves could see the truth of the city. Away from the main streets the habitation deteriorated, and within a few yards dilapidation spread like an ugly canker: building piled upon building, refuse and worse on every corner. If the roads were the arteries that led to the great heart at the Keep, then the paths were the clogged and ugly veins that led to the other organs. Less glamorous, but just as necessary for the city to function. And it was where he knew he would have to go.

Reeves hurried, head down. The way was busy with people carrying goods, some on their heads, others with horses or donkeys. Everyone looked grim and there were few, if any, exchanges. By the time he saw the rough barrier that he assumed was the eastern gate that Moga had mentioned, the path was choked with people coming and going. There was no security here; it was merely a narrowing in a defensive wall on a raised earthen rampart. He wondered for a moment as to why the gate was not manned but then realised it didn't need to be. This was a city under complete and absolute rule. There were no security issues in all of Rathkoorne. Outsiders did not exist, according to Matt and Kylah.

Not until now.

Reeves felt a moment of panic. What if they could tell? What if he stood out like a hammered thumb? But no one paid him any heed as he wormed his way through the crowds. On the other side of the gate, the congestion eased and Reeves was soon walking along broader paths where vendors sold their wares, pathetic though they were.

This, he realised, was not a part of the city where the Zatrank ventured. This was the sort of commerce that existed for the people who made the city tick. Stalls selling black bread and dead animals—possibly rats—hanging from hooks, cloth, baskets, earthenware. Reeves recalled Candin Lane, the address he'd been given, and chose a woman selling herbs as his source. He spoke briefly, slurring his words in order to disguise any accent issues.

'Yes, I know where that is,' she said, wrinkling her nose. 'Quarter of a mile to the fountain square of the Great Lindor and then west for two hundred yards. Now, get away from my stall if you're not buying.'

Reeves grunted and moved on. There were inns as he neared the square. That meant there'd be Zatrank, if previous encounters were anything to go by. He took some rear alleys until he was sure he could not be seen and headed west as instructed. There were street signs, but many had faded or were lost altogether. Not many tourists in this part of town, he surmised. His hand strayed automatically to the Seren Sea Stone. It was still there.

He didn't want to ask anyone else about the Shadow-smiths. He didn't want to raise suspicion. It struck him that this was the sort of place where it didn't pay to be too curious.

Luckily, Candin Lane still had its sign. From the look of it, it had once been a place where horses had been stabled. They looked like mews, though very run down. Reeves made his way cautiously along until he spied an old woman sweeping out dust.

'Mrs Shadowsmith?' he asked, knowing full well this was a stab in the dark, but hoping it might be interpreted as an easy mistake to make now he was in the right street.

The old woman looked up and stopped her sweeping. She studied Reeves for a long while before pointing further down the lane. 'Number 4,' she said, her eyes fixed on the magpie still in the sling around Reeves' shoulder, with a look that had 'piecrust and carrots' written all over it

He moved on. Number 4 still had all the wood in its doors, which made it stand out from the rest. Reeves knocked and waited. He knocked again and heard movement. The door stayed shut but a voice spoke from the other side of it.

'Who is it? What do you want?'

'I'm looking for Targan Shadowsmith.'

He heard an odd choking noise in reply.

'Does Targan Shadowsmith live here?' Reeves asked again.

'Who are you?' said the voice. A woman. Harsh and wavering with some unnameable emotion.

'A messenger. I have a message for Targan.'

Reeves saw a spyhole open, followed by several bolts sliding back. The door opened and revealed a woman of about forty. Like everyone else, she was too thin, her clothes loose about her as they were in almost everyone he'd met. Her features would have been handsome had it not been for the despair that dragged at her eyes above the hollow cheeks. She stood on the threshold defiantly.

'What is your message?'

'I can only give it to Targan,' Reeves said.

The woman squeezed her eyes shut. 'Then you are too late.'

'Too late? What—'

There were shouts from the top of the lane. A girl's screams, gruff voices. The girl pleading. 'No, please, no!'

Reeves' head swung around. Three Zatrank soldiers were dragging a boy out from one of the houses despite the protests of two women and a girl.

'But he has done nothing. He's a good boy.'

'De Wyville's orders. All boys between eleven and fifteen years must be seized.'

'No!'

One of the women began beating at the Zatrank's chest. He threw her off and she went sprawling on the cobbled floor.

'But why?' wailed the other woman. 'What do you want with them? What have they done?'

'It's what they might do, that's the problem.' One of the soldiers uttered a cruel laugh. 'Pick a weed when it's young. That's what I say.'

They threw the boy into a windowless cart and mounted their horses. When Reeves turned back, the woman in the doorway was bawling.

'They've taken Barnum. Poor little Barnum. He's too simple to cause anyone any harm.' For a moment she swayed, her face draining of all colour, and then she collapsed against the door jamb.

CHAPTER THIRTY-FOUR

GOGNY PAYN

REEVES GRABBED her before she fell and took her inside the house. Though there was more in the way of furnishings than at the Lathrops', they were few and threadbare. He found a battered armchair in one of the rooms and sat the woman down before fetching some water. She opened her eyes and tried to sit up, panic flaring at seeing Reeves looming over her.

He stepped back, hands up in front of him. 'I am not here to harm you. You fainted. Best you stay where you are for a while. Put your head down between your knees.'

The terror on her face faded, and she leaned back, brushing off the first aid advice. With a shrug, but with quiet respect for her resilience, Reeves offered her some water, which she sipped slowly.

'Thank you,' she whispered, her eyes still half lidded.

'What did you mean when you said, "They've got Barnum?"'

The woman was panting, but between breaths, she explained. 'You saw it. They come and take all the boys. They took Targan.' She stopped, on the verge of tears, but took more water and gathered herself. 'This has been going on for days. All boys between eleven and fifteen. All of them, taken.'

Reeves could only stare. 'Taken? Where?'

'The Keep, or somewhere worse. They tell us nothing. No reasons.'

Reeves shook his head. A great sense of dread came over him. He feared, irrationally, that somehow his presence had triggered all of this.

'What?' The woman's eyes caught something in his reaction. 'Do you know why? Do you?'

Reeves shook his head. 'No. I…You knew Targan?'

'He is my son.'

Reeves' insides swooped. 'I was sent to find Targan and deliver something to him.' He reached under his vest and retrieved the Seren Sea Stone.

Just as Matt has shown him, Reeves held the brown-and-cream whelk shell between middle finger and thumb and used the index finger of his other hand to gently press the shell's aperture. Instantly, the stone changed into the silver squid with four tentacles enclosing a turquoise heart-shaped stone.

The woman gasped, her eyes wide with wonder and fear in equal measure. She sat up and looked behind her for reassurance that someone else was not in the room before addressing Reeves again. 'You have the Stone? But it has been lost for generations. How did you…? Who are you?'

'Perhaps it's time for some introductions. I am Reeves.'

'And I am Bettany Shadowsmith. If you know anything that can shed light on any of this, please tell me.'

And so, Reeves did. At least he told her a version. A thin version, devoid of all the juicy bits. But still, hearing his own voice recount it made him realise that it added up to a strange tale indeed. He kept out the bits about the blue room for now, and the Resonaris, and slaying a Zatrank. He admitted only to being not from Rathkoorne and that he was being 'paid' to deliver. He didn't know who or what Targan Shadowsmith was, or what significance the Seren Sea Stone had.

But Bettany soon changed all of that.

She revealed to Reeves the awful truth. Well, not so much

awful as horrifying, monstrous and despicable, which might, he reflected later, have been an excellent name for a Le Liare boy band if ever they decided to release a single.

Before the Zatrank rise to power, Rathkoorne had another name in a different tongue: Hedwich. And though that older language did not translate easily, the word had a meaning that was an intangible mixture of peace and tranquillity and safety. There was no royalty, but rather a chamber of wisdom, where the chiefs of the various clans worked to retain peace and a warless existence. The great symbol of this existence had been the Seren Sea Stone, worn in a sceptre by the acknowledged leader. The last man to hold that office had been Targan Shadowsmith's grandfather.

The Seren Sea Stone contained knowledge sealed by wonderworking that its allocated holder shared with generations before. A deep and arcane link that was older than any wand lore. With Nevis Shadowsmith's death at the hands of the Zatrank, the stone had not been passed on, but somehow lost, and though an heir was usually chosen on merit, as it stood, blood remained the only link that could access its power until a ceremony of reallocation could take place.

Targanwas the heir to a powerful weapon.

But Bettany had yet more to tell as they sat in the austere surroundings of her house. 'It is difficult to imagine now that these streets once thronged with happy people. I remember it only vaguely before the trolls went on the rampage.'

Reeves frowned. 'Someone mentioned the troll wars. What was that about?'

Bettany shook her head and grimaced. 'Men's folly,' she said. 'For generations, the people of Hedwich lived in harmony with the trolls. We left them to their places in the mountains and the forests and they avoided us. We smell very bad to them. But from the east rose a coven, foreigners from Garnier. They stole troll children and began to sell a potion made from young troll blood that was supposed to reverse the passage of time. A potion of youth. Most people did not believe it, but enough did. Enough vain, deluded people wanted it and were willing to pay handsomely for it. The witches of Garnier thrived. It was they who started the hunts. Rounding up trolls, butchering them. It was only a matter of time until the trolls sought help from their northern cousins, the wights. They were organised and clever soldiers who sought quick and terrible retribution. I will always remember the day the bell tolled.'

'The bell?'

'The augur bell on the Keep tower. It is only ever rung in times of great change or danger. It rang when the wights crossed the mountains and invaded our lands. It was only through wand lore that we managed to drive them back, but we paid a terrible price. The bell has been silent ever since Erthu Le Liare took command, as he is only too fond of reminding us.'

Bettany paused, listening as somewhere another woman pleaded and screamed. She shuddered.

'The power transfer to the Zatrank was meant to be a law enacted for the purposes of war. It was never meant to be permanent. But Le Liare had other ideas. He captured and tortured the mages. Still keeps them under lock and key to do his bidding. The law remains permanent. He is unassailable and we, the people, have no choice but to comply to his will.' She glanced at the amulet in Reeves' hands before whispering, 'We thought the Stone lost for ever.'

The distant and harrowing pleas were suddenly cut off and Bettany's hand flew to her mouth.

'Do they know of Targan?' Reeves asked. 'Do they know who he is?'

Bettany shook her head. 'The name Shadowsmith is an adulteration. We dare not use our real name.'

'I like it, though.'

Reeves stood and began to pace. It didn't take a genius to work out that Le Liare had somehow found out Reeves' purpose. And since he had not told anyone, it could only mean that Milda or Raymounde had been forced to talk, though they themselves knew little. It might explain this blunderbuss approach on the part of the baron.

Reeves had heard this kind of story before. A very old story indeed. One with Herod written all over it.

Milda and Raymounde knew only that Reeves was searching for a boy of a certain age. The obvious thing to do would be to get rid of all the boys of that certain age. It was the only way to be sure. There was no need for rule or certainty when you held all the cards. So long as no one else had the joker.

Reeves stopped pacing and turned back to Bettany. 'It seems that my quest cannot succeed. I'm too late.'

'But the Stone—'

Reeves reversed the shell back to a whelk, removed it from around his neck and handed it to her. 'Best I give it to someone who at least knows what might be done with it. It is useless to me.'

'But what will you do?'

He shrugged. 'My task has ended. I was only ever the messenger.'

'But the people who sent you…can they not help us?'

Reeves shook his head. 'They dare not interfere.'

'But…'

Reeves removed the magpie from the sling. He found a tiny scrap of parchment and asked Bettany for some quill and ink. He scribbled something down, rolled up the parchment and secured it to the magpie's leg. 'I would ask one favour. Look after the bird for me. Others may come for it. A raven perhaps, or a bird of some sort, I'm fairly certain. Feed and water it, that's all I ask.'

Bettany shook her head. 'But you can't leave. We are suffering. The people of Rathkoorne—'

'Are not my problem. I'm sorry.' He turned and made his way back down the lane.

People stood and watched him go. Reeves ignored them and made for a tavern he'd seen two streets away. There, at least, he could drown his sorrows. But it felt like the eyes that followed his progress were boring holes of desperation into his back as he went.

CHAPTER THIRTY-FIVE

PICT

OUTSIDE A LITTLE HUT on the slopes of the mountains of Pict, Rimsplitter paced back and forth, the sharp wind ruffling his feathers.

'In your own time,' he yelled. 'Eff-tees.'

Inside, Bobby shook her head at the inquiring eyebrow Asher raised in her direction. 'Ignore him. You really do not want to know.'

Apart from Bobby, Asher, Kylah and Matt, Duana Llewyn and another woman dressed all in black stood watching. The woman, a senior lecturer from Le Fey Academy known as Mistress Magda, stood behind a small table upon which were four bubbling vials of orange liquid in glass tumblers. Her features, pale and unlined, belied her age and betrayed no expression. Current theories amongst the voices of the Wicca academy had her at around 600…and a day.

'Whenever you are ready,' she said to Bobby.

'Shall I go first?' Bobby reached for one of the tumblers.

Asher stayed her hand. 'No, we do this together or not at all.'

'Agreed,' said Kylah.

'Remember to take a deep breath,' warned Mistress Magda.

Asher, Kylah, Bobby and Matt lifted the tumblers, inhaled and, as one, threw the liquid down.

Although flesh and bone and skin responded quickly to the transformation, it was not a pleasant transition with several seconds of distorted morphic realignment. It meant that air was displaced and it gave the person experiencing the change a drowning sensation, before rearranged lungs could suck in fresh oxygen. Not to mention the altered perception that the new senses brought to the table.

'Wow,' Matt said, first to realign. 'Why is everything so flat?'

'You will have lost binocularity and depth perception,' Duana explained. 'Now that you have eyes either side of your head.'

Matt looked up and saw the professor flinch. 'Something I said?'

'No, it is the yellow eyes with the red rims that do it.'

Kylah strutted over. 'You look amazing,' she said.

Matt turned and studied Kylah with shocked admiration. She stood about three foot tall with pale ochre plumage and a ruffled neck. The feathers of her legs went all the way down to her feet, almost like harem pants. Her wings were a darker mottled brown and her head, extending forward from an orange crown of feathers, was black with a curved beak ending in a vicious-looking hooked bill. As Duana had already observed, her eyes, too, were encircled by a bright red rim, inside of which were yellow irises and a dense dark pupil. Matt was used to looking at Kylah's eyes, which in humanoid form were spectacular. But these were something else altogether. She was joined by two more iterations, one slightly smaller, which he took as Bobby.

'We look…'

'Different?' Asher suggested.

'You all look magnificent. Bearded vultures traditionally live in the crags of mountainous areas and you will not look out of place in Rathkoorne,' Mistress Magda explained.

'What is that I can smell?' Bobby asked.

'Something that has died, I suspect,' Duana aid. 'Your olfactory systems will be attuned to carrion, or effluent.'

'Charming,' Bobby said, not wanting to admit that whatever it was she was sensing had a certain allure.

Mistress Magda said, 'Keep together. You have seventy-two hours. Return here for the retransformation.'

'Is that an absolute?'

'Yes' Mistress Magda pointed out their clothes in heaps on the floor. 'Unless you want to transform back completely naked.'

They joined Rimsplitter outside. He took one look and began to cackle. 'Oh, my days, what an effin' bunch of bone crunchers.'

It had already been explained to them that bearded vultures usually ate the bones of dead things, cracking them open by letting them fall from a great height.

'This is a bee dream come true, this is,' Rimsplitter said. 'My own squadron. We ought to get an effin' Beecham's.'

'Beecham's? asked Kylah.

'Beecham's pill. Still. You know, a photo.'

'This is no time for frivolity,' Duana said.

'Nothing frivolous about the FF Squadron 69. Need to record them for posterity. Unprecedented, this is.'

Matt spoke up. 'We ought to have an imp-print, if only to record the fact that I have just heard Rimsplitter speak a sentence without swearing.'

'Very well,' Duana said and retrieved a black box from her bag; a feat in itself considering the box was twice as big as her bag. She placed it on a flat surface in front of the assembled crew: Rimsplitter in the middle, Matt and Kylah on one side, Asher and Bobby on the other. They all attempted a smile, but since neither eagles not vultures had any capable facial musculature, what came across was a look of pure imperious evil that would give anyone looking at it nightmares for years to come.

'Right,' Rimsplitter said when the imp inside the box had done its thing, 'test flights first. One at a time, take off and landings. And remember, you cees, you are going to stumble and eat Pict snow, but it won't take long. F4 got it sorted in ten minutes.'

The next half an hour would have filled a whole week of funny video footage and earned them all a small fortune in fees. Matt's scream as he fell off a ledge and plummeted a hundred feet before remembering that he could, in fact fly, made Rimsplitter nonsensical with mirth for a good ten minutes. But thirty minutes later, they were all competent. Bearded vultures are extremely powerful birds. And there was something incredible about soaring effortlessly over the peaks.

'It's amazing,' Matt said to Kylah when they had landed on a bare rock ten thousand feet up.

'Astonishing,' she agreed. 'Spotted the dead mountain goat, yet?'

'Thought I caught a whiff.'

'Three kilometres north, I reckon.'

'Yeah, about that.' Matt shook his head. 'How did I even know that?'

'Because it's disgustingly seductive,' Bobby wailed as she dropped in beside them.

Five minutes later with them all on the ground again, Asher shook his head. 'All I can think about is ripping away a large bone and letting it drop onto the crags below so that I can get at the marrow.'

'S'natural you inherit many of the target physiognomy's traits and sensibilities,' Rimsplitter replied. 'Effin' obvious, I'd have thought. Me, I wake up every mornin' dreamin' of ripping a lamb to shreds. You learn to live with it. Or go out and rip a lamb to shreds.'

'What now?'

'Anyone hungry?'

The chorus of 'No' that came back in response made Rimsplitter almost double up. 'Didn't think you would be, you cees. But you ought to know that the orange tinge to your feathers comes from carotenoids found in high concentration in faeces. Like it or not, you lot love Turkish delight.'

'That's reassuring. I am quite partial to a little Turkish del

—' Asher's statement stalled in response to a sharp nudge from Bobby's wing. 'Oh. I think I'm going to be sick.'

'Don't be, in case one of the others effin' eats it.' Rimsplitter cackled again.

Matt stepped forward. 'Let's get serious, Rimsplitter.'

'Okay, okay,' Rimsplitter groaned, 'I can't laugh anymore anyway. It's doin' me ribs in.' He inhaled deeply. 'Whoa. Comedy gold, this is. Right, we take our first recce. Matt and Kylah are the ones who know what Reeves looks like, so you two in the front, the others behind and me at the back on point. Now remember, stay high. We can get over these peaks no trouble. Only perch on crags or high buildings and make use of your thermals. We can stay up for hours with no effin' effort. Capisce?'

There were a lot of bearded vulture nods.

'Right,' Rimsplitter called over his shoulder as he unfurled his wings. 'Who knows the effin' theme tune to *Thunderbirds*?'

CHAPTER THIRTY-SIX

GOGNY PAYN

THE FARROWER TAVERN STOOD, or, to be more accurate, was almost falling down, next to a stable on a side street. The smell of fresh manure from the horses hung in the air like a curtain but offered a welcome freshness compared with the stench that emanated from inside the doors of the Farrower itself. The sensible drinkers—those supping ale from wooden cups—sat outside. The determined drunkards—those inured to the smell of rotting reeds impregnated with trampled underfoot horse-doings both solid and liquid carried in on the feet of punters, combined with the chamber pot shared by all in the corner of the place—hulked at tables, too drunk to care.

The tavern advertised ales and pottage, which was a bit like an everlasting stew that got added to on a daily basis by whatever was at hand. And if your fingers slipped on the stirring spoon and strayed too near the bubbling concoction, it was rumoured that you could easily add that hand and never see it again.

Reeves found a corner table away from the worst of the smell and ordered a flagon of ale. It was delivered by a surly boy of about sixteen whose features were obscured under a layer of grime so ingrained it would take a hammer and chisel to clean him up. Reeves noticed that the boy brought his cup to the table by holding the rim between thumb and forefinger. Cleanliness was clearly not the Farrower's strong point.

'Pottage?' asked the boy.

'No thanks.' Reeves had already glimpsed a bowl of steaming something brought out from the tavern kitchen and decided that he ought to give it a wide birth, if not rope it off and declare it radioactive.

He waved the boy away, filled the cup with ale, swilled the contents around and deposited it on the floor. He filled it again and took a sip. It tasted fruity and malty and might as well have been labelled headache-juice from the get-go. Reeves took some swallows, letting the wooden rim half hide his face as he scoped out his fellow imbibers.

Several shifty-looking men watched him from a table across the courtyard. They seemed particularly interested in the inked images that Ome had drawn all over his arm. Reeves held the appendage up and waved it at them.

'Resonaris rule!' he said, beaming defiantly.

The men slid their surly eyes back to their drinks.

Beneath Reeves' feet a thick rivulet of something trickled into a larger culvert running down the centre the lane. He watched as someone emerged from one of the houses and added something steaming to the rivulet from a large bucket. He hoped that it might have been hot dishwater but its amber colour did little to support his theory. Reeves wondered if the place smelled any better when it rained. At least then the flow of liquids might be swifter. He was still wondering this two flagons later when a small posse of a dozen people walked up the lane, led by an angry Bettany Shadowsmith.

'What do you think you are doing?' she demanded, looking from Reeves to the empty flagons with eyes that did not need a whetstone.

'Drinking. Or is this a trick question?' Reeves smiled back at her in the wavering way drunks do. She wasn't a bad-looking woman, despite the lines of worry on her forehead and the anger thinning her lips. The crowd of women gathered behind muttered disapproval.

'What sort of a man tries to hide in a pot of beer?'

'A very small one?' Reeves laughed uproariously at his own answer and thumped his thigh.

'A sorry excuse for a man, that's what.' Bettany's voice dropped to a harsh whisper. 'You can't walk away from this. You have just delivered the Seren Sea Stone. You must know where it came from. You must know who gave it to you.'

Reeves shook his head. 'Just some bloke. Thass all. Some broke in a blue room. S'all I remember.' He took a swill of beer.

Bettany's expression hardened. 'You're disgusting. And those pieces of wood in your hair. How did you get them? Have you been dealing with the Resonari? Have they got anything to do with the Stone?'

'Nope. But I do like the Nari. Good lot, they are. Ate wizardy grubs. Tasted like pistachio. I was surprised. Though not as surprised as the wizardy grubs, I s'pose.' Again, Reeves grinned, pleased with himself. 'They gave me this tattoo. Like it?' He rolled up his tunic sleeve once more.

Bettany pushed his arm down. 'Are you a fool as well as a coward and a drunk? Do you want to be dragged away by the Zatrank?'

'Ooh, sounds painful.'

'How can you joke when our children have been taken? Have you no heart?'

Reeves shrugged and shook his head. 'S'not my fight. I've done what I was asked to do. End of. Can I buy you a drink?'

Bettany turned to her fellow mothers. 'You see? This man is nothing but a feckless fool. I told you we would get nothing from him. Leave him to his beer.' She rounded on Reeves. 'If you stay here and attract more attention, they will come for you and throw you into the Keep's dungeons. And I have to tell you, seeing you like this, I will not stand in their way.'

'Let 'em try.' Reeves burped.

Bettany, traumatised by Targan's capture and Reeves' flippancy, finally snapped. She let fly a slap that caught Reeves squarely on the cheek with a noise like a thick bough breaking. The blow sent Reeves backwards off his chair and onto the filthy floor. Bettany stood over him. 'You should be ashamed of yourself.'

Reeves looked up. 'So, it's a no for the drink then, I take it?'

Bettany turned away so that Reeves would not see her face. Which was a shame because it was a nice face when it was not distorted by anger and disappointment. Several of the women stepped forward and spat at Reeves. He waited until they'd gone and then sat back up and used some of the remaining ale to wash his face. He noticed that the men opposite who had watched him get drunk had gone. But a moment later, he recognised one of them looking mighty pleased with himself as he led a group of four Zatrank soldiers into the courtyard and pointed.

Reeves caught the informant's eye. It slid away, as did the smirk.

Bettany and the other women stood on the corner, watching.

The Zatrank, however, were nowhere near as reticent. They marched across and stood in front of Reeves, who hid his tattooed arm under the table.

'Having a good time, are we?' asked one of the Zatrank.

'Lully, thanks.'

'Something wrong with your arm, is there?'

Reeves waved the arm holding his ale up. 'No, s'fine.'

'The other one,' said the Zatrank. 'The one with all the drawings on.'

'No. S'fine, too.' Reeves kept his arm where it was.

The Zatrank soldier took out his wand. 'Don't make me ask you again.'

'Thing is, it's paralysed. Can't move it for love nor—'

Reeves got no further. He was grabbed and yanked upwards; the table, flagon, ale and cup sent flying. To steady himself, Reeves had to grab on to one of the soldiers…with his paralysed arm.

'It's a miracle,' said the soldier, his expression wooden, his eyes taking in the elaborate designs.

'Those are Resonari markings,' said the Zatrank holding the wand. 'You one of them? Or have you been collaborating?'

'You mean this little thing?' Reeves said.

The Zatrank thrust his wand into the soft flesh beneath Reeves' eye. 'Ever seen someone with their lungs on the outside of their vest?'

Reeves shook his head.

'Well, that's what you're going to see and they'll be your lungs, if you don't shut up and start cooperating. Those markings are illegal, and you are going to have to come with us.'

The fourth Zatrank trooper now stepped forward. 'Hang about. I know this specimen. I could have sworn he was the bloke de Wyville strung up in a gibbet up country. There's something really weird about all this, Sarge.'

'Oh, good. That means we can take him straight to the Keep. They can usually get people to cough up their secrets.'

'Along with their livers and their lights,' added the fourth trooper, clearly the clown of the group.

The other soldiers all chuckled.

'I suppose that means I don' get to finish,' Reeves dropped his chin and burped, 'finish my beer?'

'Got it in one,' said the Zatrank with the wand.

They dragged him away. Reeves didn't look at Bettany as he passed her by. But if he had, he might have noticed that, though all the other women were jeering, she was merely sniffing.

CHAPTER THIRTY-SEVEN

The guards frogmarched Reeves through the streets. The little procession barely earned a glance. Reeves concluded that the lack of interest was either the consequence of habituation, or a very real sense of survival à la turning a blind eye. They climbed slowly, passing through three gates, each manned by a dozen Zatrank soldiers, before they reached an inner courtyard with steps leading up into the heart of the Keep. Getting in wasn't easy; getting out looked nigh on impossible.

In contrast with the squalid, filthy, noisy streets of Gogny Payn, the rooms and corridors he now entered oozed grandeur. The air was perfumed with incense and oils from luridly coloured candles. Fantastic, colourful tapestries and paintings adorned the walls and every alcove housed a delicate vase or a tasteful sculpture. Reeves noted all of these things as he was pushed along, knowing that they were the ill-gotten gains of a plundered people. Dictators with absolute power could be aesthetes too, or so it seemed.

After a myriad twists and turns, they came to a heavy black door guarded by two Zatrank shock troops dressed in black and gold. It didn't take an expert to work out that these must be Le Liare's elite guard.

A brief exchange of words between his captors and the

guards ensued before the door opened on to a high-ceilinged room with walls of black slate. A long walkway flanked on either side by marble pews led to a raised dais. Towering windows offered views of the mountains to the north bordering Rathkoorne and Pict, and to the south, the sprawl of the city and the plains beyond.

Reeves felt the point of a wand pushed into his back, urging him forward, his hands tied in front of him.

A man sat on an imposing ornate oak chair on the dais: Erthu Le Liare, baron supremo of Rathkoorne. On his right sat Gauinebald, fondling a black cat and giggling as the cat pawed at a piece of thick wool. He did not look at Reeves as he approached. To Erthu's left, the menacing figure of Turgiss de Wyville glared down.

One final push sent Reeves stumbling to within feet of the dais, where he stood and waited.

'Well?' said Erthu. 'Is this the man back from the dead?'

De Wyville stepped down, wand outstretched. A beam of yellow light shot out and shone into Reeves' face.

'His hair is different but it is he,' de Wyville said.

'He is a ghost,' Gauinebald called out in shrill delight.

De Wyville kicked the back of Reeves' knee and he fell forwards. 'He is no ghost,' de Wyville said. 'His bones are solid and breakable.'

'Then why is he not dead?' Gauinebald asked, grinning. 'Because I killed him.'

'Yes.' Erthu leaned forward. 'Why are you not dead? Can you tell us, ghost?'

'I am no ghost,' Reeves replied. 'Though I may, perhaps, be your worst nightmare.'

'Do you know where you are and to whom you speak, dog?' de Wyville hissed.

'All too well,' Reeves said.

'Let me kill him again.' De Wyville poked the wand at Reeves' head. It throbbed with power where it touched flesh. 'This time I will send a thousand pieces of his filthy guts to join the stars.'

Erthu sat back, a smile playing over his pale face. 'But you are missing the point, Turgiss. If this dog, as you call it, has truly survived a killing curse, we would do better to find out how and why, would we not?'

'I saw it with my own eyes.' De Wyville shook his head. 'He was dead. Let me now clear his body from where it besmirches the floor.'

'I can do it.' Gauinebald stood up. 'I can turn him to meat and the cat can eat him.'

Erthu smiled. 'Skilful though you both undoubtedly are in ridding us of problems through annihilation, one must occasionally employ different tactics. We have been given a great boon, gentlemen. Let us not waste this opportunity.' He stood and walked towards Reeves, who was still on his knees. 'You are not like the cattle we rule over. You came here to deliver a message, or perhaps a package, to a boy. What was it?'

'You've got me all wrong,' Reeves said, still slurring. 'I'm jussa bloke who likes a good drink.'

Le Liare smiled and nodded, his eyes straying to the sticks in Reeves' hair and the henna patterns on his arms. 'You have been marked by the scum that blight the land. Is this some misguided attempt by the filthy Nari to challenge my authority?'

Reeves burped and then frowned as if in recollection. 'Oh yeah. Goanna curry. Those Nari know spicy.'

Erthu snorted. 'Let the drunk sober up and then give him to Alienor. If he knows anything, she will find it. Then,' he turned to his son, 'you may kill him together with all the gathered rabble youth. I feel generous. We should gift the people a message. We must ensure it is a grand one.'

The guards yanked Reeves to his feet and marched him out through a labyrinth of passageways and tunnels, constantly descending. Reeves noticed the air change. It became colder and damper and the perfumed halls were replaced by the stench of decay and death. These were the Keep's lockups and dungeons. Vast catacombs where the dead were left to rot and which now served to imprison those who might dare question Le Liare's absolute authority.

Reeves thought he could hear chattering and crying but

when he was thrust through door after door, each one clanging ominously behind him, the noise ceased. The space was vast with at least twenty thick wooden doors in a rough semi-circle, each with a covered grill halfway down. The jailor did not wear a Zatrank uniform, but he was equally as brutal.

Reeves waited while a door was unlocked. There was nowhere to run to and so he stood.

The jailor moved aside with mock politeness to let Reeves enter. He did so, only to receive a booted shove on his back-side that sent him sprawling. The grill in the door behind let in some flickering torchlight, but this was extinguished once it thudded shut. Reeves fell onto hard stone. It was impossible to see if he was alone and so he waited while he caught his breath. Slowly, in between breaths, he heard other sounds. Some sniffling, breathing, a cough.

'Hello?' Reeves said.

'Hello?' The voice was young, male, full of fear.

Reeves turned to where he thought he could hear the voice, but there was nothing to see. He might as well have been talking to a spirit. He scrambled backwards until his arm clanged roughly against the door. His fingers felt for and found the grill's cover and he managed to push it out an inch. An oblong of light fell onto the cell floor. Reeves stuck his mouth near the opening.

'Oy, there's something else in here.'

Silence.

Reeves persisted with his mouth to the grill. 'Look, I was only minding my own business when this mad girl and a dwarf accosted me. It was them that scuppered that Zatrank nob…sorry, your colleeeeague. Sounds funny, colleeeeague. Anyway, was nuthin to do with me. Tell Eartha or whatever his, or, let's not mis-gander anyone, her name is that I don't know anything. I'm jus' Reeves. An' I could do with a drink if there's anything going.'

Silence.

'Hello, jailor boy. I know you're out there 'cos I can smell you. Like I say, it was a girl and a dwarf—'

'Reeves?' A voice, from somewhere else in the dungeon. A girl's voice. 'Reeves?'

'Oh, so you got them too?' Reeves continued to address the unseen jailor. 'Thass good, that is. Ask them some questions, why don't you.'

'Reeves?' Milda shouted. 'It's me. Raymounde is here but he's injured. They…they've tortured him. They make him dance for them. Make him hurt himself for their amusement-
-'

Reeves launched into song, 'Eyesore the night on the light la la la la la la-laaaah. La, la, la laaaaah, la la lah. Less have a singsong. I know a few good ones for this place. "Unchained Melody", thass a good one. "Breaking Out is Hard to Do", thass a good one. "Parole Devil Moon", thass a good—'

'Shut up,' the jailer ordered.

'Oh, come on, giss a drink.'

Silence.

'"Please Release Me", thass a good one.'

'Reeves,' called Milda, 'can you hear me?'

'"Silence is Golden", thass a good one.'

The jailer walked over. 'Shut up.'

'Ooh, thass rude. How about a little drinky for Reeves.'

'No grog down 'ere. An' anyway, you need to sober up for Alienor p.d.q.' He walked away.

Reeves shouted after him, '"Lock the Casbah", thass a good one.'

'Right, that's it,' said the jailor. 'I'm getting you a soberin' potion. Sod this.'

A minute later, Reeves was dragged back out, his nose pinched and his head tipped back as a steaming concoction was poured down his throat. All his digits went suddenly rigid and his brain fizzed.

'There you go,' said the jailor. 'You know, most people would have shut up and tried to hang on to these last few seconds for as long as they could. Rushin' to see Alienor is not something someone with even one sane ounce of brain juice would want to do. So, sing away, Reeves or whoever you are. 'Cos you won't be singing in a minute.'

'Now I know who you remind me of,' said Reeves, staring into the jailor's face, which was a feat in itself since the features were all on slightly different levels.

'Who?' said the jailor.

'Know anyone called Esmerelda by any chance? The bells! The bells!' cried Reeves as the Zatrank soldiers dragged him away.

He thought he heard a girl's voice wail his name just before the door clanged shut behind him.

CHAPTER THIRTY-EIGHT

Alienor Le Liare's chamber had a door, like all the other doors in the dungeon. Except that this door was painted canary yellow and had a chalkboard sign above it surrounded by wonky green and yellow flowers and the words *Home is where the heart is* handwritten, with a red stylised drawing of a heart in lieu of the word.

The three Zatrank guarding Reeves knocked hard, waited until they heard a bolt slide open and then legged it around the corner, leaving Reeves alone. The door creaked open and a face peeked out from behind it. It was the kind of face that made you stare, largely because it was as if someone had given a five-year-old a paintbox and asked them to pretend they were a makeup artist.

'You must be Reeves,' said Alienor in a quiet, high-pitched voice. The door opened wider to reveal more of the room beyond and of the woman whose face Reeves could not take his eyes away from. Her hair was braided, studded with the bones of small animals and her face had two inverted painted triangles of white beneath her stormy eyes, ending in an apex over her cheek. Here eyelids were painted black, and a single red bob of colour sat in the middle of her chin.

'Come in, Reeves,' she said and Reeves complied.

There was something about her voice, something

beguiling and irresistible. He toyed with resistance but found he could not. Whether it was the shock of not finding her to be the pantomime villain his overwrought imagination had concocted or not, he wasn't sure. But step inside he did and felt his mind blown.

The threshold gave way to a meadow. And as unlikely and impossible as that was, it was indeed what Reeves saw with his eyes and felt with his feet. Above, the ceiling had gone. In its place was a blue sky dotted with cotton clouds. Trees in full foliage rustled in a breeze that cooled the air just enough to make it pleasant. But that was where normality ended. Everything else was Lewis Carroll after several too many absinthes. A giant mushroom forest bordered one edge of the meadow. Trees had horns and made the noises of animals. Birds flew upside down, chased by cats with wings. To top it all, a couple of unicorns gambolled at the edge of a still lake.

Reeves shook his head.

'It is real,' said Alienor. 'It's my real.'

'Wow,' said Reeves.

That made Alienor smile. 'That's different. Most people bury their heads and sob when they see my world.'

'When you say your world, you mean what exactly?' Reeves asked. Despite himself and his predicament, he was genuinely fascinated by this place and this creature.

'My father has given me this space for me to live in. He said I could do whatever I wanted in here. He didn't like me changing things out there,' she turned and pointed at the yellow door, incongruous now in the landscape.

Reeves noted that there was a wand strapped to her arm.

Alienor caught his glance. 'I tie it on in case I lose it. Mostly I don't need it. What I do comes from a different place. But Father gets annoyed when I don't keep it close. Once I lost it and it took me two years to find it.'

Reeves had worked the probation service long enough to tell the difference, the real difference, between being an evil bastard and not understanding the meaning between good and bad. There were a great number of the former: the liars, the cheats, the thieves, the violent and the vindictive. But not too many of the latter, though it had always surprised Reeves how quick the former were to point out that they might have a touch of the latter if they thought it would get them a leaner sentence.

But Alienor was not trying to hide here. She was, Reeves had no doubt, the real deal.

'This is all pretty amazing,' Reeves said, tying on a fixed grin. 'And all your own work, is it?'

She nodded. 'I have ideas. And I take ideas from other people. Sometimes without them even knowing.' She smiled. Her lips were light orange. 'Would you like to walk in my animal forest?'

'Sure,' said Reeves, still unsure what to make of his situation. He could see how something like this might make your average Rathkoornians question their own sanity. But this was Willy Wonka stuff *a la* The Twilight Zone.

Alienor led him along a path bordered by flowers whose faces smiled and turned with their passage to blow perfume after them. A stream running nearby had golden fish that leapt out in graceful arcs wherever Alienor came within ten feet. They arrived at the gated entrance to the wood and Reeves looked in on an arboretum of trees shaped like giraffes and lions and wolves and elephants.

'I like it in here,' said Alienor. The wooden gate creaked open of its own volition and she stepped across and waited for Reeves to do the same. 'You first.'

Once again, any thoughts he had of resisting evaporated as one foot stepped in front of the other and Reeves found himself treading the paths with Alienor behind him, talking in her little girl voice.

'Father sent word that he wanted me to find out about you.'

'Did he?'

'He says you are very dangerous. He says that you can resist wands.'

'I don't know where he got that from.' Reeves passed underneath a huge oak tree with a curved branch arcing down like the trunk of a huge pachyderm. 'I'm just like everyone el—'

The branch swept down and curved around Reeves' waist, lifting him bodily and hanging him upside down so that his head hung at the same level as Alienor's. The sobering potion had taken effect, but not completely. It had helped to be a little tipsy in dealing with Alienor's…eccentricities. But the beginnings of a hangover had ridden on the back of the potion and now, being head down, it galloped to the front of his head and began knocking on the inside of his skull.

'What is it that you are not telling us?' she asked, smiling. She had dark smudges on her filed teeth.

Reeves hoped they were from the lipstick. 'I'm just a soldier who—' He got no further. The branch, or elephant's, trunk, depending on which way you looked at it—and Reeves was staring at it with bulging eyes—tightened some more, squeezing the breath from his lungs.

'The tree knows, because I know when you are not telling the truth.' Alienor reached down and plucked a flower. Red liquid dripped from its ruptured stem. She brushed the petals playfully over Reeves' upside-down face. They smelled of something long dead and putrid.

Reeves tried to speak, but nothing emerged other than short, strained gasps.

'Now,' said Alienor, and the crushing force around Reeves relaxed. He sucked in air. 'Answer truthfully and it will be far less painful. '

'What,' croaked Reeves, 'do you want me to say?'

'Tell me everything.'

'Everything? From the beginning?'

'Everything.'

'Okay,' Reeves said and the squeezing eased. 'I was born on 20 February, 1982…'

The vulture squadron flew high over snow-capped mountains that yielded to valleys where the monks of Pict made the fabled and much coveted digestif known as Galena Brew. It was said that the secret recipe of its manufacture was known only by two priests at any given time and that those two priests were never to be in the same room at the same time, lest some natural disaster strike them both down

It was a bright morning. Below them, white became green and then ochre as they crossed into the plains of Rathkoorne. Matt was amazed at how little effort it took for them to cover the distance so quickly.

'Yeah,' said Rimsplitter, gliding in close. 'Effin' brilliant, ain't it?'

And it was. They flew over field and farm, hamlet and forest. Birds scattered and dived for cover whenever they approached. Rimsplitter took them to a tall stand of oak on the edge of the plains, where they landed and regrouped.

'Right,' said Rimsplitter. 'Not bad, but don't get distracted by wot's dead. It's tempting to go and look, but stay high. I've got the tracer gnat with me, so when we get to within half a mile of that ess-hole Gogny, I'll let him out and follow him in. We should find F4, no probs.'

'But what do you suggest we do then?' Matt asked. 'We can't all just drop in.'

'Nah, but we'll check out the lie of the land. Maybe send the smallest one of us down to look.' He glared at Bobby.

'I'm game,' she said.

'Yeah, but you don't want to be someone's dinner,' Rimsplitter said. 'Softly, softly catchy donkey.'

'Monkey,' said Matt. 'It's monkey.'

'More meat on a donkey. You've got to start thinking big, you tart.'

They took off and stayed high. They all smelled Gogny Payn before they saw it: a mixture of rotting food and worse from the prominent city midden baking in the heat. A great dark smudge on the horizon with the Keep an angular black hulk dominating the plain.

They circled high and clear above the city. Rimsplitter let the gnat go and followed it down to make sure no swift decided to make it its lunch. The eagle's eye spotted the house the gnat entered with ease. The squadron convened, once more, atop an abandoned building.

'Okay, looks like there's a bit of a garden,' Matt said. 'Bobby, you go down and have a scout about, we'll stay here.'

'I am not happy about Bobby going alone,' said Asher.

'Nor me,' Kylah added.

'Look, we all stand out like bleedin' sheep in a wolf den. It's the only way. I'll be watching everything,' Rimsplitter said.

Reluctantly, they all agreed. Bobby took off and circled high until she was almost over Candin Lane. There she headed straight down and landed on a bird table that was at least ten sizes too small for a bird of her size. She stood and peered in through the window at a woman who seemed to be scattering breadcrumbs onto a table. Even as she watched, a magpie hopped over and began eating. The magpie looked up. On seeing Bobby, it let out a screech. The woman looked up and promptly screamed. To her credit, it lasted only a few seconds before she had the sense to clamp a hand over her face.

The back door opened and the woman emerged.

'Are you…can you…'

'The name is Roberta, but people generally call me Bobby,' said Bobby. At which point the woman screamed again.

———

In Alienor's secret garden, Reeves' promise to tell her 'everything' had now reached his late teens and university.

'Mostly, we went to lectures in the mornings and then to the union bar for a pint and a sandwich at lunchtime. That usually ended all academic endeavour for the rest of the day.'

'And you were sent to these institutions as a punishment?'

'Not at all. They are seats of learning. You had to win a place.' Reeves wriggled. The elephant's trunk branch had eased into an almost horizontal position.

'Through battling with other applicants?' Alienor sat perfectly still while some reeds behind her attempted to tease out the tangles in her hair.

'Only through exams. I was good at exams. Read the stuff the night before and regurgitated it onto the page. But like spending the night in the union bar, only with words instead of beer.'

'And did you have to pay for these university sentences?'

'Degrees, we called them degrees. No, it was all paid for back then. By government decree, though it was local government that stumped up.'

Alienor frowned. 'I am confused. Your young people go to these universities where they drink beer and sleep and obtain life experiences at the insistence of your elders?'

'Back then, yes. Unfortunately, these days they have to pay.'

'Why would they pay for being subjected to boring talks and late nights of alcohol-related misery?'

'Many of them feel it is their right and education isn't to be sniffed at.'

'But why educate the masses? Is it not enough for those in power to have the knowledge?' Alienor blinked her big eyes.

'I can guess how you might see things that way. But hegemony is not the most popular subject on most university campuses. No, they're designed to promote free speech, open thinking and discussion, unless the person demonstrating free speech offends, in which case they're not allowed a platform in case they upset the moral or emotional consensus.'

'Ah, your young people at the university have not yet been trained in combat or wand lore, then.'

'No, we give them "safe spaces" in which to mingle with people of all backgrounds in situations where they do not have to be offended.'

'And does this prepare them well for the world?'

Reeves didn't answer that one. He tried to smile instead.

'I do not think that your story of your university life is the knowledge that my brother seeks,' Alienor said and the branch in which Reeves rested tightened and tilted once more.

'No, of course not,' said Reeves. 'But it does sort of explain how it is I began to get involved with the mad and the bad…oops, that would never get me a spot in the Oxford Union debate. I meant the prison service, which is sort of how I ended up here.'

The twisting bonds of wood eased. 'You have been a jailor?'

'I'd rather say I worked with prisoners.'

'I am listening,' said Alienor and the reeds that had become frozen and rigid recommenced their gentle stroking and teasing.

I hope to God those idiots who put me here are listening, too, Reeves thought and started on an anecdote about how he broke his leg playing rugby.

––––––

BETTANY GOT over her shock pretty quickly and Bobby admired her for it. Seeing a huge bearded vulture in her backyard was shock enough; hearing it speak took surprise and horror to another level altogether. But Bettany opened the back door wide and Bobby hopped in.

'I apologise for my reaction,' Bettany said. 'It's not as if I haven't been expecting some…one.'

Bobby cocked her head. 'Really?'

'Reeves told me you'd come.'

'Then Reeves has been here?'

Bethany nodded, but there was a resigned sadness in the way that she did it that made Bobby uncomfortable. 'He made me promise to look after the magpie. He has a broken wing.'

The magpie let out a subdued chatter.

'So where is Reeves now?' Bobby asked.

Bettany's shoulders slumped. 'He has been taken by the Zatrank to the Keep. Just like my son, Targan. Like all our sons. They were taken by force, though if you ask me, I would say that Reeves almost wanted to be taken. It was as if he had a death wish.'

Bobby blinked. 'Can you as quickly as possible tell me exactly what's been going on?'

And so Bettany explained. She told Bobby about the Zatrank rounding up all the young men. About Reeves breezing in, the magpie, and finally how Reeves had gone off to drink himself into oblivion. 'All he left was the magpie, oh and the note around its leg.'

'There's a note?' Bobby asked, stepping forward and making Bettany start.

The magpie held out its foot. Bettany untied the parchment and held it open .

'Oh, Trev,' said Bobby when she'd finished reading it and clarified a few more points.

'Trev? Is that how you address Reeves?'

'It is his first name. But that'll be our little secret, eh? I think I'm going to want to pass this all on as soon as. Is it okay if you look after the magpie for a bit longer?'

Bettany nodded. 'He's quite sweet, really.'

'Oh, and the note mentioned something about a stone?'

Bettany reached for a jar on the windowsill and removed the Seren Sea Stone. She hung the 'shell' around Bobby's neck. 'This should have been our salvation,' she said. 'Targan…' She turned away, using her apron to wipe her eyes before turning back. 'I thought Reeves might have been able to do something. He had that look about him. But he simply gave up.'

Bobby nodded. 'I'll be back. I promise.'

She took off and found the others and related everything that had happened.

'What exactly did the note say?' Kylah asked.

'Ring bell. Wait. Bring stone.'

'Great,' Rimsplitter said.

'The bell must be that thing.' Bobby turned her head towards the augur bell on the Keep tower.

'But why does he want to alert everyone that there's danger?'

'I have no idea,' said Bobby.

'Could this all be part of his death wish?' Asher asked. 'Does he want to bring all of us down with him?'

Matt shook his head. 'It's becoming all too easy to have a low opinion of Reeves. But the fact is, he is our man on the ground. What choice do we have? Either we do as he asks or go back and abandon him and everyone else here.'

'Agreed,' Kylah said. 'What is the worst that can happen? We ring the bell and then circle up out of harm's way.'

'Or we could visit that dead armadillo I spotted a couple of miles to the west.' Matt made a throwaway suggestion.

'I am sort of hungry,' said Bobby.

'Give me effin' strength.' Rimsplitter opened his wings. 'I'll ring the effin' bell and then we can go and get something fresh. There's rabbits near a stream to the west. I ain't touching no armadillo, you tarts. Bobby, you wear the stone for now and try not to get too much blood on it, and definitely no crap. I seen you lot eat. Follow me.' He took off with a great swish of wings.

Kylah watched him go with a shake of her head. 'Am I really taking orders from Rimsplitter?'

'Last one to the tower's a canary,' Matt said and launched himself into space.

What Kylah said next contained only one vowel and was four letters long. Most unbefitting a lady, but a trooper's oath if ever there was one.

CHAPTER FORTY

Rimsplitter flew off towards a murky river, followed by the others. He swooped down onto a deserted bank and picked up a fist-sized stone in his talons.

'Each of you grab one,' he called as he soared back up into the sky.

The vultures circled the Keep a few times and then, following Rimsplitter's lead, dived down towards the huge bell and let fly their missiles. Each one found its mark, but the reverberations were nothing more than thin jarring clangs.

Undaunted, Rimsplitter circled above the others. 'Right, you ay-aitches, follow me.'

This time Rimsplitter landed talons first on the edge of the great bell. The momentum of the strike drove the bell away before it swung pendulum-like, back. 'Come on,' he called, 's'all a matter of timing.'

No one needed anything else explained. In turn, they all repeated the process, catching the bell as it began its swing and adding their power to it, each contact adding thrust. On the third pass a satisfying deep and sonorous 'dong' issued forth.

They continued, striking the bell repeatedly and soon, people poured out into the streets to point at the huge birds setting off the augur bell. When the Zatrank soldiers appeared on a parapet below, wands raised, Rimsplitter gave the word and they flew off and away towards the river, the bell harsh and insistent behind them.

———

IN ALIENOR'S GARDEN, Reeves heard a knock on the door. He was halfway through a story about the serial murderer he'd once had to accompany to his grandmother's funeral only to watch the man running off across the cemetery lawn with a police dog in hot pursuit.

Alienor stood abruptly. 'Can you hear it?'

'Hear what?' the still trussed Reeves asked.

Alienor opened the door. There was no one there. But faintly, Reeves could hear the deep and compelling noise of a far-off bell.

'The augur bell,' said Alienor. 'Some great change is afoot.'

Reeves nodded. 'Right then, how about I tell you how exactly it is that I came to be here.'

'I think that would be wise,' she said and walked back towards him, the door swinging closed behind her.

This time, Reeves told her about the car park, Miss Fenella Whitney, Matt and Kylah and everything else. He did not hold back one single little detail…other than that of Bettany and the magpie.

Alienor listened and nodded. 'I believe you. Your tales are too strange to have been made up. It is a shame we cannot stay in the garden to play any longer.'

Reeves felt the bonds loosen and the branch straighten such that he was deposited back on the floor on two feet.

'I would like to visit your world one day,' said Alienor.

'I'd be delighted to show you around,' said Reeves. 'Obviously, it would have to be without your wand.'

'Why would I want to give up my wand?'

'So that you would be like everyone else.'

Alienor blinked and smiled a cold little smile. 'What a strange world that would be.' She waved a hand and black tendrils shot up from the earth beneath Reeves' feet, encompassing him completely so that only his eyes and ears were visible behind the dense black covering. 'Time I delivered you to my brother.'

In the baron's courtroom, Erthu Le Liare was used to doling out judgement. Crimes needed to be punished. Though neither the judgement nor the punishment had anything to do with justice, which was an animal long since vanished from the confines of the Keep.

Reeves stood, still trussed in black tendrils, watching Erthu pace.

His mad son sat on the throne, teasing the black cat with a ball of string. Turgiss de Wyville brooded in a dark corner while Alienor told them of her findings.

It was Turgiss who spoke first when she had finished. 'This is an outrage,' he seethed. 'Some foreign power dares to threaten us. Us!'

'Maybe if you stopped randomly destroying places in foreign countries and worlds, they'd leave you alone.' Reeves' voice emerged muffled through a layer of black fronds.

'Silence,' hissed Erthu.

But Gauinebald heard and put the cat down on the floor. He got up from the chair in one smooth movement, a strange and unpleasant smile playing on his lips. 'No, let him speak. It would be interesting to hear the difference when his tongue is tied in a knot.' He raised his wand, his eyes shining in anticipation.

'Stop,' said Erthu. 'Have I not told you that we can turn this to our advantage?'

'Let me question him, sire,' said Turgiss. 'Let me learn the name of this boy he is supposed to meet.'

Erthu watched his henchman walk towards Reeves and shook his head. 'But don't you see that it is irrelevant? We do not need to know. In fact, we would be better not knowing because that way, we can justify exterminating all of them in the name of this pathetic creature. His name will be one that the good people of Gogny Payn and Rathkoorne will remember for generations as the man who caused the death of so many innocents.'

'I want to turn him inside out,' pleaded Gauinebald. 'I haven't used the Intrinsicus curse since I modified it.'

'And so you shall. In front of the whole city, along with all those snivelling boys and those he calls friends. In fact, he can watch with his guts hanging out as we deal with the vermin. A grand gesture, as I have said.'

'But what of the bell?' Alienor said. 'I heard the augur bell.'

'Birds. Yet more of his tricks,' said Erthu.

'The people will be on edge,' said Turgiss.

'Let them be. The bell augurs a great change. We will give them that change. A slaughter followed by a demonstration of our power.' He turned to Gauinebald. 'Have we a mage that is up to it?'

Gauinebald shrugged. 'We can find one.'

'Excellent. Get the word out. An execution and a culling at four today. And get the cooks to roast some fresh porcupine. I feel a hunger come upon me.'

The men swept from the room, leaving Reeves and Alienor alone once more.

'If I released you now, where would you go?'

'Back to the tavern, probably,' Reeves said.

'They would find you and kill you.'

'But at least I'd get a pint in first.'

Alienor walked languorously around him, watching his eyes. 'Why would you not run?'

'Do you want me to run?'

'Only if I could come with you.'

'Ah, I don't think we'd get very far. You're not big on rules, I don't think.'

'I can make my own rules.'

'Yeah, so I've noticed.'

'You are very different from the men my father normally brings me.'

'Glad to hear it.'

'After you are dead, perhaps I will get to know you better.'

As statements of intent went, it was one worthy of a minute's silence and that was exactly what it got. Reeves could think of nothing to say. It wasn't a threat, but the implications were beyond any and all of his conceptual abilities. Did this creature like him? If she did, she had an odd way of showing it.

'You never know,' he managed after a long while. 'But I'm dying to find out.'

Alienor stopped and looked at him. Then her lips parted and she let out a giggle. 'You made a joke.'

'That's right. I'm here until 4 pm. Tell all your friends.'

She giggled again. 'Yes, I definitely will keep you after you die. For a while, at least.'

'Lucky old me, eh?'

'Afterwards, we will go back to my garden and you can tell me all about your lovely wife.'

'Of course. You two would get on really well. Especially at Halloween.'

———

THEY TOOK it in turns to fly patrols while the others ate. Rimsplitter's prowess as a hunter was a thing of astonishing power and raw violence. None of the rabbits he brought back were long dead, most were still warm, but none of them twitching. And although the fur and raw meat did little for the meal aesthetically, thankfully, such human viewpoints had long since flown out of the metamorphic window once vulture instincts, necessarily strong in such circumstances, kicked in. And so, with the others feasting, it was Asher who landed excitedly on the riverbank full of news from his patrol.

'Something big is happening,' he said. 'People are gathering and I thought I saw a crier going about the town. Too high to hear what he was saying, obviously.'

'Do you think it has anything to do with our bell ringing?' Kylah asked, a bit of rabbit flesh hanging fetchingly from her beak.

'Coincidence, if I remember rightly, is a dirty word at Hipposync.'

'It is indeed. A cee word if ever there was one, but not in the Rimsplitter sense.' Kylah tilted her head back to ease the passage of a fleshy morsel.

'A cee is a cee in my book,' Rimsplitter said.

'Hopefully, that is a book I shall never read,' said Asher.

'So, what's the plan?' Matt asked.

'Finish up here and then go back up,' Kylah said. 'Reeves had us ring that bell for a reason. Now we've waited, as instructed. What exactly did the note say next?'

Bobby, who much against her better judgement, had eaten some entrails and found them delicious, said rather sheepishly, 'Bring stone.'

'You're in charge of that,' Matt said, eyeing the trinket around her neck.

'Let's do it,' Rimsplitter said.

'What about the food?' Matt asked.

'Let the sun ripen it a bit. Adds to the effin' flavour. Asher can eat later.'

Asher tilted his head but didn't object. A moment later, the squadron was airborne.

CHAPTER FORTY-ONE

Black stone walls overlooked the great quadrangle at the Keep. At one end a gate led out into the city, and it was through this that the people now streamed.

On a stage, the Rathbong Bongadiers were belting out a standard, dressed in fetching fatigues with boots and leather hats. Their patriotic song, 'Enemies Tremble at the Sight of My Wand', echoed around the walls to the wonderment of the assembled watchers. Around the perimeter, Zatrank guards stood to attention. At the other end, a balcony ran the length of the tallest building and it was here that Erthu preferred to stand. Sometimes, Gauinebald and de Wyville stood with him, but not today.

They had different roles to play.

Erthu looked down at the ranks of wanded guards and at his son, as wild as the heather and as idiotic as the hares that coursed amongst it. Gauinebald stood watching as they led in the seized boys, grinning and making jokes as he pointed at the ones most terrified. Terror and hopelessness were etched into every face. Many were crying. Those cries were echoed in the sobs of the gathered women, who seemed to make up the majority of the Gogny Payn unwashed who stood behind the guards, forming a barrier between onlookers and prisoners.

And then, with the quadrangle now full of hundreds of people, they led in the girl and the dwarf, followed by Reeves.

The crowd fell silent.

Erthu watched with a satisfied smile. The dwarf could barely walk; the girl however, remained defiant. But Reeves was a different animal altogether. Devoid of Alienor's all-constraining bonds, he still had his hands tied in front of him. He looked up at Erthu and mouthed something. Erthu could not make it out, but he would expect it to be derogatory.

Reeves seemed not to care. Remarkably, the man seemed fearless of his impending death. Erthu had met a few brave souls and many stupid souls, but never someone like Reeves. Perhaps he was a unique mixture of stupidity and bravery; it was all very well to not fear death, but intelligent beings would show concern about the manner of its visitation upon them. Anyone looking at Gauinebald knew that mercy was not his strong point. The boy's face gleamed with anticipation. He was more excited than Erthu could ever remember.

A timepiece on a dresser nearby showed the hour to be approaching.

It was time.

Erthu threw open the doors to the balcony and stepped out. The day was warm, the sky above covered with thin high cloud. The minute he stepped out, The Bongadiers fell silent and the air filled with wailing and pleading. Erthu raised his wand and the noise stopped. The mouths of the people still gaped, the eyes staring up at him remained full of desperation, but the clamour and lamentations that had sullied the day disappeared. Erthu pointed the wand at his mouth and then flicked it forward. When he next spoke, it was with an amplified volume that filled the quadrangle.

'Good people of Gogny Payn,' his voice echoed. He'd added in a little pious bass for effect. 'We are met on the saddest of days. For today, we are to witness the results of a heinous crime against me, this city and all of the people of Rathkoorne. A poisoner is amongst us. A foreigner from beyond the snow-topped mountains. A fell bringer of foul lies. He is a killer and spreader of vicious wickedness. One of our brave Zatrank has already become his victim. But worse than that is the seditious and evil tale he has been intent on spreading. We fear that his visitation is the result of a terrible conspiracy. For he will not have worked alone. We have two of his co-conspirators in our hands.'

Erthu waved his wand again. A thin stream of dust fell towards Milda and Raymounde and replicas of their faces leaped upwards to fill the air above them, grotesque and misshapen. The crowd gasped, Erthu having decided that gasps were admissible into his conjured quietness. It added drama.

'But worse is the gloating knowledge that he has imparted. He was not working alone. We know that there are spies amongst us. And this monster and his masters' plan has been to inveigle their way into our lives by targeting the innocent. We know that amongst these gathered boys there are those who have been turned. Agents of a foreign power set to disrupt our way of life. It is even possible that they have links to the wights whose crimes against our people are beyond description to anyone who did not experience them at first hand. And yet he will not tell us who. He refuses even under the most tactical of interrogations to divulge the identity of the foreign power he works for. He is nothing but a filthy spy.'

A murmur drifted over the assembled people.

'We will ensure that he is punished. We will execute him and his two fellow spies summarily as a message to those who dare rise against us. We have fought the biggest and fiercest of foes and won. They need to understand that we stand as one against anyone who dares challenge our borders.'

'Let the boys go,' said a voice.

Erthu allowed himself a tight smile. His control over the audience via silence charm was absolute. He had let his mind choose one to speak and he had chosen wisely, for she had voiced what the mob was thinking.

Let the boys go.

'I hear your pain,' said Erthu and the timbre and inflection were enough to melt the stoniest of hearts. 'But you must understand that amongst these boys are vile usurpers. Cuckoos sent to live amongst us like filthy weeds that will grow to choke us all. I ask you, can we take the risk? Should we spare these few in the certain knowledge that they harbour a canker?'

The crowd stayed silent.

Erthu smiled. He had them. Their memories of the atrocities and hardships of just a few years before were fresh and still aching. He'd banked on that. Played on their greater fear and won. Though there were fifty boys assembled, there were far more families in the quadrangle who had no connection to the youths. It was they to whom Erthu now appealed.

'We must be strong,' he said. 'We must be unflinching and rip the weeds out by their roots.' Something caught his eye and he looked up.

Birds circled high above. They drew closer and landed on the buildings. They were big and menacing. Vultures from the mountains. Well, well. Even the birds had heard of the impending slaughter.

Erthu smiled. 'Let it begin,' he called out across the space in front of him.

They dragged a dozen boys forward to face the Zatrank wand squad of equal number. The young prisoners wailed and fell to their knees, heads bowed.

'Oh, no,' said Reeves, walking forward. 'This isn't fair. Me first. Come on, me first.'

The crowd, released from the silence charm, muttered. The wand squad turned around.

Reeves continued forward towards Gauinebald. 'Come on, you little git. I know what you are. I know what you've done. All those innocent people, murdered from a distance. You coward. But I'm here because of one in particular.'

'Some worm I may have trodden on?'

'Someone whose name I will not tarnish by speaking it aloud. But I am here for that as much as anything. And you should be very afraid for that reason.'

Gauinebald cackled with laughter. 'My sister has made him a witless fool.'

But Reeve's dangerous grin had not slipped. 'Come on,

sunshine. You've talked the talk, now walk the walk. Come on, show me my insides, you tubby little shitheel.'

Gauinebald's face settled into a mirthless smile and he hissed out the next words. 'I was saving you until last. In fact, I will still save you until last, but perhaps only your head on a stick, alive and staring.'

Reeves' grin broadened and he tilted his head right back to allow Gauinebald access to his throat. 'Go on then. Chop it off, I dare you.'

Gauinebald held out his wand and the crowd fell silent once more. They'd seen the young Le Liare in action before. They knew what to expect.

He turned to a nearby guard. 'Get me a broom to stick his head on.'

The guard ran off.

Off to his right, Milda was crying.

'No, Reeves. No.'

Raymounde looked up. He barely had the strength to lift his head. 'Sorry,' he whispered.

Reeves eyes blazed, but all he did was shake his head. It was an odd gesture. One that might easily have been inter-preted as dismissive. But there was something in his expres-sion that only Raymounde and Milda could see. A look that made the dwarf's brows beetle in confusion.

'I did not forget you,' Reeves said and though his voice was barely a whisper, it made Ryamounde and Milda's frowns that bit deeper.

Then Reeves lifted his face to the sky and spoke clearly and loudly. 'Power through fear is a citadel built on sand. Beware the rain that falls and does not cease.'

The words echoed around the quadrangle. The crowd followed his gaze and saw four huge birds sitting on the roof lines of the buildings. Three large vultures with red-rimmed eyes and one huge eagle that suddenly opened its wings. The people fell silent because the words were somehow making them think.

Turgiss de Wyville, overseeing the execution squad lined

up in front of the boys, let out a harsh laugh. 'Words, pah! Words are no use to you now, fool.'

The birds took flight. Once more, most of them flew to the highest point of the Keep and began, once more, to hurl themselves at the augur bell.

Everyone looked.

The birds were a distraction. So much so that no one was watching the prisoners anymore. No one noticed a fourth vulture cruise over their heads. Especially since Bobby, a witch in vulture clothing, had conjured a camouflage charm. What anyone watching might have seen was the small shell on a leather thong that dropped over Reeves' head to nestle around his neck.

'The birds know,' squealed Gauinebald. 'They signal your death.' He turned back to Reeves and approached to within two feet, his wand once more at Reeves' neck.

But Reeves turned his head to contemplate de Wyville. 'Maybe against wands words are useless. But I see that your belief in your power has made you sloppy. Only you wear a knife amongst all of these hardened soldiers.'

De Wyville smiled. 'I took it from a wight when I blew him to pieces with a curse.'

All eyes in the assembled throng were now on Reeves. Some were quizzical, some pitying, some callous and uncaring. But all Reeves did was smile and speak slowly and clearly. 'The trouble with that is that all these good people probably also have knives, or sticks, or clubs, or fists, or good hard boots.'

'But we have wands,' Gauinebald said with an imperious giggle.

Reeves looked back at him and joined in the laugh. 'You do, you do. But did I not tell you what the Resonaris showed me? A repository full of wands just like yours. All without power…until I turned up. And suddenly, they did have power. Enough wands and enough power to destroy you all.' He paused and drew himself up to his full height. 'And I thought for one brief, ridiculous moment that it might have been me. That I was the source of this power. I thought that I could bring all the wands and give them to the people and they could fight you and there would be a lot of killing and bloodshed and the people would probably come off the worst. So, I didn't bring the wands, though I know where they are.'

'And now you have told me, and your head, when it is free of your body, will take us gibbering to that place.' Gauinebald grinned, his eyes glittering with a violent and dark lust.

But all Reeves did was shake his head. 'Nah, I don't think so.'

'You will have no choice, fool. Your tongue will sing. The Resonaris' treachery will give us reason to purge them once and for all from this land.'

'Yeah, nothing like a bit of ethnic cleansing to start the day off. But you've missed the point.'

Gauinebald's fixed smile faltered for a fraction of a second. This man should have been squirming and pleading for his life like all the others in all the times he had stood in this position. And yet he was not. A flicker of doubt caused him to yell over his shoulder, 'Where is that broom?'

'It wasn't me,' said Reeves. 'It wasn't me that controlled the wands. It wasn't me that switched their power on. It wasn't me who bounced the killing curse back onto your murderous, drunk, soldier. It was what I was transporting.'

'Enough,' cried de Wyville. 'Kill this fool.'

'Let him speak,' boomed a voice from the balcony above. Erthu Le Liare was watching avidly. 'It amuses me.'

Reeves grinned. 'Yeah. It's a great joke. But I don't think you're going to like the punchline.'

The crowd murmured. The air in the quadrangle crackled.

'So no, not me. Not Reeves. And no,' Reeves continued, 'Before you ask—I don't know what it is. Or what it's meant to do. All I know is, it stirred the wands in the Resonari's depository like a storm in still water. So no—as much as I might wish it were me, it wasn't. It was what I was carrying.'

He raised his head slowly, eyes locking with Erthu's.

'The thing your kind thought you'd buried for good. But

we both know the truth—just as it can awaken the wands… it can silence them.'

No wailing now. All eyes were on Reeves.

'And that,' said Reeves, 'would be a huge burden. Because only someone with the right sort of psychological makeup could do that. Someone born to wield its. Like the Shadowsmith you're so desperately trying to destroy with this trumped-up load of bollocks you're spouting.'

Erthu's expression did not change.

But a shift rippled through the crowd.

Reeves exhaled sharply. 'Or maybe even, if you were really unlucky, a foreign agent with the right sort of willpower.'

Erthu's voice rang out. 'You have heard the wild ravings of this creature for yourselves. It is time to be rid of him.'

Reeves nodded. 'Agreed. The time for talking is over. I note that I am the only one here whose hands you bothered to tie. But you,' he raised his voice to a shout, 'have no weapons. Other than wands.'

His head snapped around to the assembled boys.

Some were still shaking.

Still terrified.

But some…

Some had listened.

Some were waiting.

All they needed…was a spark.

Reeves roared. 'Targan Shadowsmith, your destiny awaits you!'

A soldier ran forward, shoving the broom into Gauinebald's hands. He snatched it and pressed his wand hard into Reeves' throat. He grinned, and whispered, '*Modenti Intrinsicus.*'

The crowd held its breath.

Nothing.

Gauinebald's eyes twitched. '*Modenti Intrinsicus!*'

Nothing.

'*MODENTI INTRINSICUS!*'

Silence.

A thick, wet plop landed on Gauinebald's shoulder.

Bird shit.

Reeves' grin widened. 'Must be your lucky day.'

And before the crowd remembered to exhale—

Reeves swung back, then brought his head forward at speed and with a sickening crunch into Gauinebald's nose.

Four vultures and one eagle broke from the augur bell and dive-bombed the Zatrank firing squad.

Reeves whirled and kicked the nearest soldier's legs out. The man fell hard, but his wand lifted and he yelled a hasty curse.

Reeves' expression had a manic edge of adrenaline-fuelled delight. 'You are pissing into the wind, my friend.' He laughed and stomped on the wand hand.

Snap.

Reeves turned.

The boys were on their feet, staring in sheer disbelief at what they'd just seen.

'What are you waiting for?' Reeves bellowed. 'A bloody fanfare? Their wands don't work. GO FOR IT!'

They did.

And so did the crowd. Or, to give it its proper name five seconds later, the mob. The Zatrank stood no chance. Unarmed and untrained in hand-to-hand combat, they were no match for the people of Gogny, who looked forward to a Friday night barney as one of their only sources of entertainment since it was free and anyone could take part.

Revenge, they say, is a dish best served cold. In Gogny Payn that afternoon, it was delivered steaming hot with bellows and screams and quite a bit of maniacal laughter on the side.

Not pretty, but very, very effective.

CHAPTER FORTY-TWO

In the midst of the mayhem, Reeves made a beeline for Milda and Raymounde and led them to a cool alcove off the quadrangle. The dwarf was in a bad way, barely able to stand. His eyelids were satsumas of purple swelling; his nose was twisted and broken. Reeves found someone with a knife to cut his bonds and then Raymounde's before laying him on some sacks.

'Who did this to you?'

'Me,' grunted Raymounde. 'I did it to myself. I had no control. It amused Gauinebald to have me attack myself once a day, even after I'd told Alienor...' He shuddered and whispered, 'I'm sorry. I didn't even know what I was telling them. I tried not to...'

'He only spoke when they threatened me,' Milda said. Vertical tear tracks ran through the filth on her face.

'But you had nothing to tell them,' Reeves said, still looking at the dwarf.

'I told them about you. That you were coming here to meet a boy.' Raymounde's distress was pitiful. 'It was me. Those kids were going to die because of me.'

Reeves shook his head. 'Don't forget, I've met Alienor too. You can't reason with that kind of irrational malevolence—it's the same with Gauinebauld. With the power they wielded, they could coerce you into revealing every secret buried in your mind. If it wasn't these kids, it'd be someone else, some other twisted misery they're warped imaginations would conjure. She's sick. Her brother's just as bad. And their father…he's their enabler, flying some bullshit expansionist flag. So don't beat yourself up—'

Reeves caught himself too late. The words had slipped out unthinkingly, and Raymounde flinched, momentarily overcome by anger and despair. But these emotions were familiar companions to the darkest, sharpest kind of humour —the type that sailed dangerously close to tragedy—and the wince soon gave way to a small, bitter, but heartfelt laugh.

'Sorry,' said Reeves quietly.

Raymounde thumped him on the thigh and, for the first time since Reeves had seen him that day, smiled. Or at least made a shape with his mouth that revealed several missing teeth. 'I see that diplomacy correspondence course was a waste of time, then.'

'I've asked for my money back,' replied Reeves.

Raymounde's giggle yielded to a wince of pain.

Reeves saw it. 'We need to get you out of here.' He stood, turning towards Milda, and froze.

Her face bore deep dark circles beneath her eyes, and she looked thinner, as if she'd lost considerable weight in just a few days. She had watched the exchange between them, her expression impossible to describe. If Reeves had been pushed, he might have called it something wavering between anguish and incredulity.

Her eyes never left his. 'You didn't speak to me in the dungeons.' Her gaze was like staring into the sun.

Reeves stepped forward. 'Milda, I'm so sorry. I—'

She shook her head. 'The boys all thought you were nothing but a drunk. For a minute, just one minute, I am ashamed to admit that I believed them.' Milda shook her head again, and to Reeves' unmitigated horror, tears began to fall from those unflinching eyes. Her lips trembled. 'But then you said, "Silence is Golden". Who would say that in such circumstances? Unless it was a message.'

Reeves tried explaining. 'It wasn't just the jailor that was listening…'

Milda silenced him with a shake of her head. 'It wasn't that you were denying us. It was that you were acting out a plan, wasn't it?'

'I'd hardly call it a plan,' said Reeves. 'More a seat-of-the-pants ghost train ride.'

Milda kept shaking her head. A tear ran all the way down to the bottom of her chin, where it glistened. 'Raymounde kept telling me that you wouldn't abandon us. That you were the only man he'd ever met who didn't care about himself, only about others.'

'He's had lots of blows to the head,' said Reeves, throwing the dwarf an admonishing glance. 'I wouldn't take anything a man with his degree of concussion has said too seriously.'

'And yet,' Milda's voice was barely a whisper, 'you are here. And they, the monsters, are running like rabbits.'

Despite the mayhem just yards away, Reeves heard every syllable. He held her eyes. 'Milda…I'm just a bloke like any other. Someone who always manages to take the wrong fork in the road. But this time, I managed to stumble back onto the right path.'

Milda was having none of it. 'How many men would protect a girl he had met for just a few minutes? How many men would fulfil a promise made to a dying man? How many men would not abandon a hopeless cause? One that isn't even yours to abandon. Not even your world's. You did not have to do any of those things. But it is you who stands before us with the enemy routed. You have given us all the greatest gift that anyone can give, Reeves. Hope.'

Reeves, who was good at compartmentalising his emotions, listened to Milda's words, searched for a quip that would dismiss it all, but for the life of him, couldn't find one. He reached out and took the girl's hands, horrified to see that they were still tied. He cut her bonds and stood back. 'I'm sorry for all your trouble, Milda. You didn't deserve any of this.'

'None of us did,' she said. 'But would it be appropriate if I asked you to do one more thing for me?'

'Anything,' said Reeves.

Milda's smile was tremulous. 'Then I think that I would like a hug.'

He swept her up. Just a slip of a girl, as light as a feather, her tears warm on his neck. Reeves did not have any children of his own, had not felt the warm and genuine touch of anyone for far too long a time. And up until that point, he had no idea how much he had been in need of this simple act of human contact. In response, the vague thoughts and ideas that he'd battled with whenever he questioned his motivation for what he'd done surged back with a vengeance.

He hated bloody villains.

Hated the Zatrank.

Hated what they'd done to others and to him in such a cowardly fashion. Revenge was a tangible and easy thing to keep hold of. And yet, in Milda's hug, something else elbowed its way to the front of his consciousness. This one act of gratitude and expression of feelings made Reeves realise that he'd done all of this out of common decency and humanity; two words that had long been banished from his lexicon.

The hug lasted several seconds and neither of them wanted to let go, but eventually Reeves stepped back. Seeing some women clobbering a Zatrank henchman into submission a few yards away, he signalled to them as they trussed the man up. 'Can you take these two to Erthu's rooms? We'll set up a field hospital there.'

'Of course, Praetor.'

'Praetor?' Reeves looked about as nonplussed as six minus four. 'Where did that come from?'

'You lead the resistance, do you not?'

'Lead? Me?' A denial that mushroomed into a guffaw.

''Tis a shame we have no healers,' said the woman, puzzled by Reeves' incoherence.

'Oh, but you do.' He held Milda by her arms in front of him. 'This is your moment, Milda.'

'Our moment, Reeves,' she said. 'Sorry. Praetor Reeves.'

From the floor, Raymounde laughed. Or at least Reeves interpreted the gurgle as a laugh. He thought about it but realised it would look pretty bad if he kicked the man while he was on the ground.

But there was more to do. 'Find them,' he yelled. 'Find the Le Liere's. Find that bastard Erthu and when you find that ogre, Gauinebauld, please, please, bring him to me.'

———

The birds wheeled above Gogny Payn, their shadows dancing across the newly liberated town like nature's victory pennants. Matt and Bobby maintained a steady patrol pattern while Rimsplitter, never one for formation flying, zigzagged beneath them like a demented wasp.

'Getting' proper narked I am, now,' Rimsplitter called up. 'Can't find that bee, Gauinebald. 'E's got to be some-where. Unless he's gone and done a disappearin' act like his sister.'

'No wandwork anymore. But he still needs legs to walk with,' Matt observed, banking left.

'Yeah, well, his legs better hope I don't find 'em first,' Rimsplitter muttered. 'I'll give 'em such a—' He stopped mid-threat, hovering on a thermal, his keen eyes catching move-ment below. A Zatrank banner, torn and muddied, was making its way across the ground toward the treeline. It could have been the wind, except this banner seemed to be working against it.

'Oy! Think I got something.' Rimsplitter tucked his wings and plummeted, the very picture of avian grace right up until he started shouting. 'Come out, come out, wherever you are, you absolute merchant banker!'

He snagged the banner with his talons and yanked it skyward. Underneath, Gauinebald's wild eyes under a cap of sweat-soaked curly hair blazed up at him, his face contorted in fury.

'Harpy! Demon! Unclean thing!' the man screamed, scrambling backward.

'Unclean? Have a look in the mirror, you tart. I had a bath last month.'

Gauinebald made to run, but Rimsplitter flew up and let the banner drop right on top of him. As Gauinebald flailed, he got more tangled with each desperate movement, until he looked like a badly wrapped Christmas present.

'Got him,' Rimsplitter screeched. 'You lot! Get your feathered backsides down here. Reeves wants a word with this specimen.'

The vultures descended, each grabbing a corner of the banner-wrapped bundle that was now emitting muffled curses and threats of eternal damnation.

'Blimey, he's a unit, ain't he?' Rimsplitter grunted, wings straining.

'What's he been eating? Bobby gasped.

'More a question of what he hasn't been eating,' Kylah said, straining upwards.

'Less commentary, more lifting,' Matt advised through clenched beak.

Bobby struggled with her corner, but they managed to get him twenty feet off the ground.

'Strewth,' Rimsplitter puffed, 'anyone spotted a good droppin'-off point? I vote we dump 'im and send for reinforcements.'

'Knoll spotted,' Matt said, 'a hundred yards northwest.'

They managed to drag their writhing cargo as far as the large grassy knoll dotted with cheerful yellow flowers.

'That looks soft enough,' Matt called out. 'On three.'

'Three,' Rimsplitter immediately shouted, letting go.

The bundle hit the knoll. Except it hit with a splash rather than a thud. The flowers bobbed merrily as Gauinebald, banner and all, flailed and splashed in the murky-looking pond.

Rimsplitter squawked. 'What is that smell?' He beat a hasty winged retreat to the edge of the raised area.

'There was this kid at school,' Matt said, 'claimed his family had a midden so old and ripe it was practically legendary. A prize midden, he called it—been slowly melting into sludge for years. They'd siphon off the liquid and spray it on the fields like it was holy water.'

A moment of silence was broken by bubbling sounds and muffled screaming. A hand appeared, then another, waving, desperate. But then both disappeared as if yanked down from below.

'OMG,' Bobby said. 'Do you think there's something living in that…stuff?'

'Things do,' Asher said with the kind of arcane knowledge necreddos had to live with.

'Things wot might have been waiting for years, dreamin' about revenge?' Rimsplitter asked.

Asher said nothing. His silence told them all they needed to know.

'Should we fish him out?' Bobby asked, though she made no move to do so.

'No way Hoze B,' said Rimsplitter. 'That's Hose A's brother, by the way.' He chortled and circled the bubbles. 'To be fair, I think he's ended up where he deserves to be. Besides, whatever else is in there won't like us interferin', eh Asher?'

'I suggest this is what we might call poetic justice,' Asher replied.

'Yeah,' Rimsplitter said. 'He treated everyone like dirt, now dirt's returning the favour.'

'That's almost profound,' Matt said.

'Don't sound so surprised,' Rimsplitter huffed. 'I can be deep when I want to be. Speaking of deep, reckon we should tell Reeves where to find his least-favourite Zatrank?'

'We will, but it looks like he's a bit busy as of this moment,' Kylah suggested. In truth, they all knew Gauinebald's fate had already been sealed. Draining the midden would take days.

'Accidents do 'appen,' Rimsplitter said. He sent Matt a look. 'Bit of luck, you spottin' that knoll, eh?'

'I'm a lucky fella,' Matt said.

'Unlike Gauinebald,' Kylah said. She too looked at Matt, and if vultures could smile, that was exactly what she was doing.

CHAPTER FORTY-THREE

A WILD AND emotional few hours followed, during which parents and children were reunited, avian-human relationships were kindled and rogue Zatrank were fished out from hiding places in empty outhouses, the back rooms of taverns and a stable. There, Erthu was busy getting away on a sleek black stallion. He'd got only fifteen yards when the animal bucked as a massive eagle appeared right in its path, heading straight for it.

Rearing up, the animal deposited its rider on the hard ground and Erthu clattered to the floor with a yelp of pain, his arm twisted uselessly by his side.

The eagle landed next to him.

'Oy mush, Reeves wants to see you. You been a very naughty effin' boy, haven't you.'

'Begone, demon.' Erthu raised his good arm in an attempt at warding off the eagle.

'That's rich, that is, coming from you. Oh good, here come the good guys.' Rimsplitter flew up and hovered, shouting at the approaching men. ''S'all right boys, he's armless.'

The screech of laughter that followed brought everyone to a halt as they stared at the huge bird.

'Armless. Ha! Sometimes I think I'm so sharp I'm going' to cut meself in bleedin' 'alf.'

SURVIVALIST INSTINCTS KICKED in and there was a degree of resistance from the Zatrank, but it was short-lived. The people rampaged through the Keep and, for the most part, Reeves let them do it. It wasn't pleasant. There was quite a bit of GBH but there were no deaths. He and the vultures saw to that. By sunset, everyone was back in the quadrangle with the tables completely turned.

Around the perimeter stood the people, three feet deep, armed with a variety of weapons ranging from rolling pins to trowels. In the centre stood the Zatrank soldiers. Truculent, frightened and bemused.

Erthu Le Liare had not taken his eyes off Reeves from the moment he'd been brought to account before him. He looked…dishevelled. As well one might after being pelted with rotting vegetables and worse.

Everyone knew he deserved to be strung up by his thumbs and allowed to rot. But that would have been the Zatrank way. And even the mob had some sense of things needing to change. And so, they looked to Reeves for suggestions.

'Alienor,' Reeves said. 'She didn't come to the execution. She's waiting for me to be delivered to her, suitably dead.' He looked up at the vultures. 'She's powerful. Even with no wand, she might dip into a darker source. Once she finds out.'

Rimsplitter landed, causing several Zatrank to cower away. 'She the witch?'

'Powerful,' Reves said.

'Where is she, then?'

'She has a place she's created, in the dungeons, only it isn't a dungeon.'

'Give me a mo,' Rimplitter took off, hovered near the vultures for a powwow.

Reeves did have some ideas, too. The city midden needed an overhaul. Gogny Payn was not big on dealing with waste or, indeed, recycling. And 'Le Liare, Sewage Treatment Company' had a certain ring to it.

That would mean that whenever anyone in Gogny performed a bodily function, they would think of Le Liare. There was definitely more than a touch of poetic justice in that. He was pretty sure that these birds that had made the impossible possible had an answer for a dethroned dictator and a mad witch. But Alienor was unpredictable and dangerous and if she found out what was happening…

Rimsplitter landed again. 'Right, 'I 'ave it on good authority from a witch wot is with us, that if you chuck this lot in with 'er and stick an iron door on the entrance, that'll keep 'er contained while we sort something permanent.'

'Wonderful,' Reeves said, but not without a touch of despair. 'All we need now is to conjure up an iron door—' he caught himself and his expression changed. Something clicked. He remembered the mages Gauinebauld had once used so callously, so carelessly as he tested his monstrous weaponry. They'd been terrified, and utterly expendable to him. But perhaps not now.

Turning sharply, he called to one of the reformed Zatrank soldiers whop had already shed their uniforms and was fighting with the people. 'You—what's your name?'

'Emmet,' the man said, squaring his shoulders.

'Emmet, are there mages held in the dungeons?'

Emmet nodded. 'There are. Gauinebauld kept them for experimentation. I think some might still be alive.'

'Then fetch them. Now. And bring them here.'

It didn't take long. Within minutes, two dishevelled but wide-eyed bearded and robed men were brought to the court-yard—blinking like they'd just emerged from years of darkness into midday sun. Reeves didn't waste time.

'We need a dungeonssealed. Properly. Containment-level magic with iron as a backup. Can you do it?'

The mages exchanged a look. One of them, a wiry man with silver-shot hair and deep lines of sleeplessness on his face, nodded. 'We can encase the whole dungeon in an iron-bound spell. Nothing gets in. Nothing gets out.'

'Good. Emmet, go with them. Make sure Erthu is gagged until he is inside with his daughter. I don't want him warning her.'

But the other mage, a younger man with a slight grin tugging at the corners of his mouth, revelling in what he could see was happening around him, held up a hand. 'There is a quicker way.' Without another word, he muttered an incantation under his breath. A brief shimmer filled the air—and suddenly, Erthu clutched his throat, eyes wide, unable to make a sound.

'Speechless,' the mage said, satisfied.

Reeves nodded his approval.

'Garam,' said the mage. 'At your service, praetor. I've waited many months to do that.'

The crowd jeered as Erthu was led away—amid boos and hisses—to be locked up with Alienor behind a hexed wall of containment iron. And there they would stay, silent and seething, while the world decided what to do with them.

RIMSPLITTER RETURNED TO A 'SUPERVISORY' role in reconnaissance, guiding fighters to where small pockets of resistance persisted. Many of the Zatrank soldiers, like Emmet, had shed their uniforms, but not all of them *looked* ashamed. Reeves and two or three of the more senior members of Gogny society stood at the front with Bettany and a boy of fifteen who had his mother's cheekbones and a mop of dark hair.

'Targan?' asked Reeves when he finally managed to get to the woman and the boy.

Targan extended his hand. Reeves took it with a nod, then turned to Bettany.

'About the pub… sorry for the act. I was a little drunk—just enough for the stink on my breath. Just enough to make them believe I'd thrown in the towel—'

He didn't finish. She stepped forward and wrapped her arms around him, cutting the words short.

'Many believed it,' she murmured. 'But in my heart… I never wanted to.'

He stood there, momentarily stunned, letting the silence settle between them.

Two hugs in one day. *Careful, Reeves,* he thought. *That sort of thing could grow on a man.*

Two very large vultures landed nearby. Reeves bent and addressed them. Four red-rimmed eyes watched him.

'Great delivery,' said Reeves and flicked the Seren Sea Stone still hanging around his neck.

'My pleasure,' said Bobby.

'She's good,' said Matt.

'I know that voice.' Reeves said. 'You're the bastard that kidnapped me.'

Matt unfurled his wings, ready for flight. Reeves waved him down.

'"Kidnapped" would not have been our choice of words,' said Matt. 'I admit that "saved" might be open to interpretation, but how about "intervention" as a halfway house?'

Reeves shook his head as he stepped forward towards the vulture known as Bobby. But he still couldn't quite manage it.

'She's kosher,' said Matt.' And a witch.'

'She's also someone this country owes a huge debt to. I wanted to shake your, erm, wing? Leg?' said Reeves.

'But you might lose a finger, I know,' said Bobby. 'The longer I'm in here, the more difficult it is to suppress avian instincts.'

Reeves slid off the amulet and held up the Seren Sea Stone so that everyone could see, turned and slid it over Targan's neck. The boy felt for it and instantly, the shell became a four-tentacled squid, appendages spread out over a turquoise heart-shaped stone. 'I suspect there may be a ceremony for this but I can't be arsed. Wear it and wear it well.'

Targan turned and waved to the crowd. A huge cheer went up. Such a huge cheer that no one noticed de Wyville lunge up from where he'd been hiding beneath an unconscious Zatrank, a blade glinting in his hand, teeth bared as he surged towards Targan Shadowsmith.

Reeves turned and knew he would be too late to stop the bastard. He let out a cry that was matched by another gasp from the crowd as a huge eagle dropped like a stone from the sky, its wicked-looking talons latching on to de Wyville's raised knife arm, while a sharp beak raked over de Wyville's scalp in a flurry of feathers.

'Oh no you don't, you Zatrank cee.' Rimsplitter flapped his wings and de Wyville's arm went up in the air, with de Wyville following, both feet off the ground. He was far too heavy for Rimsplitter to carry for more than a few feet, but those few feet collaborated with gravity to drop him and send him sprawling.

Reeves stepped forward and knelt on de Wyville's outstretched arm. He prised away the knife and shoved the killer's face in the dirt for good measure. 'Don't do that,' Reeves whispered. 'I am barely keeping this lot from tearing you limb from limb as it is.' Without turning around, he addressed the vulture. 'What's a Zatrank cee?'

Matt shook his vulture head. 'You really don't want to know. There are minors present.'

———

AFTER THAT, there was a lot of ceremonial stuff and organisational necessities. Surprisingly, a scruffy kind of municipal structure already existed beyond the Keep with councilpersons and a mayor of sorts. It was they who now came together to discuss the problem they had with how best to deal with the Zatrank. Though disavowed and, to a degree contrite, they were being held in check by mob rule. The Le Liares and de Wyville were a different problem, but locked away with Alienor for now.

Some might have said that was punishment enough.

But the troops that remained looked sullen and restless. With the power they'd had from the wands, there had been no need for a huge garrison. Still, five hundred disenfranchised men all used to having their own way was not an easy problem to deal with. And imprisoning them was not an answer either. Reeves, of all people, knew that. He needed a different solution. It came in the form of the remaining two vultures, one carrying a thin and elongated parcel wrapped in a cloth. Hovering above, Kylah dropped the parcel and Reeves caught it neatly.

He unwrapped the cloth to gasps from the crowd.

'This is not one of theirs.' He turned to Targan. 'This comes from the druid sanctuary and I suggest we return it there once this has been done. The Resonaris will guard it for you.'

'Then why do I need it now?' The boy asked.

Reeves leaned in close. When he'd finished, the boy was smiling. Reeves handed him the wand and watched as the boy concentrated. The Seren Sea Stone glowed into life and something like a wobbly wave shimmered in the air and washed out over the assembled troops. It was incredible to watch their expressions, like men waking from a dream—or was it a nightmare? And Reeves realised that indeed it may well have been that a certain percentage of these men had been bewitched against their wills by the power of the Zatrank wands.

Well, a little more bewitchery would do no harm for a year or two.

'What have you done?' asked Bettany and the question was aimed more at Reeves than her son.

Reeves winked at her and turned to address the assembled crowd. 'Put down your weapons. These men will not harm you.'

'How can you tell?' someone asked.

'Because they are no longer Zatrank.'

'Yes, they are,' shouted someone else.

'Don't be fooled by the uniforms. In fact, we'll get them to change those immediately.'

'If they ain't Zatrank scum, what are they, then?' asked another voice.

Reeves turned back and beckoned one of the soldiers,

who was now standing erect and to attention, to step forward. 'Tell them who you are, son.'

'Sir, yessir. Bonjovi, Jim, volunteer cleaner-upper and fixer to anything what is broken in the town of Gogny, sir.' The man gave a proud and heartfelt salute.

There was a silence, and then an elderly crone yelled, 'I've got a tap that's been leaking for five months.'

A burly ex-Zatrank sergeant stepped out of the ranks and turned towards the crone. 'Bil Sonder, at your service, ma'am.'

'The drains on Sowslime street are clogged,' yelled a man with a weather-beaten face.

Two men stepped out from the ranks and joined Jim Bonjovi. 'Lead us to it, sir.'

After that, there was even more mayhem than when the Zatrank were officially the enemy. Lots of things needed fixing in Gogny Payn, it seemed. The Le Liares had not been big on maintenance.

When half the Zatrank had dispersed, Reeves put his hand up and suggested they let the mayor organise the remaining workforce as to major projects. But he was quick to point out that help for individuals would be on tap—he got a laugh for that one—for the foreseeable.

The crowd dispersed, leaving only a handful of people and the menacing-looking birds in the quadrangle.

Reeves addressed Targan. 'You did well. That wand likes you.'

'And I like it,' said Targan, staring at it in his palm. 'But I don't think I should get too attached to it.'

'What do you mean?' asked Bettany.

'Dad always told me that the biggest mistake we ever made was to trust the people with wands.'

'But they are not you, Targan,' his mother replied.

'No, but I do not want to ever become them.' He handed the wand back to Reeves. 'Can this be taken back to where it came from?'

'Yes, I'm sure it can.' Reeves wrapped the wand back in

the cloth, and Kylah took off with the wrapped item in her talons.

'What about all the Zatrank wands?' asked Matt.

'I vote you collect them all up and give them to Resonaris for safekeeping. But while you have the Seren Sea Stone, I suspect you'll be safe here.'

'The stone is only special to those who can wield it,' Bettany said.

'I don't believe that for one minute,' Reeves said and laughed. When no one else laughed with him, Reeves looked at the vultures for an explanation.

'It's true,' said Matt. 'It's why you were chosen.'

'You were the right man for the job, end of,' Kylah said.

Reeves, for once, was speechless.'

Targan spoke. 'We owe you a great debt, Praetor Reeves.'

'I wish you wouldn't call me that,' Reeves said and the boy looked suitably admonished.

But Bettany was having none of it. 'This has nothing to do with your wishes. It's what the people have decided. They need a leader and Targan needs an ally.'

'There are always options for the Le Liares, but—'

Targan interjected. 'What are the options?'

'Try them. If you find them guilty, execute them for crimes against the state.'

Targan nodded. 'That is what many people want to happen, but without the trial bit.'

'You could banish them to somewhere as far away as possible and let them fester.'

'A festering wound is one that never heals,' Targan replied.

Reeves nodded. 'You run the risk of them establishing a power base somewhere else and returning for acts of vengeance, I admit.'

'And the third way?'

'Give them to the Resonaris for psychological retraining. They'll be out of public view and one day, you never know, they might even become useful members of society, if society lets them. After they're re-educated. Frankly, I think the chances are slight-to-non-existent that they end up being useful, but there are lots of crops to look after in Resonari land along the songline.'

'What if they escape?'

'They won't, because there is nowhere to escape to. If anyone can rehabilitate them, the Resonaris can.'

'Erthu Le Liare would not change in a hundred years,' Bettany muttered darkly.

'How about two hundred?' asked Reeves. 'Spent as a mule doing caravan work, or maybe a porcupine to learn survival skills, or a squirrel for harvesting techniques. And after that, in say six months or so—'

'I thought you said two hundred years.'

Reeves grinned.

'That is impossible,' said Targan.

'There's a lot about the Resonaris you don't know, obviously. In six months, give or take a couple of hundred years in Resonari time, having learned the value of living off the land and how it pays to be honest and truthful, who knows, Le Liare might even spearhead a diplomatic mission to the Northern Wights. A job that will undoubtedly challenge them and cure any and all constipation issues they may have. I suggest you have a word with the man from Uncle.'

'The man from Uncle?' Targan looked puzzled.

'My little joke. But I will introduce you to Omeolega-mundi. It's about time the Resonaris were acknowledged, and I trust them implicitly.'

'Is that really a punishment?' Bettany asked.

Reeves smiled. 'Two hundred years hard labour and philosophical rehab in six months? Sounds pretty punishing to me. All I know is that more killing isn't the answer.'

'Wise words. I will speak to the mayor and the other aldermen and discuss your suggestions, Praetor,' Targan said.

Reeves winced.

Targan and Bettany walked off to join a group of men and women who were addressing the crowd that remained.

'They seem like good people,' Bobby observed.

'They are,' Reeves said. 'All they want is a chance to live their lives.'

'Nice irony, that,' Matt observed and earned himself an incendiary look from Reeves. 'Just saying.'

'How's the magpie?' asked Reeves.

'With Rimsplitter. He's going to need some help to get back across the border since he can't fly.'

'I may just have a better idea.' Reeves swivelled on his heel and started walking.

CHAPTER FORTY-FOUR

Reeves retraced the steps he'd taken through the streets. This time there were no Zatrank guards to frogmarch him, but he was not alone. Above him, high in the clear sky, a kettle of vultures circled on the thermals. The last time he'd walked this way he'd drawn stares of pity. Now there were waves and smiles and fists held high in battle camaraderie. He walked quickly so that people saw he meant business. No one challenged him. When he arrived at Candin Lane, a crowd stood around the Shadowsmith house, listening to a huge eagle address them between chuckles.

'So then the husband says, and I guarantee you'll effin' love this, "But they're twins. If you've seen Juan, you've seen Amal."' There followed a raucous croak of laughter.

Mainly from the eagle. In fact, all from the eagle.

The crowd stayed statue silent.

Rimsplitter looked up. 'Oh my days, come on, it's a play on effin' words, you tees. Juan as in "one", and Amal as in "them all".'

Someone said, 'Are they ever reconciled?'

'Strewth, what part of that effin' joke was difficult, you cees? She has twins, gives 'em up for adoption. One of 'em goes to Rainever and is called Juan, the other one goes to Pict and is called Amal. Juan sends his birth parents an imp-pression and his mother says she wishes she could have one of Amal. But her husband says…' Rimsplitter held his wings out, nodding encouragingly.

A woman sniffed, 'Such a tragedy that she had to give up her children like that.'

'Oh my effin' gawd, come on. That's gold, that is.'

The crowd parted as Reeves walked through.

'Oh, it's you,' said Rimsplitter.

'I wanted to thank you for what you did. De Wyville is a vicious bastard.'

'That the one with the knife, was it?'

Reeves nodded.

Rimsplitter nodded in turn. 'Didn't like the look of him one bit, bee. Mind you, the other one, wossisname—'

'Gauinebald?'

'That's the one. He is proper mum and dad, that one. We caught him runnin'. We managed to bundle 'im up and haccidentally deposit 'im in the midden. For all I know, he's still there.'

Someone spoke up from the crowd, 'We caught someone climbing out of midden an hour ago. We threw him in the river. But it still hasn't got rid of the stench. He's chained up in the pub yard.'

Reeves nodded and stored away the information. 'Keep him there for now if you will.'

'Strewth, it's nice to have someone wot can speak proper English,' Rimsplitter said. ' I expect you want to see F4?'

'The magpie?'

'Yeah. He's a bit cream crackered. I'm a bit worried he's gettin' an infection. He's round the back. I'll meet you there.'

The eagle took off, causing the crowd to scatter in panic.

'Praetor, is that eagle a demon?' asked the sniffing woman.

'Only at spoiling jokes, it seems,' said Reeves.

The magpie was in the kitchen. Bettany had made him a nest out of an old blanket. The bird let out a feeble call as Reeves walked in.

'Okay, okay,' Reeves said soothingly.

'He's in pain,' Rimsplitter called from the garden.

'Trouble is your human stuff don't work so well in avian physiology.'

Reeves looked at the bird. Its eyes were no longer as sparkling as he remembered.

'Thing is we need to get him back to transform him, but it's at least a day's ride to the Pict border.'

'Maybe there is another way.' Reeves' eyes danced as he thought through his plan. 'Can you deliver a message for me?'

'At your service. We are here to help,' said Rimsplitter magnanimously.

Reeves found a bit of parchment and scribbled a note before tying it to Rimsplitter's leg.

'Right, directions?'

'Just fly east until you see a campsite that looks like a bomb went off in it yesterday. Ask for a chap called Omeolegamundi..'

Rimsplitter flew off and Reeves turned his attention to the bird and fetched it some water in a saucer. F4 pecked at it feebly. 'We'll get this sorted mate, don't you worry.' Reeves sat in Bettany's battered armchair and closed his eyes.

———

He was walking across a wet blacktop slick with puddles. The wind pelted rain into his face and he stopped to consider if this was an omen. He laughed. Omens were for people who believed in things above and beyond the grinding slog of daily life. That sort of stuff did not float his boat. There was no one and nothing that could change his circumstances.

He reached the barrier running around the edge of the roof of the car park. A metal ladder sat strapped to some brackets under a metal bar that ran at bumper level around the inside of the perimeter wall. Reeves took off his gloves and anorak and jacket and stuffed them under the bar. He climbed up above the concrete parapet, the wind causing him to sway and shudder. As he stood there, bracing himself with both hands against the curved rails of the ladder, his phone rang. That would be Demelza, full of piss and vinegar again.

No more.

He looked down. Double yellow lines marked the road edge of a narrow access lane to the hotel's goods entrance.

This time he waited until the bag lady emerged and crossed, slowly and determinedly pushing her trolly, until she was out of the way. They wouldn't get him with that little wrinkle this time. Bugger the blue room and the eagle and the vultures. Bugger them all. This was his choice. He closed his eyes and felt the pressure of his hands ease on the rails. Then he was unsupported, his body reacting to the wind that threatened with each whistling gust to blow him off. All he really had to do was succumb. Let nature take its course. He looked up and opened his eyes to feel the rain crash into them one last time.

'Trev?'

He snapped his head to the right and instantly knew he'd been wrong about his mother and Demelza and the GP receptionist. They weren't the only people who called him by his first name. But there was only one who truncated it. His eyes blinked away the Manchester rain and turned to look into the face of the girl he'd lost on a beach all those years ago.

Rhiannon.

His knees buckled and he let out a moan, his hand slipping momentarily as it reached for support before it clamped onto the slick metal and found purchase.

Rhiannon. Lithe and pretty, her hair wafting to a wind that was milder than the tempest raging around him. Her gaze was steady and she did not need to blink away the rain.

'What are you doing, Trev?' she asked.

'Giving up,' he said, teeth chattering. 'Or maybe I have already and that's why I'm able to talk to you.'

Rhiannon shook her head. 'No, you haven't. I'm here by special request.'

Reeves frowned. 'Special request?'

'Asher Lodge. Know him?'

Reeves shook his head.

Rhiannon nodded and smiled. 'Doesn't matter. I miss you, Trev.'

He almost fell then. He felt his body yield as the sheer unfairness of it all overwhelmed him. He let go one hand from the ladder rail and felt the girl he'd loved and lost grasp it. 'I miss you too,' he said.

'But you can't keep on grieving, Trev. It isn't right.'

Reeves squeezed his eyes shut and tears mingled with the rain.

'It wasn't your fault,' said Rhiannon. 'It wasn't anyone's fault.'

'Yes, it was. I let you go out onto the rocks—'

Rhiannon put a finger on his lips. 'Remember that funny lump below my left kneecap?'

Reeves nodded. 'From where you were hit by that hockey stick?'

Rhiannon nodded. 'Six months before we went to Abereiddy. But It wasn't just a haematoma. It had a different name. A nasty medical name. Osteosarcoma. Don't ask me how I know that, I just do. You get a chance at a forward look here. A glimpse of what might have been if I hadn't been swept out to sea. We would have had three years together at most.'

Reeves exhaled. He swayed and felt himself falling, but then Rhiannon's arms were around his chest, pulling him back and down the ladder to the roof. She was impossibly strong for such a slight person.

'I wanted to come back and tell you all this, Trev. I wanted you to know.'

Reeves looked at her. Her soft eyes, a smile he would die for. Because she was still smiling at him. 'It wouldn't have been the way you wanted it to be. There was nothing anyone could do.'

Reeves choked back a derisive laugh. 'Are you saying that the wave was a blessing?'

'No. How could it be when it robbed us of months of ignorant bliss? But you should not be sad for me, Trev. You should not be sad for us.'

'Shit.' Reeves tried to stand but his legs simply wouldn't

allow it. Instead, he sat in the pouring rain, shivering, with the ghost of his girlfriend watching over him.

'Just know that I will always love you, Trev.'

'Rhi—'

And then she was gone.

Reeves sucked in air and screamed at the black sky and hit the puddled floor with his open palm. It seemed to help. Behind him, the small, canopied entrance to the stairwell lit up. Reeves dragged himself upright and walked across to it as the light gradually spread and got brighter.

'Trev? Trev, are you okay,?'

Reeves opened his eyes. He was still in Bettany Shadow-smith's chair with the magpie to his left. The person gently poking him awake was Omeolegamundi.

Reeves sat up. He wiped his hands over his face and thought he felt some water in his hair. 'How long have I been out?'

'Not long, Trev. You get a visitor? The vulture said you might get a visitor.' Ome turned towards the birds.

One of them stepped forwards. 'Mr Reeves, my name is Asher Lodge. As well as being a vulture, I am an agent of the Bureau of Demonology and a necreddo.'

Reeves squinted at the bird. 'So far I have understood about 30% of what you've just said.'

'Understandably so. I am not normally a vulture. My necreddo status means that I can communicate with the dead. Whilst you were asleep, I was…contacted, for want of a better word, by an acquaintance of yours who goes…or rather went by the name of Rhiannon.'

Reeves stared.

'She was most insistent,' Asher continued, waddling in and dropping his voice. 'I do not usually succumb to such requests, but in this instance and given the circumstances she explained to me, I felt I could not refuse. I hope it has not been too upsetting.'

What, Reeves thought, *meeting the only woman I have ever loved in a dream after twenty-five years of heartbreak and longing to learn that she was going to die anyway?* 'No,' he said aloud. 'Mind-blowing, yes. Upsetting?' He considered the word for several long seconds, examining it from all angles before answering with a tight mouth, 'No. I wouldn't say upsetting.' Reeves continued staring at the bird. 'But it was real, was it? No trickery involved?'

The vulture shook its head. 'You have my word, Mr Reeves.'

For some reason, one that would not hold much water if he looked at this too closely, Reeves was inclined to believe this bird. He nodded a little nod of acceptance and…yes, and once again, surprisingly, gratitude.

'That's good, then,' Ome said, grinning. 'So, Rimmy here says you got a wonky bird?'

'Rimmy?'

Ome stood to one side. Behind him were a vote of vultures and crowned eagle.

'Kippin', Reeves? Effin' alright for some, ain't it?'

Reeves pointed out the magpie to Ome, who talked to it in a language Reeves did not understand. 'Yeah, that wing is broke, Trev,' Ome eventually explained. 'Plus, he's got an infection. Needs one of my sister's poultices and three weeks of recovery. He'll be right.'

'Can you do that?'

'Just give me a minute,' Ome said. He picked up the bird and left through a door into a passageway.

'Three weeks?' Rimsplitter squawked. 'That's a lifetime. We need to get effin' go—'

The door to the passage opened again and in flew F4, completely recovered with the spark back in his eye, followed by a grinning Ome.

'I though you said three weeks?' Reeves asked.

'Yeah, I did. But that's three weeks with my uncle at our place, Trev. Doesn't have to be on your time.'

Reeves nodded weakly and managed to mutter, 'Of course. What was I thinking.' He walked out to join the birds. 'One more thing left to deal with, then. Let's go to the pub.'

CHAPTER FORTY-FIVE

The Farrower tavern yard stank of wet straw, horse shite, and something far worse.

Gauinebauld, the ogre of Rathkoorne, was chained in the middle of it all—his once-regal clothes now stiff with dried effluent, his once-proud bearing reduced to the pathetic slump of a man who knew the tide had turned. The city midden had done its work. He'd been hauled from it, dragged through the river, and dumped here, stripped of dignity, his fine velvet sleeves now crawling with flies that refused to abandon him. Even the horses in the stables behind recoiled, stamping nervously, their nostrils flared in disgust.

A crowd had gathered. Word had spread fast—Reeves was going to confront him. They came in silence, not with pitchforks, but with a kind of heavy anticipation, like witnesses to a final reckoning. The vultures landed on the roof tiles. Even Ome stood by, his painted skin catching the sunlight, arms folded across his chest.

Reeves stepped into the yard slowly, every boot fall crunching straw and grit underfoot. He looked down at the chained man who, not long ago, had burned cities and cracked time with a flick of his wand.

'You remember a beach on a windswept coast?' Reeves

asked quietly. 'You remember the mages you've used up like firewood? You remember a girl called Rhiannon?'

Gauinebauld's lip trembled. The stink of him was nothing compared to the rot inside. His eyes, once sharp with cruel calculation, were now swollen and red, his face gaunt. He tried to speak, but only a croak emerged.

'Of course you don't. You were too full of glee at being able to destroy from a distance. But I was there,' Reeves said. 'I saw the water rise. I watched it wash her away. And I still hear the echo of her scream.'

The crowd was still. Someone handed Reeves a knife— clean, sharp, gleaming. He held it loosely at first, but slowly, he tightened his grip.

Gauinebauld collapsed forward as far as the chains allowed, grovelling, choking out words: 'Please. Mercy. I was only—only testing, following my father's orders—'

'No,' Reeves said. 'You weren't. You led. You revelled in it.'

The flies buzzed louder as silence fell again. Reeves raised the knife slightly. The crowd held its breath.

But his hand wouldn't move.

He wanted to feel rage. To let justice flow like blood. But inside, where there should have been fire, there was only ash. Reeves stared at the blade, then down at the pleading wreck of a man at his feet. And again, he found himself stuck—not out of pity, but out of something more difficult: clarity. Killing Gauinebauld would be a release. And Reeves wasn't ready to give him that.

He'd come from a world consumed and infatuated by violence. Where wars raged, crime surged. He'd fought against that. Why not fight again. He looked up at Ome waiting patiently, inscrutable as always.

'What if we didn't kill him?' Reeves said. 'What if we made him see?'

Ome raised an eyebrow. 'I'm listening, Trev.'

'No respite. No silence. No forgetting. No turning away from the consequences. Let's sentence him to relive it on the echopaths. Every day, he sees what he's done. Every death, every scream, every second of it. We make him live inside the echo of his own destruction.'

Ome considered it, then slowly nodded. 'That would be fitting. He wanted immortality. Let him have it—in shame.'

Gauinebauld whimpered now, truly afraid. 'You can't do that to me. I own you--'

'Shut up,' Reeves barked. 'No one owns anyone—don't you understand that? People are not commodities.'

The crowd shifted uneasily. Some appeared disappointed, others satisfied, but none raised objections.

'The best you can hope for now is that we let you live,' Reeves continued. 'And you *will* live. On the echopath, you'll hear the voices you silenced. Eventually, theirs will be the only voices you hear.'

'But it doesn't have to be forever,' Ome said.

'When you say "not forever"...?' Reeves muttered cautiously.

'I was thinking two, maybe three?' Ome suggested.

'Years?' Reeves looked visibly disappointed.

Ome appeared surprised. 'I was thinking more along the lines of hundreds.'

'Of course you were.' Reeves finally cracked a grin.

The knife was lowered. The sentence had been passed.

And as the chains were gathered and Gauinebauld was dragged away, screaming at the memories already clawing their way back to the surface of his feckless twisted mind, Reeves finally turned his back on him—not in mercy, but in judgment.

The crowd began to disperse and Reeves found himself in the courtyard alone with the vultures.

'Reeves. Well done,' said Kylah. 'You've delivered as promised. Now we can get you back and you're free to do as you please.'

'Even a triple back somersault off a car park roof?' Reeves narrowed his eyes.

Kylah cocked her head in acquiescence. 'Yes. And we'll make sure the coast is clear if that's what you want. A deal is a deal.'

Reeves nodded. 'It'll be good to have that choice back.'

The birds all looked at him. It was difficult to judge what they were thinking.

'What?' asked Reeves irritably.

'Nothing,' said Kylah, 'nothing. We all owe you a debt, that's all.'

'Then repay it by getting me out of here. There are some Zatrank horses tied up outside the Farrower. I'll borrow one and we can go.'

'No goodbyes?' asked Matt.

'I just need some time to think for myself. Is that too much to ask?'

'No,' Kylah said. 'It isn't'

CHAPTER FORTY-SIX

HE TOOK THE HORSE, no one objected. Praetor Reeves could do whatever he pleased. He rode out of the inner walls and through the labyrinthine shanty town. Everywhere he went, people stopped to salute him with that fist on their chest.

High above, the birds circled and kept pace. Once outside the confines of what Gogny Payn laughingly liked to call its suburbs, Reeves found a cart track and picked up speed. He didn't know what he was going to do once he got out of this place, he simply sensed a need to do something. The dream had shaken him to his core, if indeed it was a dream. Could it be true? If it was, then the idyllic existence that he'd felt he'd been robbed of with Rhiannon was nothing but dust.

His mind felt as if it was still being buffeted by the Force 8 gale on a Manchester car park roof. It was as if his whole life had been lived in error. The nights of misery and longing, the horrible mistakes he'd made in his other relationships, all were predicated on a festering sense of loss which had been compounded by Gauinebald's horrifying fecklessness. But now all that had changed because of a message from the dead.

What he could do was get very drunk in Manchester. But then he'd tried that already, and there'd be Demelza to deal with, not to mention her slimy lawyers. There'd be getting back to work. And recovering his scooter from the car park…

The car park.

Maybe he'd stop off there first, just to take a look again.

His horse stuttered and Reeves, who'd been lost in his thoughts, saw the eagle matching his pace at eye level.

'Someone following you, Reeves mate.'

He glanced back. A rider was approaching. A lone rider, and at speed. Reeves let out a sigh and reigned back his horse. He stopped and turned to wait.

The rider galloped towards him with a plume of Rathkoorne dust in its wake. When it was within a hundred yards, Reeves realised it was Bettany. She could certainly could ride a horse, that was for sure, and she didn't slow until she was within twenty yards. With the horse stationary, she slid off expertly and strode forwards to stand in front of him.

'Where are you going?' she demanded.

'I…,' His words stuttered and failed. Here he was, running away again. And without proper goodbyes to anyone. Much as he had done on that night in Manchester. 'My work here is finished,' he said, knowing they were hollow words.

'How can that be when the work has hardly begun? We have to rebuild the city and the people.'

'Your city, your people. My role was only to deliver the Seren Sea Stone.'

Bettany took a step back, horrified. 'I am sorry, I did not think…You must have people and family of your own some-where else.'

That was a difficult one to answer. But difficult didn't neces-sarily mean impossible. 'Not really,' he said. 'Not anymore.'

Reeves' horse pushed its muzzle forward impatiently. Bettany fondled it and it was obvious that she was comfort-able around the big animals.

'Then forgive me. I did not realise that you would be leaving so quickly. Targan is my son and now he has much responsibility. I know I am being selfish, but I thought you might stay for a while. We need help, Praetor.'

'I can barely help myself,' Reeves murmured.

'Please get off your horse,' Bettany said gently, looking up at him.

'Sorry, that was rude of me.' With a resigned sigh, Reeves dismounted.

Bettany watched him closely. 'I've spoken with Milda. She thinks very highly of you, although she's still somewhat confused.'

'About what?'

'Why you'd sacrifice yourself to find her.'

'I made a promise,' Reeves said simply.

Bettany nodded slowly, her eyes full of quiet understanding. 'You'll have to forgive Milda. She hasn't had the privilege of meeting someone like you before.'

Reeves shifted uncomfortably under her knowing gaze. He'd tried his best to convince everyone he had abandoned them, that all he wanted was to lose himself in drink at the pub. But he hadn't fooled Bettany, just as he hadn't fooled the serving girl who had quietly watched him pour half of each drink away into the gutter by the pub door. The Xatrank had fallen for it—but not everyone had.

'I suppose I wasn't quite as convincing as I thought,' Reeves admitted softly, eyes lowered.

'No,' Bettany said gently. 'Not to all of us. I know what you did, Praetor. So do the people.'

'I think you're mistaking me for someone, or something, else.'

'I think not, Reeves. Because unlike Milda, I have met good men. Before Le Liare spread his poison. Men who cared about the unimportant people. Small people. Worked for them and not themselves.' She reached forward and took one of his hands in both of hers. 'I know, too, that you are in pain. I read it in your face.'

'I lost some people,' admitted Reeves. 'Including myself.'

Bettany's expression softened. 'There is much to do here. Who knows, you might even find it rewarding.'

'I don't need money.'

'Who spoke of money?' Then, without warning, she leaned forward and kissed him.

Reeves had not been kissed for many years. Not like this. The pecks on the cheeks he gave and received from acquaintances didn't count. This was a proper kiss and it took him completely by surprise. So much so that he instinctively pulled back.

Confused and humiliated, Bettany turned away. 'I am sorry. I had no right.'

Reeves grabbed her arm gently and turned her back towards him. 'Maybe,' he said, 'I could find myself in that.'

He kissed her then and no one was more surprised than Reeves himself. This time, he only pulled back when he heard someone clearing their throat.

He turned to see all the vultures and an eagle standing on the empty, dusty trail, watching.

'You're a caution and no mistake. Does that mean you ain't comin' back?' Rimsplitter asked.

Reeves looked out at the hot plain stretching out ahead, and then at Bettany Shadowsmith. 'I think I might stay awhile. Would that be a problem?'

'Stay with our blessing, Reeves,' Kylah said.

Reeves turned towards the second vulture. 'How does it go again? Da, da, da-da, da, da, da-da.'

'See, I knew that motif would come in useful,' Matt said.

Kylah nudged him playfully with her beak.

'Let us know if and when you change your mind,' Matt added.

'That'll be never,' muttered Bobby, always the romantic.

———

THE SQUADRON TOOK OFF, Rimsplitter in the lead. Behind him flew the magpie, followed by the vultures.

Bobby called across to Kylah, 'Think he'll be okay?'

'He'll be fine.'

'I have a feeling this was your plan all along, Kylah,' Asher said.

"I'd love to say it was all my idea—but that'd be a lie. Saving a good man cursed by a violent rogue fae from his own worst instincts? Not my usual style.'

If vultures could grin, Kylah was doing exactly that beneath the windswept feathers of her ruff.

'Why do I get the feeling that little barb was aimed at me?' Matt called from the back.

'You're too thin-skinned, that's your trouble,' Kylah said and did a quick loop the loop to drop back and fly next to Matt.

Below them, the landscape rolled past in patches of green and gold, the border between Gogny Payn and Rathkoorne now far behind. They'd been flying in companionable silence for some time when Kylah banked closer to Matt.

'I owe you an apology,' she said.

Matt tilted his head, nearly losing the updraft. 'Now I'm really worried.'

'I'm being serious, Matt.'

'As I said, definitely worried.'

Kylah ignored his attempt at levity. 'You saw something in Reeves that none of us did. Not even me. Especially not me.'

'Ah.' Matt adjusted his flight path slightly. 'Well, misery loves company, as they say.'

'What do you mean?'

Matt was quiet for so long that Kylah thought he might not answer. When he did, his voice carried none of its usual playful tone. 'Remember the Ghoulshee-induced tsunami at the Carp Inn? The one that washed me off the bridge over the Thames?'

'Vaguely?'

'It was before I knew about you and Hipposync. A real Silvy-the-Ghoulshee-priestess moment. I was standing there, looking down at the torrent. The water was churning because of the rain.' He paused. 'I was thinking about how easy it would be to just…let go.'

Kylah's wing brushed against his, a gesture that would have been a hand squeeze in human form. 'Matt—'

'Don't worry, this isn't as gloomy as it sounds. That's when luck intervened. They sent a tsunami down the river to finish me off. But it didn't work. I got washed into a tree. And then you lot decided to come clean and explain to me that none of this was my fault. What had happened to me was not bad luck. It was malevolence, pure and simple. And joining up with you...' He gave a very un-vulturelike chuckle. 'Best decision I ever made. Well, second best.'

'Second?'

'Asking you out was the first. Even if you did say no three times.'

'Four,' Kylah corrected.

They flew on for a while before Kylah spoke again.

'You saw yourself in Reeves?'

'Parts of him. The isolation. The feeling that nothing really mattered anymore. But mainly I recognised what he could become, given the chance. Just like someone once did for me.'

Kylah's feathers rustled. 'I was wrong about him. And I was wrong to ever doubt your judgment. You still need a bit of reigning in, but you're good, Matt.'

'Thanks for that.'

'I mean good, as in good and evil. That's a potent weapon.'

'You weren't wrong to doubt. I just got lucky.'

'No,' Kylah said firmly. 'You have insight that I sometimes lack. And compassion that I admire more than I've ever told you.'

'Careful,' Matt warned. 'All this praise might go to my head. These thermals can only lift so much weight.'

'When we're back in our own skin,' Kylah said, her voice taking on a tone that had no business coming from a vulture's beak, 'I'm going to show you exactly how much I appreciate you.'

'Oh?' Matt nearly lost his altitude. 'Are we talking about

another medal ceremony? Because the last one was a bit OTT—'

'Shut up,' Kylah purred, 'this ceremony will be strictly private. And definitely against DOF regulations regarding proper conduct between agents.'

'We're going to break some rules, are we?'

'There will be no rules.'

Matt's resulting wobble had nothing to do with air currents. He spoke up so the others could hear. 'You know, I think we could make better time if we flew a bit faster.'

'Race you?' Kylah suggested.

They shot forward, their shadows merging into one as they carved through the golden evening air, leaving their doubts far behind them.

Bobby flew close to Asher. 'What you did for Reeves, and for his girl, that was very kind.'

Asher rode the thermal and, after some consideration simply said, 'Sometimes the dead need to have the last word.'

Bobby let her wing touch his momentarily.

'Come on, you lot,' said Rimsplitter from the front. 'Keep up. I ain't never seen a worse bunch of effin' slugs. I'm starvin'.'

'Me too,' said Bobby. 'I could eat a scabby donkey.'

'Funny you should say that. I just spotted one on the edge of that rocky outcrop five miles back. At least five weeks dead,' Matt almost whispered. Well, it was a shout at a quarter of a mile up, but you get the gist.

'Nicely slow barbecued by now,' Kylah added.

'We couldn't, could we?' Bobby said.

'Guilty pleasure,' said Asher and dived towards lunch.

'You total bunch of Ethans,' said Rimsplitter.

F4 chattered. It was magpie for 'Ethan's?'

'*Mission Impossible.* You know, Ethan Hunt. Rhymes with—'

F4 chattered again.

'Punt, yeah, that's right, punt.' Rimsplitter glared disbelievingly at the magpie. 'You got to get out more, Piano, mate. You and me need to have a natter. Now let's follow these merchants and see wot they get up to. Honest to God, it's like takin the bleedin' space cadets to Bognor.'

F4 chattered some more.

'Space cadets? You know, the kids in the class where you could dare to do anythin', like eat a live worm.'

F4 chattered again.

'Yeah, I know you could eat a live worm, but you wouldn't when you weren't a magpie, would you?'

The conversation continued in much the same vein as the eagle and the magpie followed the vultures down through the clear blue air towards a very unappetising-looking carcass.

———

REEVES STOOD on the plain as dust-devils rose and fell, watching the birds fade into the distance before turning back to Bettany.

'I lied when I said I wanted you to stay only to help my son, Praetor,' she said.

'You can drop that Praetor stuff, for a start. The name is Reeves.'

She reached up and brushed a speck of dirt from his cheek. The gesture was small, almost nothing—tender, instinctive. But to Reeves, it struck like a thunderclap.

A simple touch, one that would mean little between people accustomed to closeness, felt to him like a miracle. It had been years—so many, he'd stopped counting—since anyone had touched him with such quiet care.

It was nothing. And it was everything.

The warmth of her fingers lingered, stirring a hollow ache deep in his chest. A sudden tide of sorrow rose within him, sharp and unexpected—a grief for all the years he had gone untouched, unnoticed in that way. But riding just behind it, swift and shivering, came something else: a flicker of hope.

The longing for what had been met the fragile promise of what might still come, and for a moment, it felt like plunging into icy water—shocking, consuming, and impossibly alive.

'Do you not have another name, Reeves?' Bettany asked.

Reeves shook his head. 'One day, I might let you call me something else.' He turned away and contemplated the huge horse next to him, not wanting her to see his confusion.

'Would you like me to help you get back in the saddle, Trev?' asked Bettany.

Her teasing challenge somehow flushed away all of his pain in a heartbeat. He did not know how she did this, but he sensed in a vague and ephemeral way that it had everything to do with the unwritten alchemy that bound people together.

He turned back, grinned and kissed her again. It felt good. 'I think, Bettany Shadowsmith, you may well already have.'

CHAPTER FORTY-SEVEN

Four days after returning from Rathkoorne and with the transmorph spell well and truly reversed, Duana Llewyn called the task force together for a debrief. As before, they met in Pict to accommodate Rimsplitter, who did not do offices, or indeed inside in general, at all well. Once more, they convened outside the shepherd's hut. But instead of mugs of tea, Duana had commissioned Ned to provide a high tea of crustless sandwiches, Victoria sponge and champagne.

She held up a bubbling glass in a toast. 'To the spectacular success of the FFs,' she said.

Four other people raised a glass and a crowned eagle dipped its beak into a goblet.

'Oh my days, not a bad drop of Scotsman, Prof,' Rimsplitter said, champagne dripping from his beak.

Asher frowned in deep thought and then, with a look of intense concentration, said, 'Flying Scotsman, steam train, champagne.'

Bobby beamed at him and squeezed his arm in encouragement and they all toasted, except Rimsplitter who'd toasted already.

Duana nodded. 'Not a bad drop of Scotsman at all. You all deserve it and I now have a framed imp-pression of the squadron in my office in pride of place next to the desiccated head of Jordog the Appalling. I have to say I had my doubts when the suggestion was made for a vulture squad, but it proved to be a stroke of genius.'

'I 'ave me moments.' Rimsplitter preened himself.

'Um,' said Bobby, 'wasn't it Matt's idea?'

'Yes, it was,' Kylah said, glaring with something approaching admiration and a twist of apology at Matt. 'You trusted your gut, Agent Danmor. We ought, perhaps, to add that to the manual.'

Matt raised an eyebrow but got no chance to respond.

'Yeah,' said Rimsplitter scathingly, 'his idea, but my implementation. Ideas is one thing, makin' them 'appen is another.'

Matt nodded. 'There are some ideas so wrong that only a very intelligent person could possibly believe in them.'

Rimsplitter nodded. 'There, see. He knows.' He cocked his avian head in a way that suggested suspicion. 'That's a bit deep for you, you tee.'

'Actually, that was George Orwell,' Bobby said.

'Fat bloke wot did the *War of the Words* and *Citizen Crane*, I know,' Rimsplitter nodded in the self-assured way only the really ignorant can.

Matt opened his mouth to speak but promptly shut it again. Some battles are simply not worth fighting.

'I have to say that, despite my better judgement, I quite liked being a vulture. Flying is amazing.' Kylah beamed.

Rimsplitter strode across to what was left of a small goat and started ripping off bits of flesh. 'Don't mind if I finish me breakfast, do you?'

No one answered.

'Flyin' is just the start,' he added between rips. 'There's aerial acrobatics, too. When you get really good you could even try some in-flight entertainment while whistling "Somewhere Ogre the Rainbow", know what I effin' mean?' Rimsplitter winked.

Kylah coughed back a tiny morsel of Victoria sponge that suddenly appeared in the back of her throat. 'Unfortunately, I think I probably do.'

There was, of course, so much wrong with Rimsplitter's sentence it was impossible to know where to begin, since it left little to the imagination. And Kylah had come to realise it was nigh on impossible to judge whether he butchered the song title deliberately, or not. Still, it had a certain *je ne sais quoi* ring to it, under the circumstances. To distract herself, she turned to the professor. 'How are they getting on over there, Duana?'

'Remarkably well. The old order has been re-established. Targan Shadowsmith has been accepted and inaugurated. Sweeping changes are afoot. Of course, the Northern Wights were quick to try and seize the opportunity. A change of leadership often leaves a power vacuum.'

'Have there been incursions?'

'Only one. A battalion of wights marched across the border and met little resistance other than a family of Resonari. Reports are that the whole battalion disappeared for two whole days. On their return they all appeared to have aged by at least four years. As yet, we have had no further reports of any hostilities.'

'And Reeves?' asked Bobby.

'Ah yes, the enigmatic Mr Reeves—'

'Oy, this is supposed to be a celebration, you cees,' Rimsplitter butted in. 'We are not 'ere to talk shop. We should have a singsong. I know some good vulture songs. How about "Green, Green Ass of Skome"? Skome's a desert, see, and there was this mule caravan wot got lost. Fed a vulture colony for months, it did. Legendary.'

'Is it compulsory?' Asher asked.

Rimsplitter cocked his head in a way that they all knew was the precursor to an argument.

'No. Course not. I could always tell you some jokes.'

'"Green, Green Ass of Skome" it is, then,' said Asher and raised his champagne flute.

———

AT ABOUT THE SAME TIME, another meeting was taking place in an office overlooking the River Thames. Magister Hamage sat sipping tea from a mug with a logo that said *Shh, there's gin in here.* Opposite him, the DG of MI5 sipped tea from a china cup.

'Are we to assume that the Zatrank threat is well and truly negated?' the DG asked.

'It is, Sir Bernard. Your man did very well.'

'I'd hardly call him our man. After all, from what I read, he was a slightly reluctant volunteer.'

Hamage nodded and took another ginger snap from the plate and studied it. 'These are really very good. Ernest Porter recommended them and he, as we all know, is an aficionado. Oh, yes, reluctant Reeves may well have been, but he outdid himself.'

'My understanding was that he was unstable.'

'And all the better for it, in my opinion. By definition, to be unstable means that one also has a state of stability from which one veers in the first place. Mr Reeves appears to have found a degree of enviable equilibrium and he is not a man who appreciates that state being disrupted. Neither in himself, nor in others. As Erthu Le Liare has found out to his cost. Reeves is going to be decorated, you know. We're giving him the Mauve Entrail, presented only to those who distinguish themselves in the service of their fellow men, or women, or…other creatures are available, as my politically correct secretary is always telling me to add to my letters. Mr Reeves is that rare breed that knows the difference between what is right and what the people in power think is right, which is often not the same thing at all. It is called the perspective of justice and is a very dangerous gift to possess. I am looking forward immensely to watching him wield it.'

'Even in your world?'

'As someone else much more famously said, the jurisdiction of a good man extends to the end of the world. And I interpret that as including any world that'll have him. Oh, and Rathkoorne has reverted back to its old name, Hedwich.'

'Should we offer Reeves something? An OBE, perhaps?'

'That is up to you. However, I do not think that he will be

returning at any time soon, though he now has dual citizenship. Seems to have established himself as a peacekeeper.'

'What about the other barons? Any signs of military moves?'

'All quiet. Nary a whimper.'

'Strange. I thought they'd be the first to rattle sabres.'

'They tried—briefly. But the people moved faster. Tired of noble games, they organised themselves, stood their ground. No violence, no grand declarations. Just a firm, quiet refusal. And that, it seems, was enough.'

'And Reeves?'

'He was behind it—coordinated the whole thing. And there's talk he's grown rather close to Ms Bettany Shadowsmith.'

'Really?'

'Mmm. A very capable woman, by all accounts.'

'Best of luck to him, I say.' The DG picked up a ginger snap and dunked it in his tea.

'Indeed.' Hamage nodded, staring into the bottom of his teacup. 'Very useful having an established presence in what is a highly volatile part of the southern peninsula. I have a feeling that we both might be needing Reeves' services again at some time in the future.'

The DG paused and cocked his head. 'Is that what the tea leaves are telling you?'

Hamage looked up. 'What? Oh, no. Reeves will write his own story, I am sure of that. The tea leaves, on the other hand, suggest something else altogether. Are you a betting man, Bernard?'

'Not really.'

'Pity. I happen to know that Sweetex Ginger Crumb is running in the 4.15 at Doncaster. Ah, well. We can't all be winners.'

———

IT WAS Moga Lathrop that saw them coming. At first, they were mere dark specks in the distance, a shimmering movement in the heat haze on the horizon. But as they neared, he could make out two horsemen and a Zatrank carriage. When they finally rounded the bend that confirmed their destination could only be the Lathrops' farm, Moga threw down his hoe and ran. His mother and sister were inside, his father at the rear, tending to their own meagre crops.

'Father! Father! Zatrank!'

It was a week after the uprising. Rumours of trouble had leeched into the countryside. But they were just that, unsubstantiated rumblings. Information was a form of power, and limiting it—and learning not to trust it—had become a way of being in Rathkoorne. It was all very well the city was going through change. What happened there had little impact in the countryside, where every day was a matter of survival. The city dwellers could have their politics and smoke it.

Welwyn appeared from the rear of the farmhouse just as the Zatrank carriage skidded to a halt on the parched earth. Prandy, with Robyn clutched tightly to her skirts, came out and stood in the doorway.

Both horsemen dismounted. The door of the carriage opened and three burly men exited, leaving only the carriage driver.

'Are you the Lathrops?' he called out from his seat.

'I am Welwyn Lathrop. What brings you here?'

'Urgent business and a message.'

'For me? There must be a mistake. We are but simple farmers. Our quota is not due for another month—'

One of the men stepped forward. 'Stand clear of the door, please.'

Welwyn turned towards his wife and nodded. Prandy stood aside but he caught in her face a reflection of the expression that he, too, was wearing. Fear had given way to wary confusion. All thanks to a word. The 'p' word. No Zatrank they had ever come across had even hinted at politeness, never mind actually said 'please'. Welwyn heard heavy boots crossing the rooms of his house, a faint scraping, and then the man emerged holding the portrait of Erthu Le Liare.

'Ah,' said Welwyn, 'you're probably wondering why he was facing the wall...'

The soldier walked back to where his compatriots stood in a line in front of the carriage.

'We were thinking of doing a bit of whitewashing,' explained Prandy. 'Didn't want to get any splash—'

The driver cleared his throat. He had a bit of parchment in his hand and unfurled it to read.

'To Welwyn, Prandy, Moga and Robyn. These men you see before you are volunteer cleaners and fixer-uppers. They have come to the farm to run it, put in some irrigation, and renovate and decorate the house. You are not to stay while all this is going on, and you are therefore ordered to take a holiday.'

'A what?' asked Moga, looking up into his father's face.

'It's a kind of...rest,' he whispered, terror in his eyes. 'Where you don't do anything but enjoy yourself.'

Moga stared at his father uncomprehendingly. His expression was that of someone having just been told that the ground was made of pudding and that the rivers ran with milk.

'You are ordered to pack some essentials and return to Gogny Payn in the carriage, where you will be put up in the Keep. There are some very nice rooms there.'

'But,' Prandy protested, searching frantically for the right words. 'Who? Why?

'Is this some trick?' Welwyn asked, weakly.

'It's no trick,' said the driver. 'He said you wouldn't believe us. He told us you'd need proof.'

'Proof?' Prandy breathed, confusion piling on top of confusion.

The Zatrank holding the portrait of Erthu Le Liare placed it carefully against the wheel of the carriage and, with one stamp of his boot, kicked through Erthu Le Liare's face. He then broke the frame in two, then four, then eight.

The Lathrops stared with eyes as large as the harvest moon. A time they normally dreaded, because, if bright enough, it meant work could carry on long into the small hours.

Robyn giggled nervously.

'Father, I don't understand,' Moga implored.

'No, I don't suppose you do,' said the driver. 'We were told to show you the orders.'

Moga, the only one as yet capable of moving since his parents were paralysed by incredulity, and his sister was doing a great impression of a limpet, stepped forward and took the parchment from the driver, still standing to attention.

He peeled the curling paper open, reading, sun blazing down on his head, until he got to the bottom of the page, where he blinked several times before he managed to drag his eyes back up to his astonished parents.

'He signed it,' Moga whispered.

'Who?' Welwyn asked. 'Who signed it?'

'The Praetor, of course, who else?' said the driver.

'The Praetor?' Prandy remained confused.

'There is a note at the bottom before the signature,' Moga added, his mouth slowly shaping itself into a bemused grin. 'It's to me and it says, "My good friend Moga, come and see the city as it should be."'

'But what does that mean?' his mother asked.

'It means Reeves,' said Moga looking up into his bewildered family's faces, and the grin that had been vying for supremacy over incredulity finally blossomed into a full-blown, unabashed, laugh of sheer delight.

ACKNOWLEDGEMENTS

As with all writing endeavours, the existence of this novel depends upon me, the author, and a small army of 'others' who turn an idea into a reality. A special mention to Bryony Sutherland for editorial guidance through the labyrinth. The Hipposync Archives are a work in progress and who knows where the next turn might lead. Special mention goes to Ela the dog who drags me away from the writing cave and the computer for walks, rain or shine. Actually, she's a bit of a princess so the rain is a no-no. Good dog!

But my biggest thanks goes to you, lovely reader, for being there and actually reading this. It's great to have you along and I do appreciate you spending your time in joining me, the scribe, and the team at Hipposync and in New Thameswick, where anything is possible.

CAN YOU HELP?

With that in mind, and if you enjoyed it, I do have a favour to ask. Could you spare a moment to **leave a review or a rating**? A few words will do, but it's really the only way to help others like you discover the books. Probably the best way to help authors you like. Just visit the book's page on Amazon and leave a few words, or a rating, if you have the time. Thank you!

FREE BOOK FOR YOU

Visit my website and join up to the Hipposync Archives Readers Club and get a FREE novella, ***Every Little Evil***, by visiting:

https://dcfarmer.com/

When a prominent politician vanishes amidst chilling symbols etched in blood, the police are baffled. Enter Captain Kylah Porter, an enigmatic guardian against otherworldly threats. With her penchant for the paranormal and battling against cynical skeptics, she dives into a realm where reality blurs. Her toxic colleague from the Met is convinced it's just another tawdry urban crime. But Kylah suspects someone's paying a terrible price for dipping a toe, or something even less savoury, in the murky depths of the dark arts.
She knows her career and the missing man's life are on the line. Now time is running out for the both of them…

Pour yourself a cuppa and prepare for a spellbinding mystery.

By signing up, you will be amongst the first to hear about new releases via the few but fun emails I'll send you. This includes a no spam promise from me and you can unsubscribe at any time.

AUTHOR'S NOTE

Once upon a time, in the swirling mists of the last century, my journey into the fantastical began. A devotee of the greats like Tolkien, I found myself drawn deeper into Terry Pratchett's Discworld and Tom Holt's tilt at the modern—the holy trinity of the Ts, if you will.

Two decades ago, I embarked on what I now affectionately call "the archives." But alas, life's currents swept me into real world. I found myself scribbling away in different genres. Don't get me wrong, I still do that. But those archives? They never stopped whispering my name.

Somewhere Ogre The Rainbow began life as a hero's journey. And it ended up that way, too. Reeves was meant to be an ancillary character, but he ended up taking over the narrative as, sometimes, characters simply do.

The question is, are there any other files in the archive? There might be. Let's just say I am having a rummage as you read this, so … watch this space is all I am prepared to say at this juncture.

All the best, and see you all soon, DCF.